5.0 Nautical Miles
Not for navigation

Toba Inlet

British Columbia Mainland

Pendrell Sound

East Redonda Isl.

Prideau

Waddington Channel

Roscoe Inlet

Black Lake

West Redonda Island

Deer Passage

Raza Island

Rendezvous Islands

Reversing Rapids

Von Donop Inlet

Ha'thayim

Cortes Island

Sutil Channel

Calm Channel

Stuart Island

See Inset

Sonora Island

Thurston Bay Lagoon

N E S W

Chatam Point

1.0 Nautical Miles
Not for navigation

British Columbia Mainland

Arran Rapids

Big Bay

Stuart Island

Yuculta Rapids

Dent Island

Devil's Hole

Dent Rapids

Sonora Island

Cordero Channel

3D satellite charts for this area are available at www.whiskeygulf.com/onscene.

WHISKEY
GULF

WHISKEY GULF

A Charlie Noble Suspense Novel

CLYDE FORD

Vanguard Press
A Member of the Perseus Books Group

Published by Vanguard Press
A Member of the Perseus Books Group

Designed by Jeff Williams

Set in Adobe Jenson Pro by the Perseus Books Group

Library of Congress Cataloging-in-Publication Data
Ford, Clyde W.
    Whiskey Gulf / Clyde W. Ford.
      p. cm.
    ISBN 978-1-59315-522-3 (hardcover : alk. paper) 1. Private investigators—Fiction.
2. Inside Passage—Fiction. 3. Wilderness areas—British Columbia—Fiction. I. Title.

PS3606.O724W47 2009
813'.6—dc22

2009004087

Vanguard Press books are available at special discounts for bulk purchases in the U.S. by corporations, institutions, and other organizations. For more information, please contact the Special Markets Department at the Perseus Books Group, 2300 Chestnut Street, Suite 200, Philadelphia, PA 19103, or call (800) 810-4145, ext. 5000, or e-mail special.markets@perseusbooks.com.

10 9 8 7 6 5 4 3 2 1

To Chara:
No gulf too wide for our love to span.

ACKNOWLEDGMENTS

Natasha Kern, my literary agent, who helped chart the course that made this book possible. Roger Cooper, Georgina Levitt, Amanda Ferber, Peter Constanzo, Francine LaSala, Annie Lenth, and the rest of the fabulous crew at Vanguard and Perseus. And, to Chara Stuart, whose love is the wind in my sails.

PROLOGUE

MAYDAY. Mayday. Mayday."

The thin voice, crackling with static, whispered to Donald McCaffrey. He leaned forward, pressing two fingers to his earbud. He took in a deep breath, squeezed the Transmit button slowly, summoning forth an inner calm.

"Vessel calling Mayday, this is Comox Coast Guard Radio."

He waited, breathing in and out, a tense silence. Static popped in his ears like the sound of distant gunfire. A tiny plume of steam rose from his coffee cup. He held his breath, felt his jaw tense.

"Mayday. Mayday. Mayday."

Static engulfed the call, as though it was coming to Earth from a distant planet. Don dropped his head and exhaled.

"Vessel calling Mayday, this is Comox Coast Guard Radio."

"Mayday. Mayday. Mayday. This is the sailing vessel *Rebecca Anne . . .*"

Don closed his eyes briefly, nodding his head. He ran his fingers through his thinning gray hair, following the contours of his scalp. The caller sounded like a woman.

"*Rebecca Anne.* This is Comox Coast Guard Radio."

Nothing.

Suddenly, words broke through the static like the sun's rays piercing through an overcast sky.

1

"Comox Coast Guard, this is the sailing vessel *Rebecca Anne*."

Don punched the air with his fist. "*Yes*." He let go a tense victory whisper.

"*Rebecca Anne*. State the nature of your emergency."

"This is the sailing vessel *Rebecca Anne*. The sailing vessel *Rebecca Anne*."

She hadn't heard him.

"I say again, ma'am. State the nature of your emergency."

Don leaned back and closed his eyes again. He sifted through the darkness, imagining that he could hover above the Strait of Georgia like a gigantic eagle surveying everything below.

"Comox Coast Guard, this is the sailing vessel *Rebecca Anne*. We believe we've hit an uncharted rock. We're adrift without an engine. We've damaged our hull. We're taking on water fast."

Her voice sounded stressed, but not panicked. The transmission, though still peppered with static, came through more clearly than the others. Don lowered his shoulders.

"*Rebecca Anne*, Comox Coast Guard. Ma'am, do you have a bilge pump aboard?"

"Roger. Our bilge pump is on continuously. My husband is operating a handheld pump. So far we are able to keep up."

Don nodded. This woman communicated clearly.

"Ma'am, do you have a GPS unit aboard? And can you give me your present location?"

Don reached around to massage the back of his neck, then he picked up a pencil.

"Comox Coast Guard, our present location is . . . " She paused. "Forty-nine point thirty-three degrees north. One-hundred twenty-four point zero-five degrees west."

Don scribbled.

"*Rebecca Anne*, copy."

Don spun around to a computer, typed in the coordinates. A chart flashed onto his large LCD screen. A red *X* pulsed below and to the right of the Ballenas Islands, which were inside a red polygon marked WG. He tapped on the screen with his pencil. ·

"Ma'am, could you please stand by."

He didn't wait for her response. He popped out his earbud, picked up a red telephone handset, and punched in four numbers. A moment later, a man answered.

"Winchelsea Control, Herndon."

"Comox Radio Operations Center calling to confirm the status of area WG."

Herndon's voice tightened with impertinence. "Whiskey Gulf is active today from 0700 to 1800 hours."

Herndon hung up.

"Thank you," Don said to the empty line. He dropped the receiver into its cradle, peering at the time at the bottom of his computer screen, then at the wall clock. Both read 1112. He pushed his earbud back in.

"*Rebecca Anne.* Ma'am, what was your last port of call and time of departure?"

"We departed Pender Harbor at 0600."

Don copied down the information.

"And your destination?"

"Nanaimo."

Background conversation aboard the *Rebecca Anne* filled the spaces between the static, but Don couldn't decipher the words.

"Ma'am, how many people are aboard and what are their names?"

"Two people. William and Rebecca Anne Kinsley."

"Can you state the make, model, and length of your vessel? Also, its hull color?"

"We're a blue and white, custom Bob Perry design, forty-foot sailboat."

"*Rebecca Anne,* stand by please."

Don bellowed, "Peter! I have a forty-foot sailboat that may have hit a rock, adrift, and taking on water east of the Ballenas Islands. It's—"

From across the control room, a deep, measured voice answered, "How far east?"

"Within the boundaries of Whiskey Gulf."

Peter's voice rose. "Shit. Do you have the exact coordinates?"

"On my screen."

"And you've called Winchelsea Control to tell them?"

"I called for a status check only. Can you take over channel sixteen? I'm switching this call to twenty-two alpha. Then I'll call Winchelsea Control again."

"Picking up sixteen right now," Peter said.

"*Rebecca Anne*, Comox Coast Guard. Can you switch and answer channel twenty-two alpha?" Don said.

"Comox Coast Guard, switching twenty-two alpha."

Don dialed in channel 22A. He tapped the floor with his foot. He sucked in a breath.

Static came first. Then, "Comox Coast Guard, *Rebecca Anne* answering channel twenty-two alpha."

Don exhaled deeply. "Ma'am, please stand by. I'm transferring this call to Winchelsea Control. They will coordinate a rescue."

Sweat from Don's palm greased the handset. He punched up Winchelsea Control. Herndon answered again.

"I have an emergency and I need to speak with the Range Control Officer immediately," Don said.

A cascade of off-key electronic tones sounded before a man with a high-pitched nasal voice answered.

"Lieutenant Andrews."

"McCaffrey from the Comox Ops Center. I have a sailboat that may have hit a rock, adrift and taking on water within the boundaries of area WG."

"Damn!" blasted through the receiver.

Don pulled it away from his ear.

"Fucking makes my day," Andrews said. "Zero visibility. No recon flights. Deck's too low to scramble helos. Gimme the GPS coordinates of the target's location. I'll see if I have them on radar."

Don's foot tapped faster, as if it had a mind of its own.

"We've got all sorts of boats on the water this week. Joint antiterrorism training exercise with the Americans and the Bahrainis. High-speeds zooming all over the damn place," Andrews said. "Can't tell if it's them near one of our target retrieval vessels. I'll call the joint ops CO and advise him. We'll coordinate from here."

A loud click sounded at the other end of the line. Don hung up.

"*Rebecca Anne*, Winchelsea Control has been advised of your status. They should be with you shortly on twenty-two alpha."

"Roger. *Rebecca Anne* is standing by . . ."

Static completed her sentence.

"Break. *Rebecca*. *Rebecca*. *Rebecca*. This is Winchelsea Control."

Don punched the Transmit button.

"Break, Comox Coast Guard. Vessel's name is *Rebecca Anne*. I say again, *Rebecca Anne*."

"*Rebecca Anne*. *Rebecca Anne*. *Rebecca Anne*, this is Winchelsea Control."

Only a few static-filled hisses replied.

"*Rebecca Anne*, Winchelsea Control on channel twenty-two alpha."

Don jabbed the red Transmit button with his thumb.

"Break. *Rebecca Anne*, this is Comox Coast Guard."

Silence. Don blew out a breath and shook his head. His foot and his leg now bounced.

"*Rebecca Anne*. This is Comox Coast Guard."

"Comox Coast Guard . . ."

Don shook his head.

"Comox Coast Guard, this is Winchelsea Control. We cannot raise the *Rebecca Anne*. Joint Operations Command has been advised. They will coordinate search and rescue."

"Winchelsea Control, roger your last. Comox Coast Guard will be standing by sixteen and twenty-two alpha."

Don released the red button. He sighed. Then he squeezed it again.

"*Rebecca Anne*, this is Comox Coast Guard."

Don closed his eyes and reached out in his mind to the *Rebecca Anne*. He loved to sail the strait. He imagined Rebecca and William Kinsley trying to manage a sailboat taking on water in zero visibility with no engine and no wind. He squeezed the red button hard.

"*Rebecca Anne*, Comox Coast Guard. Comox . . ."

A hand tapped Don's shoulder lightly, then grasped it firmly. He looked up into Peter Braithwaite's round, red, bearded face. Peter shook his head. Don sighed, then nodded. Peter lifted his hand, then turned to walk away. Don winced. The feeling, he imagined, was like a lone doctor yelling, "Clear!" and planting two defibrillator paddles to shock a patient's chest after everyone else knew the patient was gone.

He dialed in channel 16.

"Break. All stations. All stations. All stations. This is Comox Coast Guard Radio. This station has received a distress call from the *Rebecca Anne*, a forty-foot sailing vessel with a blue and white hull and two persons aboard. The *Rebecca Anne* was reportedly adrift and taking on water approximately four miles east of the Ballenas Islands. Any mariners with additional information about the sailing vessel *Rebecca Anne* are requested to contact Comox Coast Guard Radio, VHF channel one-six. Comox Coast Guard Radio out."

Peter hollered from across the room, "Take a break. I'll fill in for you."

Don hesitated to answer.

"That's an order," Peter said. "Even if you are the shift supervisor. Take a break."

"Roger that," Don said.

He pulled his earbud out and let his head bounce against the leather chair back. He rose from his chair and walked to the door of the control room, holding his cold cup of coffee. The continuous marine weather forecast played on speakers outside the control room door. The forecaster's deep voice echoed down the cavernous cinder block hallway. With his back against the wall, Don paused to listen. The weather broadcast ended with an additional recorded message:

"Military exercise area Whiskey Gulf is active today from 0700 to 1800 Pacific Time with surface, subsurface, and air-launched torpedo fire. Area Whiskey Gulf is considered extremely hazardous and all mariners are advised to stay well clear. Any vessels with concern, contact Winchelsea Control, VHF channel ten."

Chapter 1

THE *NOBLE LADY* CURTSIED to starboard as I sat with my feet propped up along the bench behind the galley table. My head rested against a forward bulkhead. My finger ached too much to pull back a curtain. Besides, Kate said she'd play nursemaid and bring over lunch. I thought about popping another of the painkillers the doctor had given me. But I don't like pills, so I didn't.

The cabin door swung open and Kate ducked under the doorway. She wore navy blue trousers, a short-sleeved navy blouse, and a navy blue baseball cap emblazoned with the Coast Guard insignia and surrounding that the words, "USCGC *Sea Eagle*." She also wore a huge smile.

Then she took one look at me and her smile wilted. "Ouch," she said.

I nodded. "Yes, ouch."

She closed her eyes slightly and pouted. "I'm sorry," she said. "Let me serve lunch, then I want to hear all about what happened. I stopped by Thai Haven and got your favorite dish."

"Black beans, broccoli, and shrimp?"

"Yes."

She dropped a plastic bag onto the galley table, then walked over to the cabinet.

"No plates," I said.

Kate turned around with a puzzled expression on her face.

I held up my injured hand. "Hard to do dishes with this."

She frowned, then nodded. "Poor baby. I guess so. Well, then we'll just have fun eating straight from the box."

Kate looked at me sheepishly. I hadn't lowered my hand.

"Poor Charlie. Do you want me to feed you?"

I frowned and reached for the plastic bag. I growled, "Just give me some food, woman."

Kate snatched the bag before I could reach it. She laughed, making that soft gurgling sound, almost a coo, which always made me smile, and which helped ease my pain.

Kate unfolded the flaps of a white box, peeked inside, then promptly slapped it down in front of me. She opened another box and placed it on her side of the table. A third box she set in the middle. She laid out forks and napkins.

I sniffed the sweet, piquant aroma emanating from my dish. "Four stars?"

"Ban said, 'This for Mr. Charlie, must be four stars.' I think she likes you," Kate said.

I chuckled. "I was one of her first customers. She was very direct. 'You have girlfriend?'"

"And you like women who are very direct," Kate said, "don't you?"

"I do. And I seem to recall another very direct woman who insisted that I should not drink a bottle of wine alone."

Kate grinned. "And look how far my directness got me."

I picked up a fork with my right hand, but the bandage on my ring finger got in my way. So I switched to my left hand. But I didn't make a good switch-eater, so I went back to my right hand. I grabbed the fork like a saber. Then I raised the box of rice to my mouth and shoveled some in. Before chewing or swallowing, I also shoveled in some shrimp, vegetables, and black bean sauce. What the hell. Not elegant, but I wouldn't starve.

"What happened?" Kate asked, nodding to my finger.

I sighed. "I was in a dinghy helping Ben polish the side of his boat facing away from the dock. When I finished, I came back into the dock. You know how the wooden edges of the docks are splintered in many places?"

"Yes."

"I propped my hand on the edge of the dock to hoist myself out of the dinghy and a sliver of wood jabbed under the nail of my ring finger, embedding itself more than a quarter of an inch down into my nail bed."

"Ooooh." Kate shuddered, squeezing her eyes closed momentarily.

"To make matters worse, the sliver broke off when I jerked my hand back so I couldn't pull it out."

"Oh, Charlie."

"Ben poured two microbrews down me, and then drove me to the emergency room. A man came in after me with a gunshot wound, another with a bad gash from a falling window pane. A woman in premature labor was rushed ahead of everyone. So my sliver hurt like hell but triage put me in last place. I sat there for four hours. The ER doc used a tiny pair of forceps and managed to pull the sliver out. My finger gushed blood. Of course, the damn wood is treated with creosote, and it's dirty, so he was worried about an infection starting under my nail. He gave me antibiotics and painkillers and sent me home."

"Will you lose your nail?"

"I hope not."

"And infection?"

"Hopefully the antibiotics will take care of it."

Kate gasped as though she'd just remembered something. Her hand flew to her mouth. "Oh Charlie, your guitar. My god, you can't play now."

I studied the bandaged ring finger of my right hand. "I don't know how long I'll have to stop. But I called Mr. Oller, and he told me how to keep practicing."

Kate grimaced. "What? You practiced anyway? Are you a cantankerous sick person?"

"A what?"

"You know, someone who doesn't follow doctor's orders. Doesn't take medications. Ready to leave the hospital before being discharged."

I laughed mischievously. "Doesn't follow orders." I pointed my bandaged finger at Kate. "I seem to recall a superior officer's similar words a few years ago, which is why I'm now in civvies."

Kate held up her hand. "That's fine with me."

"What's fine? That I'm now in civvies?"

"No, that you're cantankerous when you're sick or injured. Haven't you read that cantankerous patients recover quicker and live longer?"

"I hadn't read that."

Kate swallowed some food, then screwed up her face. "I don't understand how you practiced with your finger bandaged."

I helped myself to another mixture of rice, vegetables, and shrimp, and held up my hand while I chewed.

"Ah," I said, "the secrets of a master teacher."

"Mr. Oller had you play with only your thumb, index, and middle fingers?"

"No. Django Reinhardt may have been able to pull that off, but not me. I practiced with all the fingers of my right hand, even with my ring finger in a bandage."

"Okay. Okay. I give up. How?"

I tapped the side of my head. "I practiced here, with my mind. Mr. Oller had me sight-read a line, then hum the melody. Sight-read a line, then close my eyes and imagine playing it."

"And that's practicing?"

"Did you ever take a Coast Guard Situational Awareness class?"

"Yes."

"And do you remember the part about—"

Kate snapped her fingers. "Mental rehearsal. Rehearsing a mission in your mind enhances your awareness, and prepares your body by stimulating the same areas of your brain involved in the actual execution of the mission."

"You took the class."

"Mr. Oller's a smart man."

"Which is why he's my teacher."

"So what are you practicing on your virtual guitar?" Kate asked.

"Two pieces by John Dowland," I said. "Queen Elizabeth's Galliard and Lady Hundson's Alman."

Kate smiled. "It amazes me that you like music from the eighteen hundreds," she said.

I shook my head. "Dowland lived during the time of Elizabeth I. Shakespeare's Elizabeth. The Virgin Queen. The fifteen hundreds."

"All the more amazing."

"There's something haunting about the music. Fascinating and beautiful. It captures me, transports me back in time."

"And you play it so well."

I tipped my imaginary hat to Kate, then bowed my head. "M'dear lady, of such compliments I fear I am unworthy. For the worth of my playing 'tis a treasure known only to the ears of such a beautiful listener as you. And others, with ears less sweet, but perhaps sharper of musical discernment, might presently beg to differ."

Kate laughed so hard she nearly choked on her food. Several drops of red curry sauce splattered over her blouse. She looked down. Then she picked up a napkin and dabbed at them. She wiped them off, but they left grease stains.

"Do you need something to take care of the stains?"

She waved me off. "They're working blues," she said. "And I'm in the engine room this afternoon. Believe me, they'll be a lot grimier when I'm finished."

"The engine room of the *Sea Eagle*?"

"No, the *Etheridge*."

"The *Etheridge*? She's here? In Bellingham?"

"At dry dock in Fairhaven."

"And Jeffrey Leighton?"

"You know Captain Leighton?"

"I served under him as a junior officer in District Seven, on a cutter charged with drug interdiction out of Miami. I heard he took command of the *Etheridge* about two years ago."

"He seems like a great guy. It's obvious the ship's crew respects him."

"Jeff commands respect because he gives it. What are they in for?"

"The *Etheridge* took part in joint exercises in Canada that ended last week. Apparently, she sustained some damage to her bow prop. Maybe caught part of a deadhead in the blades. One of the computerized gunnery guidance systems also needs recalibration. And I'm part of a team working on the port engine."

"Which one, the diesel or the turbine?"

"You know the ship?"

"Four mains. One locomotive engine and one 707 jet engine on each side."

"You know the ship." Kate pushed her box of curry away. "We're working on the port diesel."

I checked my watch. "And you have to be back on duty at what time, Lieutenant?"

"Fourteen hundred hours, Commander." She checked her watch. "Which leaves me—" She grabbed her baseball cap and flung it at me. Her long dark hair fell in an unruly mass around her shoulders. "—over an hour to nurse you. Now are you going to be cantankerous with me, too?"

"Depends."

"On what?"

"Whether I approve of your technique."

She slowly undid the topmost button of her blouse.

"So far I approve."

She undid the next button down.

"My cantankerousness is slipping away."

She unfastened a third button. My hand shot up. "Stop."

Kate frowned. "What's the matter?"

"Nurse Kate, I have suddenly come down with a new complex of symptoms."

"And what would those be?"

I put the back of my hand to my forehead. "Fever. Lightheadedness. And a sense that I may soon need mouth-to-mouth resuscitation. I am also acutely aware that more than my ring finger is now throbbing."

"I see my technique is having the desired effect?"

"It is."

Kate started for a fourth button, when someone knocked on the galley window. She flinched. We shot a quick glance back and forth. Kate's face turned bright red and she quickly buttoned her blouse. "Expecting company?" she asked.

I whispered. "No. Let's not answer it. They'll go away."

Two more knocks followed.

"Mr. Noble," a voice outside said. "Mr. Noble, it's Arthur Grodin from the Kulshan Yacht Club."

Kate looked at me. I shook my head.

Art knocked again. "Mr. Noble, I'm sorry to bother you, but it's urgent."

Kate pointed at her cap and motioned for it. I shook my head. She nodded emphatically. I handed her the blue cap. She tucked her hair underneath it, then tugged on the bill. She left me still shaking my head as she walked out the cabin door. The latch on the entry gate rattled, and the *Noble Lady* dipped.

"Hi Art," Kate said.

"Lieutenant Sullivan . . . I didn't . . . I mean, I'm sorry . . . I mean, if I had known . . . I wouldn't have—"

Kate chuckled. "Don't worry, I was just checking in on my patient."

I stifled a laugh.

"I don't understand," Art said.

"Charlie injured his hand."

Art gasped. "I hope it's not serious."

"He lodged a splinter deep into his nail bed."

"Ouch," Art said.

"An ER doc removed it last night. But now he's in pain, aching, and throbbing." She articulated her last few words slowly, intending them, I'm sure, mostly for me.

"I'm glad it wasn't anything more," Art said.

"He'll survive," Kate said.

"Well, perhaps you could tell him that I'm here because the yacht club desperately needs his help. Two of our members have gone missing."

"Missing?"

"Yes. William and Rebecca Kinsley were headed south from Pender Harbor to Nanaimo aboard their forty-foot ketch, the *Rebecca Anne*, when they apparently developed engine trouble. They radioed a Mayday to the Canadian Coast Guard but they haven't been seen or heard from since."

"Usually in cases like this, the missing boat is discovered at a port other than its intended destination."

"Yacht club members have monitored VHF radio for over a week. Canadian Weather Radio has placed an announcement at the beginning of its continuous marine forecast requesting that any mariners with information about the *Rebecca Anne* contact the Canadian Coast Guard. To our knowledge there have been no sightings. Bill and Becky were experienced sailors. They had a world-class bluewater boat. They knew these waters well. We're very worried and we'd like Mr. Noble's help in finding out what happened. We've convened a special meeting this evening to discuss this matter. I came over to ask him if he would attend. Of course, this is business and we'll pay him for his time."

Kate opened the galley door and stuck her head in. She looked at me, raised her eyebrows, then cocked her head. I shook my head. Kate narrowed her eyes and frowned. I sighed and then nodded. She slipped back outside. The plastic enclosure on the fantail crinkled as she pulled it back.

"He'll be there. What time?"

"Eighteen-thirty. Thank you so much. I feel better already knowing that Mr. Noble will help."

Art's footsteps faded down the dock. Kate stepped back inside. She frowned. "You should call your agency the RIA, 'Reluctant Investigations Agency.'"

"NIA not RIA."

"What?"

"NIA. Noble Investigations Agency." I held up my hand. "Just before I did this I'd hired a Web designer to create my new Web site, www.charlienoble.net. It's called the 'Noble Investigations Agency.'"

Kate shook her head. "But you didn't want to help out the Kulshan Yacht Club. How noble is that?"

I shoved my hand at Kate. "I'm recovering from my wounds, or did you already forget?"

She shook her head and a tight smile spread over her lips. Then she checked her watch. "So much for Nurse Kate's long-lasting pain relief."

"Then I guess I will just have to live with these aches and throbs a little longer."

Kate's smile turned into a mischievous grin. She pursed her lips, then sucked a finger into her mouth. She slowly withdrew it. "I do have a quick fix that might offer you temporary relief." She beckoned me with her finger.

Her quick fix worked.

Chapter 2

QUARK, THE YELLOW LAB, sprawled out along the bottom step of the Kulshan Yacht Club's entrance. She raised her head as I approached and looked me over quickly. She let out a soft sigh, then dropped her head back down. Her down-turned eyes and droopy ears sent the sad message, "I've been abandoned. My owner doesn't love me."

I reached down to pet Quark. She rolled her eyes up toward me, then she rolled them away. Vince Marcellis's booming voice sounded on the other side of the door. Quark barked, then turned away from the sound of her owner with a look of aloof disdain.

At the top of the steps I turned around. Off to the right, behind Bellingham, the crown of Mount Baker glowed golden orange in the waning rays of the evening sun. To my right, an old wooden boat, at least one hundred feet long, dwarfed smaller vessels sitting in a boat-yard. The big boat reminded me of an aging diva in her dressing room before a performance, primping with restorative touches of makeup to transform herself into a beauty queen. The boat showed missing planks and large areas of bare wood. Only love, I thought. Older wooden boats can be so much work, it takes great love—and on second thought, great money—to restore and maintain them.

I twisted the doorknob and stepped inside. No one seemed to notice. Glances bounced back and forth between Vince Marcellis and Art Grodin, sitting next to each other at the head table. I stood by the door.

"It's golf," Art said. "G-O-L-F." He pronounced each letter slowly.

"No, Art," Vince said. "It's pronounced *gulf*, as if there were a *u* instead of an *o*." The former aerospace engineer stroked his graying beard as though it lent him more credibility.

Art held up a yellowed paper. "Here, see for yourself. I have a copy of the NATO phonetic alphabet." He pointed to the paper. "Alpha. Bravo. Charlie. Delta. Echo. Foxtrot. Golf! Technically, it's Whiskey *Golf* not Whiskey Gulf."

"Sorry, Art," Vince said. "The correct pronunciation is 'gulf' not 'golf,' according to the International Civil Aviation Organization."

Finally Art looked up. He ran his hand through his full head of silver hair.

"Welcome Mr. Noble."

I waved him off. "Charlie, please."

"Well then, welcome Charlie. Please have a seat at the head of the table with Vince and me. You were in the Coast Guard—maybe you can settle this. Is it Whiskey Golf or Gulf?"

I walked over to the head table and pulled out a small metal chair. I took a seat next to Vince. I knew him well enough to know he didn't like to be challenged on points of fact, particularly nautical facts.

"Hi Charlie."

Vince sounded slightly aloof and disdainful, much like his pet.

I scanned the expectant faces of the thirty people sitting in front of me on either side of the U-shaped arrangement of wooden tables. I debated whether I should wade into the midst of this verbal duel.

Finally I said, "You're both right."

Art and Vince shot wrathful glances my way.

"What do you mean, we're both right?" Art said. "Either it's 'golf' or it's 'gulf.'"

"When the International Civil Aviation Organization published the latest revisions to its Radiotelephony Procedures," I said, "it listed G-O-L-F as the correct spelling. But G-U-L-F as the preferred phonetic pronunciation."

Vince and Art turned to each other and glowered.

Vince grumbled, "You got a reference for that?"

"The Aeronautical Mobile Communications Panel, Working Group C, Third Meeting, October 2001, Anchorage, Alaska."

"You're pulling my leg?" Vince said.

"I attended the meeting as a Coast Guard observer."

"See," Art said. "He's a really smart guy. That's why I wanted Charlie to help us find Bill and Becky."

Vince mumbled. "He's got a good memory. I'll give him that much."

"I thought this was a meeting about a missing sailboat," I said. "What does Whiskey Gulf or Golf have to do with—?" I sucked in a breath. Before I'd even completed the sentence, I'd answered my own question.

"The Canadian Coast Guard reported the last known position of the *Rebecca Anne* several nautical miles east of the Ballenas Islands," Art said.

I nodded. "Which placed her within Canadian area WG," I said.

"That's right," Vince said. "We think she was trying to cross the strait through the thousand-yard safe transit corridor south of the Ballenas Islands, and north of Whiskey *Gulf*"—he pronounced the word slowly, then craned his neck around to Art and grinned—"on a day when it was active. They lost their engines. They had no wind. They drifted into Whiskey Gulf and haven't been heard from since."

Art blurted out, "Wait. Aren't we getting ahead of ourselves with Charlie? Why don't we first ask if he's willing to help us. Find out what his rates are. And then bring him up to speed about what we know."

I held up my hand to a few grimaces at the sight of my bandage. "Why don't you tell me what you know, and then I'll tell you if I can help out."

Many people nodded. Art looked around the room.

"Who wants to start?" he asked. A few people raised their hands. Art pointed to a couple at the end of the row on my left. "Mark, you and Linda cruised with Bill and Becky just before they went missing. Why don't you begin?"

Mark, a rotund man with thinning dark brown hair, stood up. He must have been six foot five. He wore khaki shorts, white socks, and sandals. His bright red face and red arms protruded from beneath a white polo shirt.

Before Mark began, I held up my bandaged hand with a small digital voice recorder in it.

"I injured my hand the other day, so I can't take notes. I hope no one minds if I record what is said here?" When no one objected, I motioned to Mark. "Please, go on."

"I'm Mark Yeager. My wife, Linda, and I cruised in Desolation Sound with Bill and Becky for two weeks. Our last anchorage was in Von Donop Inlet. We had sunny weather for the entire time. I had to get Linda back to Nanaimo to catch a ferry, so we left a day before Bill and Becky, who wanted to stay to kayak into the reversing rapids. We anchored off Newcastle Island across from Nanaimo and waited for them. But they never arrived."

"Mark, did the Kinsleys' boat have any mechanical problems during the trip?" I asked.

Mark waved my question away. "Minor. During the trip up, Bill noticed he was losing coolant."

"What kind of engine?" I asked.

"Perkins . . . I think the *Rebecca Anne* had a Perkins 4-108. Anyway, we pulled into Herriott Bay on Quadra Island, where he discovered that his fresh-water pump was leaking. He called over to Vancouver Island and a shop there put a new pump on the next ferry. I think Bill had the old one removed and the new one installed within two hours. He knew his stuff, and he didn't have a problem after that."

"Medical problems?" I asked. "Did either Bill or Becky show any signs of illness during the trip?"

"They were fit." Mark laughed. "A lot more fit than me. Linda and I trailed along as they walked from Von Donop into Squirrel Cove. We had to turn back because we couldn't keep up. Bill and Becky didn't even break a sweat."

"How old are they?" I asked.

"They're both in the middle to late fifties," Mark said. "You know, I listened to part of the rescue call on channel sixteen. It was never a clear call, lots of static. The Comox controller had difficulty keeping in contact. They reported their position east of the Ballenas Islands in zero visibility fog, light drizzle, and no wind. The controller switched them over to Winchelsea. That's when the Canadian Coast Guard lost them."

To Mark's left, an elegant woman, whose dark gray sweater matched her hair, raised her wineglass as if to toast.

"Linda?" I asked.

She nodded. Mark frowned.

"Did Bill and Becky have any relationship problems that were evident during your time with them?"

Mark answered, "No—"

"Yes," Linda said. Mark frowned.

"Linda?" I asked. She cut her eyes at him, then stood up. Mark sat down.

"We were anchored in the Octopus Islands. Mark and Bill went fishing. Becky and I decided to take a dinghy into shore and walk up to Nelson Lake to go swimming. Becky started telling me about how much stress they were under. I said, 'Here we are in all this beauty, and you two are feeling stressed?' And she said, 'Yes.' Of course, I asked why, but Becky spoke in vague terms about Bill's work, their house, their family, and making ends meet. I got the feeling she didn't want me to probe any deeper, and I didn't."

I turned to Art. "What kind of work did Bill do?" He opened his arms to those in attendance.

Vince broke in. "He was a former aerospace engineer, too. Worked at a NASA facility in Florida before they moved up here. I believe he now works . . . er, worked as an engineering consultant. I don't think she worked."

"How long have the Kinsleys lived here?"

A woman with silver-blue hair raised her hand. I recognized Art's wife, Connie. "They joined the club five or six years ago, and they'd been living in town for about a year before that. They bought a place in Sudden Valley."

"And family? Anyone know anything about the rest of their family?"

Heads turned toward each other. A buzz rose around the room. Lots of heads shook.

"No family that I ever heard them talk about," Connie said, "though I'm sure you all noticed that Becky spoke with a slight accent. Kinda Canadian but more British."

Art moaned. "Connie, dear, what kind of accent is that?"

"Well, I just don't know what to call it, but Bill said she was Lebanese."

Vince blurted, "She wasn't Muslim, was she?"

"You know, Vince, there's a strong Christian community in Lebanon," Art said.

"That so? Well then—"

I cut Vince off. "Linda, you're sure Becky mentioned her family to you?"

Her face reddened. "No, I'm not certain, but I think she did."

"Has anyone from the American or Canadian governments contacted anyone here about the Kinsleys yet?"

The room hushed. Then Mark stood up. "I reported them overdue when I cleared customs in Roche Harbor. A customs officer took my report. He said he'd pass it on to the Coast Guard. But they haven't contacted me."

"Who can tell me more about the *Rebecca Anne*?"

Vince chimed in, "Forty feet overall, thirty-four point eight at the waterline. Bill told me they had her custom built while they lived in Florida. Shoal draft with a drop-down daggerboard gave them either three feet or ten feet of keel. Fiberglass construction. Rugged. A pilothouse. Ketch-rigged. A real bluewater boat. All the lines came back into the pilothouse. The latest electronics: radar, GPS, plotter, computer navigation system, SSB radio, VHF. Bill and Becky both had their ham radio licenses. They knew what they were doing on the water. They'd sailed their boat through the Panama Canal and up the West Coast by way of Hawaii to get here."

"And they did have an inflatable?" I asked.

"A brand new inflatable with a ten-horsepower outboard," Art said.

"SOLAS equipment?" I asked.

"They had more Safety of Life at Sea equipment than most boats crossing oceans," Vince said. "A life raft. A sea anchor. Survival suits."

"Did they have an EPIRB?"

Vince did a double take. He looked at Art. I looked at Mike. Mike looked at Linda.

"I don't know," Mike said. "I can't recall whether I saw an EPIRB or not."

"That would be good to know, wouldn't it?" Vince said. "I hadn't thought of that. If they had an EPIRB it should have gone off if the boat sank."

"Canadian Coast Guard didn't say anything about picking up a signal from an emergency position indicator radio beacon," Mike said.

"Could mean lots of things," I said. "If they had an EPIRB it could have been destroyed. It could have failed to deploy."

Art whistled low. "Or the *Rebecca Anne* may not have gone down."

"Which brings me to my next question," I said. "Anyone know if either Bill or Becky had any reason to run or to hide?"

"As in running from the law?" The raspy smoker's voice belonged to a woman I knew only as Cynthia.

"Or from creditors. Alimony. Child support payments. Did they have any enemies?"

Art chuckled. "Bill and Becky? 'Bout as American as apple pie. Everyone liked 'em. Don't seem like the kind to make waves to me. Bill didn't like to talk politics much. Most people here know I'm the radical of this club. I'm not Republican, and proud of it. Bill, on the other hand, never wanted to talk politics. Kinda got the feeling he was more the Republican, conservative type."

"Hell, Art, half the people in here are the Republican, conservative type, but we still manage to get along," Vince said.

Cynthia blurted out, "Well, I beg to differ."

Art seemed to sink into his chair as though he wanted to disappear.

"Beg to differ how?" I asked Cynthia.

"I think Bill and Becky did have something to hide."

"Why do you say that?"

"Call it a woman's intuition, but something wasn't right. In the five years or so they were members of this club, how many of you ever went inside their home?"

Club members exchanged glances but no one raised a hand.

"I used to ask Becky if she wanted to play bridge or go for a walk with us girls or join our book club. She always had an excuse. She never participated. Then one day about two years ago, I was in Sudden Valley at another friend's house. I decided to drop in on the Kinsleys, you know, just for the hell of it. Driving up to their house, I passed a black SUV with a group of men leaving the Kinsleys' home."

"Cindy," Art said, "none of that proves anything. It—"

"Art, hold on. I haven't finished. Try Googling the Kinsleys, Mr. Noble. Know what you'll find?"

"What?"

"Nothing. Absolutely nothing. I find that strange, don't you? He's supposed to be a consultant, yet there's nothing on the Internet about it."

"Cindy, honey, you've been watching too many conspiracy movies," a woman said.

"Mary, dear, I didn't say there was a conspiracy. I just said something hasn't been right with them and this supposed disappearance is the icing on the cake."

"You sound like you don't believe they disappeared?"

"Six or seven years ago a sailboat washed aground in Chuckanut Bay. People thought the owner had fallen off and drowned. For several weeks they searched the bay for his body but found nothing. A year later, he turned up in Idaho, with a new name, a new wife, and a new family. He'd staged the grounding to hide his disappearance. He wanted to start a new life. Who knows, maybe the Kinsleys did the same thing."

"Then where's their sailboat?" Vince said.

"Maybe they scuttled it and headed to shore in their dinghy," Cynthia said.

"But their last reported position was in the middle of Whiskey Gulf. That's a long way from shore."

"That's if they told the truth about their position," Cynthia said.

"Well, as the designated radical of this group, I also think there's something nefarious going on here," Art said. "And I do think it's a conspiracy. Whiskey *Golf*"—he emphasized the *o*—"was active the day the Kinsleys attempted to cross. What if they did have engine problems? What if they did drift into Whiskey Golf? What if their boat was hit by a torpedo?"

"But the torpedoes aren't armed, are they, Charlie?" Vince asked.

"To the best of my knowledge they're not," I said. "Still, Art has a point. Each torpedo has a guidance system that could lock on to a boat."

"Or it could have been an errant torpedo," Art said.

"Hmmph. Errant torpedo?" Vince waved Art off.

Art cut his eyes at Vince. "It happens," he said.

I held up a hand to both men. "It happens," I said.

"They wouldn't stand a chance," Art said. "And, if they were hit by a torpedo, I bet the Coast Guard's covering up what they know."

A man with a trim white beard spoke out. "Art, now *you* sound like the one who's been watching too many Tom Clancy movies."

"Curt, do you have a better explanation?"

"No," Curt said, "and I thought that's why we brought Mr. Noble here tonight."

"Mr. Noble's presence doesn't stop me from—"

The chatter grew louder in the room, and I whistled above it, then called out, "Wait."

The room fell silent.

"It does no one any good to speculate without all the facts," I said. "Let me talk to the Coast Guard here and in Canada. Let's see what they say, and what evidence they have before we jump to any conclusions."

"Vince," Art said. He nodded in my direction. "As vice president and treasurer, please tell Charlie what financial arrangements we've made to accommodate his fees."

Vince cleared his throat. "We're not a wealthy club but we've created a special fund for the Kinsleys and seeded it with a few thousand dollars. We intend to pay for your investigation from that fund."

I held up a hand. "Let's wait until we see if there's anything to investigate before we talk about payment."

Art thwacked a polished wooden block with his gavel. I flinched, and so did several other club members.

"It's getting late," Art said. "I'm calling this special meeting of the Kulshan Yacht Club to an end. Charlie, thank you for agreeing to look into the Kinsleys' disappearance."

A buzz of conversation rose in the clubhouse. I stood to leave. Quark barked when I opened the door. She jumped to her feet and wagged her tail. I patted her a few times. But she didn't take her sight off the clubhouse door. I made my way toward the asphalt walking trail that lead back to gate 9. I hadn't got very far from the clubhouse when I heard a voice call out, "Charlie, do you have a minute?"

I turned around to see Cynthia hurrying my way. When she reached me she grasped my uninjured hand.

"I know you must think we're all a bunch of crackpots," she said. "But there is one thing I didn't say in there. I didn't want to say it in front of everyone else. About three years ago, William Kinsley took out a million-dollar life insurance policy on his wife."

"How do you know that, Cynthia?"

She grinned. "Bellingham's such a small town, you know. My

sister worked for the insurance agency he used. She remembered me telling her about a couple that had sailed their boat through the Panama Canal to Bellingham. Apparently, the insurance agency had never dealt with such a contingency before and the policy excluded any benefits being paid if Rebecca's death happened in the open ocean more than five miles offshore."

"Which wouldn't exclude the Strait of Georgia."

"No, it wouldn't."

Chapter 3

I CHUCKLED THINKING ABOUT the scene I'd just left. I know the words "yacht club" conjure images of glitz, glitter, and snootiness in the minds of many; visions of self-titled commodores and vice-commodores, well-heeled men and women in full dress uniforms or cocktail gowns who take their stations a little too seriously and spend more time meeting and drinking than boating.

I've known yacht clubs like that.

But most clubs are like the Kulshan Yacht Club, a collection of ordinary men and women with an extraordinary love for boats and the camaraderie that love engenders. Most yacht clubs boast their own cast of characters like Art, Vince, Connie, Cynthia, Mark, and Linda; men and women who stay young at heart by boating whenever and wherever they can.

Beneath their deep concern for fellow yacht club members—and their outrageous assertions—every question and suspicion raised tonight about the Kinsleys harbored enough plausibility to warrant further investigation. I decided tomorrow I'd pay a visit to my former CO, Captain Jeffrey Leighton. If he'd just come back from joint training maneuvers in Canada, perhaps he could tell me what really happened in Whiskey Gulf.

The walking trail back to gate 9 skirted the harbor where boats floated in a sea of light reflected from the city. Beyond the harbor, the dark void of Bellingham Bay loomed. And beyond the bay, lights twinkling throughout the islands appeared to float in space.

I hadn't yet reached gate 9 when it occurred to me that I might find Kate aboard the *Noble Lady*. I don't know if it was wishful thinking or a sense that something other than her pleasure had been left incomplete at lunchtime. I walked down the main ramp at gate 9. The entry gate was closed and latched, the plastic enclosure rolled down, when I'd left it up. I stuck my key into the door and unlocked it. For a moment, I stood just inside the galley.

"Kate, I'm glad you came back."

She called to me from the stateroom. "Damn." I thought I heard tearfulness in her voice.

"Are you all right?"

"No. I'm not."

"I'll be in there in a minute," I said.

"Charlie, don't turn on the lights, please. Just come in and hold me."

"Are you hurt?"

"No. Just come. I need you."

Orange light from the sodium lamps along the dock, filtered through the *Noble Lady*'s blinds, pointed my way through the galley and down the steps into the stateroom. Kate sat on the berth with her legs out and her back propped against the side wall of the boat. Outside light, peeking through a porthole, painted a wavy iridescent circle on the front of Kate's body over her heart.

I joined her on the bed. She grabbed my arm and leaned her head on my shoulder.

"What's the matter?"

"Work. The guard. Everything."

"What happened?"

"The new engineering officer of the *Etheridge* arrived today."

"And that's a bad thing?"

"In a manner of speaking, yes. His name is Christopher Stanwood III."

"A lieutenant?"

"Yes."

"I don't know him."

"I do," Kate said. "We graduated from the academy together."

"So you have a history with this Lieutenant Stanwood?"

"Yes."

"And may I assume that this history is as more than just classmates?"

"Yes, you may, and you would be correct."

"Is this the Chris that—"

"Yes, the Chris I was engaged to. The Chris who walked out on me after we'd set our wedding date and planned our honeymoon."

"And you would like me to go over to the *Etheridge* and give Lieutenant Stanwood a sound thrashing?"

Kate sniffled. "It's not funny. Really it's not."

"Tell me more."

"Captain Leighton took the *Etheridge*'s officers out to dinner at Boundary Bay Brewery to celebrate Chris's arrival. I joined them. Some of us walked back. Chris walked with me. We fell behind the others. We stopped and sat on a bench overlooking the bay. Chris apologized for his cruelty. He broke down crying, begging me for forgiveness. I told him how angry I was back then, how he'd crushed me by walking out on our relationship. He said he'd been in therapy for the last three years. I also told him that I was in a relationship with someone I loved deeply. He said he simply wanted to express his deep regret for hurting me, and if there was any way possible he wanted to be friends. Then I started crying."

"Because—?"

Kate sniffed back tears. "Even though it has been more than three years since Chris walked out on me, I finally heard from him the feelings I never heard when we were together. That made me feel both guilty and good."

"Good?"

"Because I deserved to hear them."

"Guilty?"

"Because Chris still has the power to evoke strong feelings in me, when I'm in a relationship with a man I love."

"And you believe only the person you love should have that power?"

"I may believe that but my emotions obviously believe something else, and for the next two weeks I have to work under Chris's supervision. I'm also scared."

"Of Chris?"

"No, of me. Scared that there are more unfinished feelings between us."

"He certainly left in such a way that would produce unfinished feelings. Should I be worried?"

"Are you?"

"At the moment I'm not because you're being very honest and everything you're saying seems very natural." I put my good arm around Kate and pulled her even closer. "I was married to a woman who left me prematurely when she died, remember? It took me more than five years, and meeting you, to come to terms with all the unfinished feelings I had for Sharon."

"God, the past can be a bitch."

"The past can be a bitch, but it doesn't have to be the basis for the future," I said.

Kate started crying softly. I kissed her on her forehead.

"Do you love me?" she asked.

"Yes."

"Will you hold me all night?"

"Yes."

Kate whispered in my ear. "Can we make love?"

"Yes."

She pulled me toward her and we kissed. Salt from her tears lingered on my lips.

KATE HEADED BACK for duty early the next morning and left me a note with Leighton's number. After a fruit and protein smoothie for breakfast, I called my former CO.

"Scuttlebutt was I'd be getting a call from an old friend, Commander," Leighton said. "You interested in a VIP tour of the USCGC *Etheridge?*"

"Yes, I am."

"Drive down to Fairhaven Dry Docks. When you get to the front gate call me again and I'll sign you in. Crews are everywhere working on the ship, so wear closed-toe shoes. We'll grab a hard hat for you when you get here."

Before leaving, I unraveled the spool of gauze on my ring finger. The flesh underneath my nail had turned an angry blue. I walked down into the head, grabbed a medicine kit, and replaced the gauze with a smaller adhesive bandage looped over the tip of my finger.

A crow perched atop a sailboat's mast cocked its head and eyed me as I walked by. At the bottom of the ramp, a mother goose gathered her goslings and hurried them off down a fairway as I approached. At the top of the ramp, I stopped to look back out over the water. Far in the distance, at the southern end of Bellingham Bay, flat calm water gave rise to dark green humps of islands. Beyond the islands, the pale blue morning sky had been painted with wispy strokes of orange and pink above the jagged dusky blue peaks of the Cascade Mountains. And even further away, the sharp silhouette of the Olympic Mountain Range cut a sawtooth pattern over the horizon.

Closer in, I could see Fairhaven on the other side of the bay. The *Etheridge* towered above the blond concrete walls of the dry dock. Her black smokestack aft stood in sharp contrast to her gleaming white hull. I couldn't see a cloud anywhere in the sky. The snowy dome of Mount Baker peeked over dark green foothills behind the city.

I set off and forty-five minutes later I neared the gates of the Fairhaven Dry Docks. I called Jeffrey Leighton, then walked through the first set of gates and over to the guard station. The guard, a burly guy with a no-nonsense stare, stepped out.

"You got a pass?" he asked.

"He does now," a voice behind me called out.

When I spun around to see Jeffrey Leighton, my mind instantly superimposed a fit young man with dark brown hair just the other side of regulation length atop the equally fit but graying figure walking toward me. Both had the same sparkle in their blue eyes, even if the crow's feet on one had clawed deeper. Jeff Leighton also now walked with a more pronounced limp. I seem to recall that Jeff favored khaki pants and a striped, open-collar shirt as an off-duty uniform, both of which he wore today.

He gave me a lazy salute, which I returned.

"You're looking well, Commander," Jeff said. "It seems like just yesterday that I welcomed you aboard a cutter in Miami." Jeff extended his hand toward me. I grasped it and we shook. Then we both clasped each other's forearm with our opposite hand and pulled ourselves in for a partial hug.

"Funny how memory eclipses time," I said.

"You're looking well, too." For a brief moment, Jeff stared at me with a faraway look. Then he snapped back.

"Memory eclipses time." He nodded. "Good turn of phrase, Commander."

"Jeff, I'm no longer in the guard. So unless you want me to call you 'sir,' you'll have to call me Charlie, not Commander."

"Roger that, Comm—" Jeff chuckled, "Charlie."

I stepped into the guard booth and signed my name on the entry roster. The guard sat on a stool with his legs propped against a wall reading a paperback. I twisted my head to see the wall clock next to him, then twisted back around and copied the time down. I also grabbed a yellow hard hat from a box of hard hats sitting by the door.

Without lifting his head from his book, the guard said, "Sign out when you leave." Jeff had already starting walking. I took a few hurried steps and joined him. The bow of the *Etheridge* rose like a steel mountain above us, the black numbers 715 painted on her white hull.

We reached the edge of the concrete canyon the *Etheridge* sat in, where the gangway led up to the main deck, and a stairway led down to the dry dock floor underneath the ship. I peeked over and down.

"Let's see. The *Etheridge* is a Hamilton-class High Endurance Cutter, 378 feet in length. Forty-three feet wide, weighing in close to 3,250 tons. Maybe sixty feet from the deck to the top of her aft tower, with a fifteen to eighteen-foot draft."

Jeff laughed. "Wow, time really hasn't eclipsed your memory, and she looks a whole lot bigger out of the watuh." The missing *r* replaced by a nasal *a* in Jeff's "water" reminded me that he came from Bedford, Massachusetts, and generations of seamen who'd bullied the British, harpooned whales, and commanded Coast Guard or Navy vessels since the early eighteen hundreds.

"Wanna peak under her skirt?" Jeff asked.

I grinned. "Sure do."

We took the wooden steps down. Above us, metal screeched beneath the high-pitched whine of drills and grinders. A blowtorch's hiss had me looking up to a cascade of sparks fluttering over the ship's railing then vanishing against the sunlight. I tapped my hard hat down onto my head.

Perched atop large wooden blocks, the *Etheridge* looked like a behemoth ballerina on point. Along either side of her keel, thin metal stands cradled the hull, like pairs of hands raised overhead, palms up. Thick cables trailed from her sides, steadying her in dry berth.

Jeff patted the hull. "When you're rolling in forty-foot seas, it's a comfort to remember what's underneath you."

"Even rolling in four-foot seas, it's a comfort to think about what's under me," I said.

"What is she?" Jeff asked.

"A Willard 36 Aft pilothouse."

"Classic," he nodded. "We always did have the same good taste in boats. I look forward to retirement. Susan loves boats, and we've agreed that we'll purchase a trawler and keep her out here. Cruise the Inside Passage during the summer." We walked aft, along the port side of the ship, stepping around one of the metal stands.

"Aren't you nearing the end of your command?"

Jeff stopped, and turned back to me, a look of surprise spread over his face. "That's what I liked and hated about you when you were my executive officer."

"What?"

"You always had such a goddamn good memory, and you acted like everyone else did, when in fact most didn't, especially me. We locked horns a couple of times because of it."

I chuckled. "You mean that time you thought we could take that cutter in closer to shore than I did. I insisted that the chart of the Keys showed an incorrect depth. I'd read it somewhere, maybe in a Notice to Mariners."

"You said, 'Sir, I believe we should anchor here.' And I said, 'Helmsman, take her in another hundred yards.' To which you jumped up from your seat and said, 'Begging your pardon, sir, but in a hundred yards we will hit bottom. Recommend that we come to full stop now.'"

"I guess I did say that, didn't I?"

"And a moment later the depth sounder warning went off. I yelled for 'All reverse full.' You'd just become my XO, and I was ready to read you the riot act for questioning my judgment. Hell, you saved my six, which is all a long-winded sailor's way of saying, yes, I leave command of the *Etheridge* at the end of the month."

"Will you miss her?"

"When I entered the guard, all I ever wanted to do was command a high endurance cutter. I did that for two years. Now it's someone else's turn at the helm." He nodded. "I'm ready to really go cruising."

"I know the feeling," I said. "It's actually harder living aboard a boat. I wake up each morning fighting the urge to cast off and head out to sea."

"I would have done the same thing," Jeff said.

"What? Fight the urge to cast off?"

He shook his head. "No, made the same decision you did to leave the guard."

"If I had to do it over, I would not have gone into Coast Guard Intelligence," I said. "It was always better for me at sea."

"The brightest and the best," Jeff said. "You wowed everyone back in D.C. with the way you outfoxed drug dealers while under my command. They thought a bright young officer under their direct command would make them look good. And I guess you did until one admiral's idea of looking good and your honor as an officer collided."

I laughed. "Did it ever collide."

"Like I said, I respect you for what you did and I would have done the same damn thing." A quarter of the way toward the stern we passed a gaping hole in the keel. "I don't know if it was deadhead or floating debris with metal in it," Jeff said. "But somehow we sucked something through the cage protecting our bow prop and damaged the blades. We pulled into dry dock so they could be repaired. And since we're on the hard we're taking care of some other maintenance needs." At the stern of the *Etheridge*, we stood beneath one of her two massive propellers, polished to look like huge shining, bronze four-leaf clovers sticking out from the end of gleaming stainless steel stems. We turned to walk back to the bow along the port side.

"A disabled sailboat drifted into Whiskey Gulf during your joint exercises," I said. "The couple aboard called in a Mayday. Canadian Coast Guard lost radio contact. Nothing's been heard from the *Rebecca Anne* since. Do you know what happened?"

Jeff's body went ramrod straight. He stopped, then turned to me. A steely look set into his eyes. "Commander, would you like to see the rest of my ship?" Before I could answer, he pivoted and walked away.

Chapter 4

THE HONEYCOMBED aluminum gangway swayed beneath us. I climbed behind Jeff to the main deck. At the top of the gangway, a boatswain's mate dressed in dark blue sucked in a breath and pulled a cord, ringing the ship's gong.

Ding-ding . . . Ding-ding.

The boatswain's mate sang out, "Attention, Captain arriving." But the *rat-tat-tat* of an air-driven wrench drowned out his words. The young man's heels clicked. He snapped to attention, offering Jeff a crisp salute, which he held until Jeff returned it.

"At ease, Johnson," Jeff said.

The young man smiled. "Welcome aboard, sir."

Jeff spoke over his shoulder. "Need I remind you to watch yourself stepping through doors and climbing ladders?"

"So noted," I said.

I gave extra attention to lifting my foot over the raised steel lip of a doorway just to one side of the boatswain's mate. Then I followed Jeff down a narrow passageway forward. Along the way, he tugged sharply on the long metal locking arms of the doors we encountered, before jerking the huge steel plates open. After stepping across each threshold, I turned to yank the doors closed behind me, then as if playing a succession of one-arm bandit slot machines, I pulled the locking arms over to dog the doors down. We climbed up several metal ladders with mesh treads before walking through a final doorway into the bridge.

Huge windows lined three sides of the cavernous command center. Video monitors dropped down from above the forward windows. A bank of radar screens and instruments sat atop metal consoles in the middle of the space. Instruments also crammed several cubbyholes off the main bridge. I looked for the ship's wheel but didn't see it. Then in the middle of the main instrument bank, I saw the small joystick that guided this giantess through the water.

Two lone chairs stood forward of the instruments, one far to port, the other far to starboard. I took the starboard chair. Out the window ahead, a long, thin, black cannon barrel stuck out from a large rounded white turret, pointing straight at a metal building onshore. Jeff walked over to the port chair, spun it to face him, climbed in, then spun around forward. He stared out the window.

"You're in my seat," Jeff said.

I swiveled around to face him.

"You would have made a good command officer."

"I'm sure I would have enjoyed it."

"I try to stay in my chair as much as I can when we're underway. I don't like to micromanage my crew. I lay out our objectives, and then let them sort out the best way to achieve them. Builds character, morale. Makes for good officers to follow after me."

"It's why I enjoyed serving under your command. Something out of the ordinary happened up north, didn't it?"

"Something out of the ordinary always happens when you're in command of a 378-foot ship with a crew of two hundred." Jeff tapped his thigh with his finger. "They called the mission 'Gulf Freedom.' The *Etheridge* was part of a Coast Guard task force practicing with our Canadian counterparts for deployment to the Gulf. Basically, the group will have ships from many countries, intercepting and inspecting tankers that move through the Gulf. A contingent of Bahraini naval personnel also accompanied us during the training.

"Personally, I'd prefer to conduct training exercises offshore, away from civilian populations and recreational traffic. Sure, we set out nets to catch the fish. The sea bottom in Whiskey Gulf is one huge mud field, which makes retrieving the bottom fish easy. But, damn, we've got nuclear subs in the area, and high-tech untested weapons systems being used for the first time. The idea of Jack and Jill out for a summer cruise in their fiberglass boat less than a mile from all of this firepower is frightening and sobering."

Jeff tapped his thigh faster.

"Something go wrong?" I asked.

"You investigating this sailboat's disappearance?"

"I am."

"I heard you were working as a P.I. It's a far cry from being an officer for Coast Guard Intelligence Service."

"Yes, but at CGIS I always worked for the chain of command. Now, I'm the only link in that chain. I get to call my own shots, to have my own successes and mistakes, and take responsibility for them. Couple on that boat belonged to the Kulshan Yacht Club here in Bellingham. Club asked me to investigate the incident."

Jeff took in a breath. "If a major incident happened between a civilian and a military vessel, don't you think the U.S. or Canadian governments would report it?"

"And what if an incident involving a small sailboat isn't considered major?"

"You're parsing words."

"And you're bullshitting me."

Jeff's jaw tightened. "No, I'm trying to navigate a course between my duty as an officer of the United States Coast Guard, and my admiration for a former officer who once served the guard well. I think you know all substantive communication about an operation is classified."

"An emergency call was taken by the Canadian Coast Guard from the *Rebecca Anne*. The vessel gave a GPS location within Whiskey Gulf. The call was handed over to Winchelsea Control, but radio contact was lost before Winchelsea Control could make contact. And the *Rebecca Anne* hasn't been heard from or seen since."

"You're the investigator," Jeff exhaled sharply. "Have you checked into the fundamental assumptions here? If all you have to go on is an emergency call, do you even know the vessel was stricken and that it was within Whiskey Gulf? What were the conditions the day the sailboat was lost?"

"Fog. Zero visibility."

Out the window, I watched a crane lift a large piece of equipment housed in a metal cage. It looked like the *Etheridge's* bow prop engine minus the propeller blades.

"Pea soup fog," Jeff said. "No planes or helos flying. Send out a patrol boat to the last known location and maybe the crew can't see anything. Perhaps radar shows several small targets in the area. No means of independent visual verification. How convenient."

"Convenient? For whom?"

The crane dropped the object into a crate on the back of a flatbed truck, and the truck drove off.

"Whoever wants the truth to remain hidden."

"And someone does?"

Jeff shook his head. "I don't know. But if someone did, the conditions were perfect that day."

"And you tried? You sent out a patrol boat to the *Rebecca Anne's* reported location?"

Jeff pursed his lips. "The operational details of a mission are classified." He stood up with his gaze still fixed somewhere out the window. He pivoted around without making eye contact. "Thought you might like to see our engine room. We've got a crew working on one of the diesels."

I'd forgotten the treachery of climbing down a ladder between the decks of a large cutter—the treads aren't more than a foot wide, and the angle of the ladder is nearly vertical. I started by facing forward and tried to place a foot on the tread of each step while holding onto the side rails, but I nearly tripped. Jeff had already scurried down ahead of me. I thought about turning around to climb down, before an old habit kicked in. Facing straight ahead, I pointed my foot down at forty-five degrees. Then I caught the leading edge of each tread in the middle of my sole and caught up to Jeff.

We walked quickly through a maze of passageways and doors, past a crew practicing with foam firefighting equipment, and another sorting through a mountain of paper charts. We passed the scullery, where a seaman lifted a door and pulled a tray of plates from the steamy jaws of a dishwashing machine. And when we entered the mess hall, the aroma of cooked tomatoes and melted cheese wafted my way, suggesting pizzas for lunch.

At the far end of the mess hall, we climbed down a few ladders further into the bowels of the *Etheridge*, then took a narrow catwalk between the four leviathans that powered the ship.

Jeff called out above the hum of machinery. "We're either going to repair or replace a water-cooling jacket in one of the diesel's cylinders."

We stepped over a metal bridge above the huge propeller shafts and entered the engineering control room where a group gathered around the main console. I didn't see Kate. Jeff walked over to a young officer in the middle of the group. He pulled him away from the console and toward me.

"Chris, I want you to meet Commander Charles Noble, retired. Commander Noble once served as my XO in District Seven." Jeff turned to me. "Lieutenant Stanwood is my new engineering officer. We just welcomed him aboard yesterday."

Lieutenant Christopher Stanwood III wiped his hand with a rag and reached out toward me. We shook. I'd call him a pretty boy, with his dark hair, dreamy hazel eyes, and cleft chin. And while I'm not accustomed to checking out men, I believe most women would consider him quite pleasing on their eyes. Stanwood made of point of allowing his handshake and his gaze to linger just a bit longer.

"Know much about Fairbanks-Morse opposed piston diesels and 707 jet engines, Commander?" Stanwood asked.

"You mean, the Hamilton-class CODOG system?" I said.

Stanwood's eyes flashed wide. He stepped back. "Sounds like you do know something about combined diesel or gas propulsion."

"Not as much as a good EO like you should know."

"Good?" Stanwood laughed. "Haven't been here long enough to get rated by most of the crew. One of the cylinders on the port diesel is overheating and we're concerned about a crack or some other problem with the water-cooling jacket."

He spoke with a hint of condescension and the practiced air of a patrician, which suggested that Stanwood might be a name affixed to the founding documents of this country.

"Mr. Stanwood, I just checked the—" Kate breezed into the engineering control room. She halted abruptly and her gaze ping-ponged between Stanwood and me. Her faced reddened. She also noticed Jeff standing behind me. Her hand flew up into a smart salute.

"Pardon me, sir," she said.

Jeff saluted her. "As you were, Lieutenant." He turned to me. "Commander Noble, I'd like you to meet Lieutenant Katherine Sullivan, on loan to us from Station Bellingham while we're in for repairs."

Kate reached out to shake my hand.

Stanwood chuckled. He pointed back and forth between Kate and me. "I believe you two know each other already."

"It's a small Coast Guard community up here," Kate said.

"Lieutenant Sullivan is a fine engineering officer," Jeff said. "She helped the previous EO track down the overheating problem."

Kate looked at me and I read in her eyes the not-so-cryptic message, What the hell's going on here?

"In fact," Stanwood said, "I'd like to convince the captain to ask Station Bellingham to loan us Lieutenant Sullivan for an extended period of time. I'd like to see her as part of my crew as we take the *Etheridge* over to the Gulf. Given her talents and abilities, I think a long deployment would be great for her. Don't you agree, Commander?"

So much for the reformed bad boy.

"I'm sure Lieutenant Sullivan has a very good sense of where her talents and abilities are most needed," I said.

I stared at Stanwood without flinching. He grinned. Kate steamed. Jeff seemed clueless.

Kate turned to Stanwood. She barked, "I need to recheck the valve clearances on that cylinder." Then, turning to me, "Nice to see you in engineering, Commander." Finally, she saluted Jeff. "By your leave, sir."

He returned the salute and Kate stepped quickly from the engineering control room.

"Carry on, Mr. Stanwood," Jeff said.

Jeff pivoted and walked out of the control room. Standing on the catwalk between the diesels, he stopped and turned to me.

"Did I miss something in there?"

"Lieutenant Sullivan and I have been dating for the better part of two years," I said. "Lieutenant Stanwood's an ex who left her at the altar some years back."

Jeff chuckled. "His poor decision, your good one. Congratulations. She sure seems like one hell of a woman. But as far as requesting her transfer, the lieutenant's way out of line. The *Etheridge*'s a warship not a buddy-boat. Seems I need to have a man-to-man with my new EO soon."

We threaded our way back through the labyrinth of passageways, doors, and ladders to the main deck exit. The boatswain's mate came to attention as we stepped out. Jeff walked over to a railing and leaned both elbows on it. He bent over and propped his chin on his hands, folded in a prayerful position.

"What do the Canadians have to say about the sailboat?" he asked.

"Haven't asked them."

"Maybe you should."

"Maybe I will."

Jeff stood up from the railing, and reached out to shake my hand.

"Thank you for visiting the *Etheridge* during the last weeks of my command."

Jeff saluted me briefly, though he didn't wait for my salute before dropping his hand, then disappearing through a massive steel door.

LATER THAT EVENING, I sat in bed, reading the latest issue of *PassageMaker* magazine. A feature article titled "Navigating Through Fear" caught my attention, in part because Eugene Wendell had written it. I recognized him as the African American author living aboard his boat at gate 6. I'd met him a number of times around town. I liked what he said in the article, that admitting fear is a first step in managing it. The more you keep it in, the more control it has over you.

The *Noble Lady* rolled slightly to starboard. I checked the clock. At this hour it'd better be Kate. A key scraped into the cylinder of the cabin door's lock. The door opened, then slammed against the outside of the boat, then slammed closed with a loud thud. Kate marched into the stateroom. I looked up from my magazine.

"Were you checking up on me today?" she asked.

"What?"

"What the hell were you doing in engineering? And what was all that male head-butting about?"

"I called Jeff Leighton to visit the *Etheridge*. We walked around the ship and I asked him about the sailboat that disappeared in Whiskey Gulf. He took me on a tour and insisted that I see the engineering section. He introduced me to Chris."

"Oh." She looked away. "Are you jealous?"

"No."

"Then why'd you get into that verbal scuffle with Chris about my career?" She patted her chest. "I'm not some object for the two of you to toss between you like a football."

I narrowed my eyes. "He started it."

"That's not what Chris said. He said you were rude to him before

I entered the control room. Are you concerned about me being around him?"

I set the magazine down on my lap. "I wasn't until you burst in here on the attack. Are you okay?"

Kate sat on the edge of the bed. "No. I'm confused."

"About?"

"Chris."

"Uh-huh."

Kate rubbed her forehead. "He said he wanted to be friends, and then this evening, when I got back to Station Bellingham, a bouquet of roses was waiting for me. I smiled thinking that you'd sent them, but Chris had sent them. He called me and apologized for what happened in the control room. Then he said he hadn't been completely truthful. He still had strong feelings for me, and wanted another chance."

"And you told him—?"

"That I was in a relationship with someone I loved."

"And he said?"

"He wasn't giving up on winning me back."

"And that's why you're confused?"

"No. I'm confused about why Chris's come back into my life at a time when I love being with you, and I'm confused by all the conflicting emotions that have suddenly emerged as a result."

"Did you ever stop loving Chris?"

"I tried calling him, writing him. I tried to see him. But he managed an assignment in Asia and I never got the chance to tell him how much I'd loved him and how much I'd been hurt by his leaving me."

"Did you ever stop loving him?"

Kate bit her lip. "I don't know."

"Was another woman involved with Chris leaving you?"

"He now says there wasn't, but I've always wondered if there was."

"And in regard to us, is there anything you need to say or do?"

"No . . . Yes . . . I mean . . . Damn, not at this time." Kate pounded the bed. "I feel so goddamn guilty about everything. About the way I'm treating you. About the feelings that have come up since Chris reappeared. Hell, I've got to work around him for the next two weeks." Then instantly, her eyes welled up, and she burst into tears. "I've got to go. I'm sorry. I've got to go. I love you, but I can't stay." She shook her head, bit her lip, trying to fight back tears. "I don't feel good enough about myself to stay."

She stood, then like a tempest, swept out of the boat as fast as she'd swept in. I sighed, then picked up my magazine and continued to read about how one navigates through fear.

Chapter 5

AT FIVE-THIRTY the follow morning, I stood outside on the observation deck of the ferry *Queen of New Westminster* as she sliced through the dark green waters of the Strait of Georgia, bound for Nanaimo from Tsawwassen, British Columbia. Early morning sun rising in the distance off her port side framed snowcapped Mount Baker in a golden orb. To starboard, north along the Inside Passage, the morning light slowly revealed the separation of sea and sky. Straight ahead, the mussel-shell blue silhouettes of islands hovered, superimposed on the rough-hewn, mountainous body of Vancouver Island.

This beauty all-around notwithstanding, it challenged me to ride the ferry, which made this forty-mile crossing in a mere two hours. Traversing a body of water that I knew so well from more intimate slower speeds left me feeling guilty, as though I'd crossed paths with a former lover and only managed a weak hello. I needed more, needed to feel the ocean under the keel of my boat, to grasp the wheel and sense the fiberglass and metal as extensions of my own body, to feel my vulnerability when a wave picked up the boat and tossed her about like a child's toy.

An hour into the passage, I sauntered back inside for some coffee.

I took a cup with me to the newsstand, where I purchased the *Vancouver Sun*. I folded the paper under my arm and found a seat in the forward cabin. Sipping coffee and staring out the window, I laughed at two harbor seals splashing in the water far below. They stopped to watch the ferry pass, curiosity filling their monkeylike faces. I raised my cup to my lips and opened the newspaper, but a headline at the bottom of page one nearly had me choking on my next sip: ENGULFED IN MYSTERY: SAILBOAT DISAPPEARS IN WHISKEY GULF. After the byline and the Who-what-when-where-why opening, the article continued,

> The disabled and distressed American sailboat with the couple aboard drifted into Whiskey Gulf. Comox Coast Guard radio originally handled the distress call. But contact was lost after turning the call over to Winchelsea Control, which coordinates military activity in Whiskey Gulf. Neither the sailboat nor the couple have been seen or heard from since. What happened in Whiskey Gulf? And why aren't Canadian or American authorities being more forthcoming about the sailboat's fate?

The article, written by a reporter named Maya Shimazu, went on to publish a transcript of Comox Coast Guard Radio's contact with the *Rebecca Anne*. Reading through the call, my heart went out to the controller, who sounded so professional despite his obvious frustration at being unable to raise the couple on VHF again.

The transcript also confirmed that the Kinsleys were indeed experienced sailors. Rebecca spoke calmly and with precision, even as her awareness of their danger grew. Furthermore, Winchelsea Control had transferred the call to the Joint Operations Commander. I rushed through the remainder of the article. Apparently, Maya Shimazu hadn't discovered the Joint Ops Commander either.

But the United States military loathes the idea of another country having any control of its forces, which would argue for an American serving as the JOCO. I didn't see an admiral making his way up here just to coordinate a training exercise, and that meant the CO of the largest vessel most likely took the command. At 378 feet, that pointed to the *Etheridge* and Jeffrey Leighton. I took another sip of coffee. So Jeff had actually told me in the only language he could that he'd sent out a search and rescue team and apparently they came up empty.

Two hours later, I drove off the ferry at Duke Point, and headed north past Nanaimo for the one-hour drive to Comox and the Comox Marine Communication and Traffic Safety Center on the Canadian Forces Base Comox. I'd visited CFB Comox several times while in the guard. My then Canadian counterpart, John Driggs, still held his position as an intelligence officer at the base. I parked my car outside the entryway guard station, and waited for Driggs to meet me with his car.

Two MPs cradling rifles stood in front of a long yellow and white hinged metal arm that blocked the entrance to the base. Behind the guards a woman stuck her head from a glass kiosk, checking the ID of entering vessels. Between the guards, a uniformed officer argued with a young Asian woman. And behind the young woman, a small group of protesters paraded in a tight circle carrying signs that read, "Nukes Out of Nanoose Bay," "Take the Nuclear Noose Away from Nanoose," and "Tell the U.S. to Eat Sushi. Don't Let Them Nuke Our Salmon." I chuckled. I like protesters with a sense of humor.

The young woman arguing with the officer wouldn't relent. He walked away. She craned her neck forward and yelled. At a distance, I couldn't make out what she said, but it got his attention, though. He pivoted, pointed his finger at her, and scowled, at which time she raised a camera to her eye. The officer rushed toward the barrier. The young woman backed away. He stopped just short of jumping over. The two armed guards exchanged glances and a few words with the officer before he walked away. The guards remained stone-faced, at attention.

The young woman spoke briefly with one of the protesters, then continued walking toward a car several spaces down from me. A decal on the side of the car read *Vancouver Sun*. I hopped out of my car and walked over to meet the young woman. She stood about five feet five and wore blue jeans and a white sweatshirt. Silver earrings with ebony and ivory carvings of the yin-yang symbol dangled from beneath her short-cropped black hair, which curled around behind her ears. In all, she had the look of an Asian pixie.

I took a chance. "Are you Maya Shimazu?"

She reared back and squinted. "And you are? . . ."

I held up my hand. "An American investigating the disappearance of the *Rebecca Anne*."

Words left her mouth with a staccato pace. "You mean because Americans were lost at sea something finally happened here in Canada that caught the attention of the American press? Who do you work for?" She laughed disdainfully.

"I don't," I said. "I'm an investigator, not a reporter."

She cut her laugh short, and stared at me with intense dark eyes. "Military intelligence?"

I chuckled. "No. A private investigator hired by friends of the Kinsleys to find out what happened." I saw Driggs pull his car up next to mine. I dug in my pocket for a business card, then handed it to Maya Shimazu. "Call me soon," I said. "I'll drive up to Vancouver to meet with you."

Maya didn't say anything. She looked at me quizzically. But at least she took my card. I walked back over to Driggs's car and got into the front passenger seat. The guards raised the yellow and white barrier, and the woman in the kiosk waved us through.

"She's a firebrand all right," Driggs said.

"Who, that reporter?"

"Maya Shimazu, Investigative journalist, *Vancouver Sun*. Covers mid Vancouver Island. Political beat. Government corruption. Scandals. She did a couple of articles on the environmentalists protesting the presence of U.S. nuclear subs in Nanoose Bay and Whiskey Gulf. Now she thinks she's onto something big with this missing American sailboat. Probably hopes to break a story like what happened in

Hawaii when the USS *Greeneville* blew her main ballast and struck that Japanese fishing vessel, the *Ehime-maru*."

"Could that have happened in Whiskey Gulf?"

Driggs shook his head. "No. The range is small and tightly controlled."

"Were subs operating the day the sailboat went missing?"

Driggs frowned, rippling the sea of freckles that dotted his face. "Better ask the Yanks that question, Commander. You know the drill. I can't discuss operational details of exercises in Whiskey Gulf." Then he smiled. His red hair and mustache lent him a disarming boyish quality. "Don McCaffrey was the watch supervisor. He also handled the call. I'm sure he'll be glad to talk with you."

"What do you think happened?"

Driggs smoothed out his mustache. He slowed down, then stopped in front of the Comox Marine Communication and Traffic Services building. He let his head fall back softly against the head restraint.

"I think we've been snookered by a very smart couple in some kind of trouble who needed to disappear. They let their friends go south ahead of them. They probably went north. They knew that Comox Coast Guard Radio covered a wide area and called in reporting a false emergency and an incorrect location. Maybe they scuttled the boat and took a dinghy into shore. By now, they've probably left the country and are sitting on a beach in Mexico or the South Pacific, drinking piña coladas."

"Yeah, but you could have easily triangulated their position to find out if they were telling the truth about being in Whiskey Gulf."

"Ask Don. I don't believe they did."

We both got out of the car and inhaled the sharp sweet smell of cedar. Before entering the building, I peered out from the high sandstone bluff we stood on. The Comox MCTS station had a commanding southeast view of the central Strait of Georgia. Boulders littered the sun-spangled emerald water nearly a mile out from the base of the bluff. Beyond the boulders, a line of three red buoys bobbed, marking the narrow course across the infamous Comox Bar. On the other side of the bar, sand built gradually into a spit, which became tiny Sandy Island, adorned in its middle with a tuft of trees. Looking further south, the island bodies of Denman and Hornby lay together like two outstretched fingers separated by slender Lambert Channel.

I turned back to the MCTS building, where Driggs stood holding the door open. Inside, a mass of frigid air met me. We climbed a staircase to the second floor. Then we slipped into a conference room with a highly lacquered wooden table and a wall of windows that framed picture-postcard views east to Lasqueti and Texada islands, and beyond to the snowy tips of the mainland British Columbia coastal range.

I'd just taken a seat when the door opened and a tall, gaunt man entered.

"Don McCaffrey," he said.

We shook hands.

"Charlie Noble," I said.

"Charlie Noble?"

The corners of Don's lips curled up in an all-knowing smile. It happens in a tiny fraction of the general population, and only in about ten percent of boaters I meet. I smiled, in part because this recognition usually meant I'd just met someone who loved boats and the lore of the sea as much as me.

"My dad cooked on a merchant vessel and named me for the galley stovepipe on a ship."

"All these years I've known you, I didn't realize that," Driggs said.

"I read the *Sun's* transcript of the emergency call you took from the *Rebecca Anne*," I said. "Was that the entire call?"

"Every word," McCaffrey said.

"How'd Maya Shimazu get it?" I asked.

"SOS, the environmental group she often reports on, continuously monitors our calls," McCaffrey said. "They'd—"

"SOS?" I asked.

"Save Our Strait," Driggs said.

McCaffrey continued. "As I was saying, SOS would love nothing better than to catch us in an emergency involving Whiskey Gulf, which proves their point."

"Which is?" I asked.

"That Whiskey Gulf is an accident waiting to happen," McCaffrey said.

"So they record an emergency call from a sailboat that drifts into Whiskey Gulf and pass along the recording to Maya Shimazu," I said. "She investigates and tries to find out what happened to the missing sailboat."

"And her reports grip British Columbia for several weeks. Sells a lot of papers."

"If that emergency really happened," Driggs said.

"You're not convinced, are you?" McCaffrey said to Driggs.

"Are you?" I asked McCaffrey.

"I've worked calls for almost twenty years. I've run that call over and over in my mind for more than two weeks. Today I'm sure it was a genuine emergency. Tomorrow I'll be convinced it wasn't. The woman I spoke with was calm and collected. Maybe too calm, too collected. She gave GPS coordinates, which placed the boat in Whiskey Gulf."

"Which could have been faked," Driggs said.

"Yes, they could have," McCaffrey said.

"Did you triangulate her signal?" I asked.

McCaffrey sighed. "I was about to do that, but when I realized they could actually be in Whiskey Gulf it seemed most prudent to let Winchelsea Control take over. We lost contact after that so we couldn't triangulate the call. But it came in from somewhere below Chatham Point. That much I'm sure of, because of which antenna showed the highest signal strength."

"Have either of you listened to the ship-to-ship and ship-to-shore communication tapes from the joint exercise right after contact with the *Rebecca Anne* was lost?"

McCaffrey shook his head. "Out of my league."

Driggs chuckled.

"That mean you have?" I asked.

"That's a security matter, which I can't confirm or deny," he said.

McCaffrey pounded the table. Driggs flinched. "Hell, John, a damn sailboat's been lost with two people aboard. Winchelsea Control should at least release the tapes for us here at MCTS to review."

"Yeah, and start an international incident between Canada and the United States," Driggs said. He turned to me.

"Charlie, you know what goes on behind the scenes. Washington pays Canada for the use of the Whiskey Gulf and then demands total control. Those tapes have communication Washington would consider a matter of national security, especially since the *Etheridge* was entertaining a group of dignitaries from Bahrain who'd come to marvel at American naval weaponry. The U.S. is probably pissed as hell that the transcripts of the MCTS call were published in the *Sun*." McCaffrey rolled his eyes.

"One thing in those transcripts bothers me," I said. "The caller reported taking on water and thought they'd hit some kind of obstruction. That area is well charted. It stretches my imagination to believe there are any uncharted rocks out there."

"Yeah, I've thought about that, too," Driggs said. "Possibly in the fog, they could have gotten too close to one of the Ballenas Islands and hit a rock there. But from where they called that would have meant they'd drifted for several hours."

"My thoughts exactly, and that's hard to understand because if I hit something, lost my engine, and started taking on water, I'd radio Mayday immediately," I said.

"Unless they hit a floating obstruction out in open seas," McCaffrey said.

"Zero visibility. No wind," I said. "You're a deep draft forty-foot sailboat motoring. Even if you could drive the boat at hull speed, the most you'd expect is eight knots. But it's zero visibility. Any experienced mariner would keep a constant lookout and go dead slow. So let's give them six knots. They can't put a hole in their hull by striking a floating object at that speed. It's too slow."

"Unless it was a widow maker," McCaffrey said.

"A widow maker?" I asked.

"A huge deadhead, maybe a log the tide's lifted off the beach. The weight, the water saturation, the action of the current, sucks the log deep under the water. It's like a slingshot pulled back. Get that coming up at you, and it'll put a hole in your boat. Just like a torpedo," McCaffrey said.

Driggs's jaw flexed as I scribbled down *widow maker.* "There's one other thing I wanted to ask about," I said. "So far no one's mentioned the P word." Driggs frowned.

McCaffrey shrugged, "Piracy? I hadn't thought about that, but I suppose it's a possibility." He nodded. "We've had some incidents over the years. Armed robbery against pleasure boats for sure. We get a handful of those each year. But outright piracy where you board a boat and steal it? Kill the couple and throw their bodies overboard? Seems unlikely. That said, we do have a file of missing vessels marked, 'Unsolved.'"

I also jotted down *unsolved* and stood up to leave. "Thanks for your help," I said to McCaffrey.

"Say, if you do discover what happened to the *Rebecca Anne* and her crew, will you let me know?" McCaffrey asked. "This incident has really bothered me."

"I will," I said.

John Driggs drove me back to my car. The protesters had left the guard station. Before stepping from John's car, I turned to him, "What's the chance of me talking with Winchelsea Control about this incident?"

"Zero," Driggs said.

I nodded. "You know it really pisses me off being around people who know more than they're willing to tell."

Driggs laughed. "Weren't you once an intelligence officer, Commander? And isn't that the definition of the job?"

I shook my head and stepped out of his car. I fumbled in my pocket for my car keys, and hit my finger in the process. It stung, and when I pulled the keys out I noticed blood seeping through the bandage on my finger. I reached into my pocket this time with only my thumb and index finger, pinching my cell phone between them to get it out. I turned it on, and my screen showed a call had come through while I sat talking with Driggs and McCaffrey.

I checked my recent call list. The call came from a Canadian number I didn't recognize. I opened the door and sat behind the wheel. After a few moments, I called the number.

"Hello."

I recognized Maya Shimazu's voice.

"Mr. Noble, debris from the *Rebecca Anne* may have been found."

Chapter 6

I AGREED TO MEET Maya Shimazu in Comox Harbor, a deep hole within a vast shallow mud flat. I got there early and ordered a grilled salmon burger and fries to go from a pub just up from the harbor. Wooden timbers creaked beneath me as I ambled along the harbor's elevated boardwalk, carrying my lunch to a bench with a panoramic view across the flats of a powder-blue sky, meeting the snowy white mountaintops of Vancouver Island.

I'd nearly finished my burger when a small burgundy and white boat with a large outboard engine threw a huge rooster tail as it rounded Goose Spit, then settled down entering the harbor and gliding to a stop at the front of a long finger pier. The boat had a small inflatable dinghy tied upside down on its roof. The skipper shoehorned her smartly into a tight space between two larger fishing boats. I let out a little chuckle when Maya Shimazu stepped away from the helm, jumped off, tied up the boat, and marched up the dock.

I walked toward her. When she saw me, she waved.

"Where'd you find debris from the *Rebecca Anne*?" I asked.

She frowned while shaking her head. "Rather not talk about it here. Why don't we go down to my boat?"

I grabbed what remained of my burger and chips, and followed Maya Shimazu down the ramp.

I stopped before going aboard. "Twenty-five-foot C-Dory with a 200-horsepower Honda four-stroke."

Maya nodded. "You know boats, eh?"

"Yours?" I asked.

She shook her head. "With that 200 Honda, I couldn't afford it. Can you believe the paper actually bought it so I can run down stories out in the islands? Best of all, they pay for gas. It's got a full galley, enclosed head, diesel stove that's also a heater, a v-berth that's plenty large for someone as small as me. With my laptop and a wireless Internet connection I can work from just about anywhere. I have an apartment in Vancouver, but this time of year"—she pointed across the flats to the mountains—"I'd much rather stay out here on the *Samurai Princess*." She pointed to the boat's name emblazoned across the transom in black and gold letters with an Oriental-style font.

Maya stepped aboard. I ducked under the door frame and into the cabin. I took a seat at the small galley table. She sat at the helm and swiveled around to face me.

"Tell me more about the debris from the *Rebecca Anne*."

She sighed. "Truth is I'm actually not certain what we found is from the *Rebecca Anne*."

I slapped the table. Maya flinched. "Then why'd you waste my time and lie to me?"

I winced. My injured finger stung.

"I didn't lie. And you'll have to decide if meeting me here was a waste of your time."

She hopped down from the helm, reached into the v-berth, and pulled out two jagged pieces of fiberglass, each about three feet long and two feet wide. She held up one for me to see.

I shrugged my shoulders. "That could be from any boat."

"Floating around near the Ballenas Islands?"

"Who found it?"

"SOS—"

"The group Save Our Strait?"

"An American who knows something about the world north of the border. What a rarity. SOS members around Whiskey Gulf regularly monitor beaches and near coastal waters looking for anything out of the ordinary that might suggest an incident has taken place and gone unreported. SOS has found stranded whales and dolphins washed up ashore, schools of dead fish, large oil slicks, military debris, even errant torpedoes that have run aground."

"Proof of sinister activity in Whiskey Gulf?"

"No, but the sightings appear to increase when Whiskey Gulf is active or when American nuclear subs pass through Nanoose Bay. Today, a group monitoring the waters near the Ballenas Islands found floating chunks of fiberglass tangled in seaweed. I got the call right after I ran into you at CFB Comox. The SOS team said they thought they sighted more, but they had to return to Parksville, so they couldn't continue their search."

"More debris? Where?"

"Around the Ballenas Islands." Maya pointed beyond the harbor. "Care to have a look with me, Mr. Noble? I'll have you out there and back in no time."

Maya stepped to the helm and I stepped from the cabin to untie the *Samurai Princess*. When I pushed her away from the dock, she glided like a feather over water, and I had to leap aboard before Maya left the harbor without me.

We rounded the breakwater and Maya slowly brought the *Samurai Princess* up to speed. By the time we reached Goose Spit, we threw a rooster tail behind us almost as high as the boat. Maya carved a deep turn to port and headed us over the Comox Bar. Just past the red spar buoy, she peeled away to starboard, veering off the designated route followed by most boaters. Our GPS read twenty-five knots. I stood behind Maya, holding on to an overhead stainless steel bar.

"I take it you have local knowledge?"

She raised her voice above the roar of the engine and the slap of the hull on the water. "Been this way many times."

Goose Spit receded quickly from view. Maya made a sweeping turn to starboard that headed us down the Strait of Georgia, whipping past Denman and Hornby islands to our right and Lasqueti Island to our left, with barely enough time for me to recall memories of being any of these places at slower speeds. And, while cruising the Strait of Georgia just a foot or two above the water at twenty-five knots certainly made for an intimate, intense voyage—unlike taking the ferry—traveling at these speeds smacked me as an over-the-water quickie.

The bump of the Ballenas Islands rose rapidly on the southern horizon. From our approach, this island group appeared as one. I punched in WX on Maya's VHF radio and twirled the volume knob up a half-turn. Environment Canada's forecast called for heavy fog north of Nanaimo in the late afternoon. At the end of the forecast came a warning: "Whiskey Gulf is active today from 0600 to 1800 with surface, subsurface, and air-launched torpedo fire. Area Whiskey Gulf is considered extremely hazardous and all mariners are advised to stay well clear. Any mariners with concerns contact the Range Control Officer, Winchelsea Control, channel ten."

I turned the radio down and back to channel 16. Maya stared intently at the water straight ahead. She had no choice. Hitting even the smallest log at twenty-five knots could result in the biggest disaster. She called out without turning. "Ballenas. You know what the word means?"

"I don't."

"From the Spanish *ballena* for whale," she said. "The first Spanish mariners probably encountered a pod of orcas here."

As Maya swung the *Samurai Princess* east around the northern tip of North Ballenas Island, I thought of Raven. "And the native name for the islands?"

"My friend, Huntington Tommy, a Nanoose elder, tells me they are called *tiqw*." The word left her lips with a short guttural plosive. "But I'm sure I'm not pronouncing it right."

She eased the throttle back and gentled the C-Dory through a low-speed starboard turn into the eastern opening between the islands.

"Which means?"

She pointed ahead to an islet blocking the western entrance. "Tight."

I chuckled. "A canoe would have difficulty entering that way."

"In heavy fog, even the entrance we came through would feel tight."

The channel between the islands enlarged to a wider bay formed by the south portion of North Ballenas Island, the north portion of South Ballenas Island, and the whole of West Ballenas Island. Maya drove the *Samurai Princess* in close to the sandy beach on the south side of the bay. She cut the engine, then flipped a switch to raise it. After that, she stepped outside, and shuffled along the narrow side deck, moving hand over hand with the help of the stainless steel railing affixed to the boat's roof. When she got to the bow, she pulled a small anchor from its chocks, and tossed it overboard. First came a *kerplunk*, then a splash, then she let out about thirty feet of rope. She shuffled back to the cockpit, stopping to untie the dinghy from the railing on that side before moving to untie it on the other.

I stepped out from the cabin and into Maya's command.

"Haul the dinghy back, then let the stern fall down into the cockpit."

I hauled.

"Then, push the bow over the side but make sure you hold on to the painter."

I pushed. But I jammed my injured finger into the dinghy while pushing. I winced.

"You okay?" Maya asked.

She left the dinghy perching precariously atop the boat's side rail, and reached quickly for my hand.

"Looks nasty," she said. "It's bleeding through. Got a first-aid kit inside. I'll get the dinghy into the water, then find a bandage."

She took the painter, then positioned her hip midway along the inflatable's side and bumped it overboard. I teased the bloodstained bandage from my finger. She tied the painter to a cleat, then stepped back inside the cabin, emerging with a first-aid tin and two oars.

"Hold your finger out," Maya said.

She unwrapped a small adhesive bandage, held my hand, and gently fitted the bandage over the tip of my ring finger. The warmth of her touch and the softness of her skin lingered.

Maya climbed over the side and into the dinghy, locking the oars in place. I followed, taking the small seat at the bow as she rowed us to shore.

We pulled the dinghy up the gravel beach and tied it off to the end of a driftwood limb. I walked left, Maya right. I headed inland to the high-water mark, kicking through seaweed as I went. I stooped for a white object amidst a clump of partially dried seaweed, which turned out to be a plastic yogurt container. Further along, I picked up a clear plastic bag with half a banana floating in salt water. I emptied out the water. The gravel beach ended at a tree-topped rock wall. I spun around and headed back toward the dinghy, carrying the plastic bag with the banana and container inside.

Maya shook her head as she approached. I pointed to North Ballenas Island.

"Based on the orientation of this bay, we might have better luck over there."

An apparition of fog trailed us across the narrow channel. Fifty yards offshore from North Ballenas Island, a floating patch of brown seaweed held a jagged white object. I pointed to starboard. Maya veered that way. I scooped the piece of fiberglass from its nest, then inspected it in light now dimmed and diffused by fog. A layer of fiberglass weave showed through a hardened shell of epoxy on one side. And on the other side a layer of white gel coat gleamed, untarnished by exposure to the sun or the sea. I ran my fingers over its rough edges, frayed with strands of fiberglass hanging out.

"Something?" Maya asked.

"Something, but exactly what and from where I'm not sure."

"Let me pull in to shore," she said.

I pointed to the mist now swirling around the *Samurai Princess*. "Fog's rolling in. We should cruise instead of anchoring. See if we can spot any more debris from the dinghy."

I got Maya to row the dinghy in a search pattern parallel to the shore, beginning fifty yards out, then moving ten yards in with each pass. The fog continued to thicken. We came across several more pieces of fiberglass, all showing similar patterns of construction and destruction to the first. Above its frayed edge, one chunk did have a line of dark blue paint. When I scratched the paint with my fingernail, it flaked off in a way that hinted it may have been a layer of bottom paint. Another fiberglass fragment displayed brown stains that reminded me of explosive burn marks.

After our last pass, Maya rowed us back to the *Samurai Princess*. We threw the fiberglass pieces into the cabin and hoisted the dinghy onto the top deck. Then she weighed anchor and headed us out from the bay.

At the opening into the channel between the islands, Maya started to turn north toward Comox, hesitated, turned slightly south, then hesitated again. She shifted into neutral.

"Two-mile visibility and dropping," I said.

"I've got radar, GPS, and a good radio. Thought maybe we should scoot outside of South Ballenas."

I checked my watch.

"Whiskey Gulf's still active for almost three hours."

"There is a safe corridor," she said.

"One thousand yards offshore from Ballenas?"

"Yes. I can set the radar to one mile, and we can stay within the second range ring from the island."

"Fog's rolling in fast."

Maya draped her arms over the black leather steering wheel, and rested her chin on them. She twisted back toward me. Her dark brown eyes sparkled. "We've come a long way to turn back now."

"Eighth of a mile rings?"

"Yes."

"A thousand yards is about a half-mile, which gives us a quarter-mile cushion." I held up a finger. "One pass west. Another back east. Then we're outta here."

She smiled. "Deal."

Maya eased the shifter forward and we nudged along the South Ballenas coastline until making our turn east. Fog had now reduced visibility to less than a mile. I stepped beside her and counted green range rings on the radar screen. The beginnings of a knot tightened my stomach. Traveling this corridor between Whiskey Gulf and South Ballenas Island in the fog didn't offer much comfort with surface, subsurface, and air-launched torpedoes less than a thousand yards away.

On our first pass, Maya brought us close by the rocky southern shore of South Ballenas Island. We saw nothing, then turned 180 degrees and moved about one hundred yards offshore. Through the fog, South Ballenas now looked like a dark silhouette lit from behind a white curtain. We hadn't gone far when I grabbed binoculars from the galley table and peered out the window behind Maya.

I pointed. "There. Fifty yards to starboard. Seagulls can't sit on water."

Maya slowed the boat down. She put her forehead to the window, and shielded her eyes from the diffusion of light created by the fog. "Looks like a log with birds."

"Look closer."

I handed her the glasses. She raised them briefly, then thrust them back at me. She spun the wheel and gunned the engine momentarily. The seagulls paced nervously before screaming at us, then flying off. We circled the log. It had trapped a fishing net, and within that net lay the largest piece of fiberglass we'd seen today.

Something had broken apart out here.

I stepped outside the cabin and slid the boat hook from its holder. Slowly, Maya edged us closer to the log. I stretched out and snagged a burl with the hook. A healthy tug pulled the log closer to the boat, but it also pulled the light boat much faster toward the log. Our hull thumped against it and Maya shut down the engine. I reached down and grasped the section of fiberglass, which on the inside looked like the others. Then I flipped it over to examine the gel coat.

"You might want to see this," I said.

Maya pushed open the cabin door. I held the fiberglass while she ran a finger over the remaining spots of paint on the smooth gel coat surface.

"Whiskey-November-7-7-2-5-6-Xray-Bravo," she said. "Look like that to you?"

I nodded. "It does."

"What do you want to bet that's the registration number of the *Rebecca Anne?*"

"Fiberglass hull. Washington registration number. Debris drifting just beyond Whiskey Gulf. I'd be hard pressed to find a simpler explanation."

I set the fiberglass piece inside the cabin next to the others. Maya turned 360 degrees in the cockpit, staring into a dense fog that had now enveloped us in near white-out conditions.

"Time to head home," she said.

"Roger that."

She ducked inside the cabin. I dug into the floating log with the boat hook, then pushed hard. Maya waited until we'd glided well away from the log before starting her engine. But she hadn't yet shifted into gear when a sharp whooshing sound rose then fell out of the fog and a ripple raced through the water thirty yards off our starboard side.

I yanked the cabin door open. "You see that?"

"No. What?"

"Whatever raced by the boat just under the water about thirty yards to starboard."

"Dolphin?"

"Never saw a dorsal fin."

"Could be a boat's wake moving through the water."

She shifted into gear, then held down an arrow key until a glowing green line on the radar screen aligned with the glowing green eastern tip of South Ballenas Island. She moved us slowly along that line.

A few minutes later, another *whoosh* came from our left and a rippled trail of water uncovered from the fog, racing ahead to cross twenty yards in front of our bow before making a sharp turn to starboard and disappearing into the whiteness around us.

Maya screamed. "No!"

She slammed her fist into the wheel. I shook my head in disbelief.

Maya's voice quivered. "Oh my god, that was a torpedo."

Chapter 7

MAYA LUNGED FOR MY ARM and pulled me closer to her trembling body. She shifted the engine out of gear. My thoughts raced.

Head back to the log and drift with it? What if the log's been targeted? Head into the closest part of South Ballenas Island? What if someone's tracking and firing at a moving target? Wait. I checked the radar range rings. Then I ripped the VHF mike from its holder and jabbed a button repeatedly until the LED channel selector read 10.

I fired off words. "Winchelsea Control. Winchelsea Control. Winchelsea Control. This is the motor vessel *Samurai Princess*."

The controller spoke slowly and calmly. "*Samurai Princess*, this is Winchelsea Control channel one-zero."

But my speech did not slow to match his. "Winchelsea Control. We are a twenty-five-foot vessel with an outboard"—I checked radar again, then did a quick mental computation—"about three hundred yards offshore. We have witnessed two torpedoes moving in the water less than fifty yards from our position."

"*Samurai Princess*, copy. Can you report your present location from GPS?"

Maya pointed to the black-on-white numbers in the small GPS screen.

"Winchelsea Control, Four, niner, point three, three. North. One, two, four, point one, four. West."

"*Samurai Princess*, copy. Please confirm. Forty-nine decimal thirty-three degrees, north. One hundred twenty-four decimal fourteen degrees, west."

"Winchelsea Control, roger your last."

"Sir, those coordinates place you well within the thousand-yard 'safe transit' corridor. Suggest you may have seen a surface anomaly. Perhaps a boat wake."

"Winchelsea Control, sir, this is Lieutenant Commander Charles Noble, retired, United States Coast Guard, aboard the *Samurai Princess* with extensive experience on torpedo-launch vessels."

Maya's eyes grew big.

"Sir, those were two fish in the water, not surface anomalies."

"Roger, Commander. Checking with the Range Control Officer."

Maya whispered indignantly. "You didn't tell me you were Coast Guard."

I placed my hand over the mike. "*Was* Coast Guard."

"Still, you didn't tell me."

"Does it matter right now?"

"Commander Noble, the Range Control Officer reports no errant torpedoes from any surface, subsurface, or air-launched sources presently in range. Requesting you switch to channel twenty-two alpha and report in to Comox Coast Guard. Comox Coast Guard has been alerted and will track your progress to port. Winchelsea Control out."

Static crackled.

"Break. *Samurai Princess*, Comox Coast Guard. Switch and answer channel twenty-two alpha. That's twenty-two in the USA mode."

I reached for the button but Maya beat me to it. She punched it until the VHF display read 22A.

"Comox Coast Guard, *Samurai Princess* answering on twenty-two alpha."

"Commander Noble, this is Don McCaffrey from the Comox Ops Center. Understand you just ran into some unexpected turbulence near area WG. What's your current destination, Commander?"

I looked at Maya but spoke to Don. "Comox."

Maya nodded.

"*Samurai Princess*, roger. Assuming you do have radar and GPS, Commander, with all this fog, any chance of me talking you into diverting to Nanaimo? It's only ten miles away, not forty."

I looked at Maya again. She sucked in a breath, hesitated, then nodded.

"Comox Coast Guard, *Samurai Princess*. Don, we do have radar and GPS and the *Samurai Princess* will divert to Nanaimo."

"*Samurai Princess*, roger. Commander, requesting you report in on twenty-two alpha at the Horswell Channel light, then again past Departure Bay at the yellow channel light near the entrance to Newcastle Channel, with a final report when you are at anchor or in port."

"Comox Coast Guard, roger. Reporting in at Horswell Channel light, yellow entrance light at Newcastle Channel, then at anchor or in port."

"*Samurai Princess*, roger. Commander, Vessel Traffic Services, channel eleven, will advise of any opposing traffic into Nanaimo. Comox Coast Guard Radio out, standing by channels one-six and twenty-two alpha."

"*Samurai Princess* out, switching to channel one-one."

With the VTS channel selected, I hung up the mike.

"Is your GPS also a chart plotter?" I asked Maya.

"You seem too young and too smart to be retired from the Coast Guard," she said. "I'm guessing there's much more of a story behind it."

"And you're too young and too smart to spend your days running around in a small craft through these islands," I said. "I'm guessing there's much more of a story there as well."

"Touché." She nodded, then let out a short laugh.

I laid in a course on the GPS while Maya piloted the *Samurai Princess* at a much slower speed in the thick fog. After calling in to Comox Coast Guard at Horswell Channel, Vessel Traffic Services put the ferry *Queen of Victoria* ten minutes out from Departure Bay. So we turned to starboard, toward Departure Bay, but held up near Jesse Island while a huge green blip glided by on our radar.

One half-hour later, having called Comox Coast Guard Radio twice more, the *Samurai Princess* bobbed at anchor in the fog of Mark Bay off Newcastle Island. Maya rummaged through her small refrigerator.

"After today, I need a beer. How about you?"

"I do."

"Only have Guinness."

"Sold."

She handed me the cold can of Guinness and she didn't bother with glasses. She took a long swallow, then sighed.

"My v-berth's made for two. You can spend the night if you want. I've got an extra sleeping bag. I'll run you back up to Comox in the morning. Or I can call my friend on the island who'll drive you up to Comox tonight. You can take the passenger taxi from Newcastle Island over to Nanaimo to meet him."

I raised the can of Guinness to my lips. After a swig I pulled it away. "Or we can go over to Protection Island Pub by dinghy and discuss it over dinner."

Maya swallowed another mouthful. "Roger your last."

So we hauled down the dinghy and wove our way through fog around boats at anchor until we came to the dock in front of the Protection Island Pub, less than a half-mile away. We swung open the pub's door to the sounds of sea shanties sung by a couple on stage. An older, plump bearded man squeezed the bellows and pressed the keys of a concertina, while his slender female companion strummed a mandolin. They sang the tale of an Irish fisherman who went to sea one foggy morning, never to be seen again.

I ordered a crab cake dinner, Maya the baked black cod. Before our dinners arrived, we raised glasses of merlot to toast our escape from Whiskey Gulf.

"You believe the range control officer?" she asked.

"That they had no errant torpedoes? Yeah, he could have been telling the truth. What if those fish were exactly where they were meant to be?"

"Outside of Whiskey Gulf? How would they reclaim them? Thought there was a net stretched between buoys they fired the torpedoes at, and robotic submersibles that pull the fish from the area's soft bottom after they fall? So where were those fish headed?"

She swirled her wineglass, then sipped from it.

I stared into the middle of my glass, and for a moment my thoughts drifted to Adam Webster, head of the Naval Underseas Weapons Engineering Station in Keyport, Washington. Then I raised my head. "I don't know why those fish ran near us. I don't know where they came from, where they were headed, or why. But I intend to find out."

"From whom?"

"My sources."

Maya laughed. "Two investigators." She shook her head. "We're more alike than I first realized. So do you also have sources that can analyze the fiberglass we recovered?"

"I do."

"And considering that we were both nearly killed by the same torpedoes, will you share the conclusions of your sources with me?"

"I will, if you will find out what vessels were active in Whiskey Gulf today."

"I don't know if my sources will be able to reveal that information."

"I'm sure you'll manage to persuade them."

Our waiter, who could have passed for the male singer's twin brother, set our plates down before us. Maya flaked off a piece of cod, then hesitated with her fork in midair.

"Do you really think that sailboat was struck by a torpedo and sunk and the incident covered up by our governments?" She slipped the cod into her mouth and swallowed.

I broke off a piece of crab cake, then swished it around in the sweet spicy sauce that came in a small bowl. "There's a preponderance of circumstantial and physical evidence to suggest that."

She smiled. "Are you married?"

"You have just changed the subject."

"Yes, I have," she said.

I shook my head. "No, but in a relationship."

"What's her name?"

"Kate. And you?"

"My fiancé is named Roger, and he's who I will call if you need a ride back to Comox tonight. Though he would need to drive up from Duncan. And I would very much appreciate it if you stayed aboard tonight." Maya stabbed a baby carrot with her fork. "As much as I love spending time alone on the *Princess*, I'm feeling rattled after our near miss today."

I washed down a mouthful of crab cake and rice with another sip of wine. I tapped my foot to the rhythm of the couple on stage, who sang a rollicking ditty about a formidable woman who lived along the Welsh coast and rowed to the rescue of her husband and his crew, caught on their whaler in a gale.

Maya turned toward the performers. My gaze drifted over the flesh of her neck, glowing golden in the pub's soft lights. It wandered further down her body. My pulse quickened. For a brief moment, I took the measure of two people brought together by circumstance, then bonded by a shared close call with death. I weighed that part of me obviously attracted to Maya Shimazu against the part of me surprised, even a little hurt, by Kate's strong emotional response to Christopher Stanwood III. When Maya turned back toward me, the soft gaze in her eyes had me wondering if she'd not made similar emotional calculations.

"Duncan's a long drive," I said. "Would Roger be upset if I stayed?"

She shrugged her shoulders. "I don't know. It's not a bridge we've crossed before. And Kate?"

"I would need to call her and find out."

"Roger deserves a call, too."

"Perhaps we should wait until we're back on the *Princess*, or, hearing the reverie of this pub, our partners may have less sympathy for our predicament."

Maya laughed. "Roger that."

When we finished our meal, I paid the bill. Maya left a ten in a bucket at the feet of the performers. Then we made the short dinghy ride back to the *Samurai Princess*.

KATE'S VOICE ROSE. "Lemme get this. You're on a small boat anchored in Mark Bay about to slip into the v-berth with another woman? This *is* one of those conversations I need to sit down for. Give me a moment . . . Okay, now I'm sitting. And you are sure this predicament you are in with this woman has nothing to do with the sudden appearance of one Christopher Stanwood III in my life and my resultant emotional turmoil?"

I stood outside in the cockpit of the *Samurai Princess*, gazing at the lights of Nanaimo shining through the thinning fog. "Maya Shimazu is an investigative reporter for the *Vancouver Sun*. She invited me out in her boat to look for debris from the wreckage of the *Rebecca Anne*."

"All of which sounds perfectly reasonable. Did you find any debris?"

"We did, including a piece that may contain the *Rebecca Anne's* registration number."

"It sounds like you and Maya had a successful day. Does the debris provide you with a clue to what happened?"

"At the moment it only offers more questions, but after we recovered the last piece of debris, two torpedoes nearly missed our boat."

"And you were outside the boundaries of Whiskey Gulf?"

"Clearly, though we were in heavy fog."

Kate sighed. "It stretches my credulity to believe that someone would fire a torpedo at a small boat. But, the *Rebecca Anne* suddenly disappeared in Whiskey Gulf, and I don't believe for a moment that you would lie. In fact, the torpedo is far more alarming than this woman you are about to sleep with. Charlie, what the hell have you gotten yourself into?"

I cleared my throat. "As I recall, it was you who suggested it would be less than noble of me to turn down the request from the Kulshan Yacht Club to investigate the couple's disappearance."

Kate sighed again. "And I may live to regret that I did. How many sleeping bags are aboard Maya's boat?"

"Two."

"And you will sleep in yours, and she in hers?"

"We will."

"And your zippers will be zippered up?"

I laughed. "All of them."

Kate laughed, too. "Maya sounds like someone I would enjoy getting to know. I trust you, you know that, but we do need to talk."

"Yes we do, but not now."

Kate sighed. "I feel terrible that I'm grappling with my unruly emotions while you're dodging torpedoes in Whiskey Gulf."

Chapter 8

ROGER PACED THE DOCK as Maya and I pulled into Comox early the following morning. He stood about my height but slimmer. He had long shaggy dark hair that fell below his ears and gave him the look of a rock star. But a pen clipped to his shirt pocket and a thick book under his arm suggested an engineer. Then, again, the suntan line on his arms above the cut of his short sleeves argued for someone who spent time outdoors.

Roger sized me up with a handshake. I asked about his drive north. He laughed and told me he'd come in his floatplane, hoping to capture Maya for few days and whisk her off to a remote inlet near Tofino along the west coast of Vancouver Island. So much for telling a rock star by his cover.

Maya and Roger strolled off arm in arm to breakfast, while I headed over to my car. All I remember about my night on the *Samurai Princess* was waking up to the sounds of Maya interrogating another woman in her dreams, asking where this woman had met me and how long we had been together. I shook Maya to wake her so we could both get back to sleep. Funny, when I told her about the incident as we cruised up from Nanaimo this morning she didn't remember any of it. But she did remember waking me up in the middle of the night while I was talking to myself, though she graciously declined to tell me what I'd said.

AFTER CROSSING THE BORDER, I stopped at the *Noble Lady* for a shower, a shave, and lunch. Then I hopped back in my car and drove an hour and a half south to Edmonds, Washington, where I waited forty minutes for a ferry to Kingston. While en route to Edmonds, I called Adam Webster. We'd only spoken a few times since Sharon's death, though we'd spent four years together at the academy.

In chemistry lab, Adam was the cadet who concocted the mixtures that exploded, while the rest of us struggled simply for ours to change colors. And when most cadets put together FM radio receivers from off-the-shelf kits for an electronics project, Adam constructed a home-brew transceiver that he mounted on a remote-controlled helicopter and connected to two small infrared cameras. He launched his surveillance helos at night, and flew them past the open windows of the dorms at the women's college across the road, while we gathered around his video monitor to watch.

So when most of our class trundled off to sea, the navy swooped up our nerdy classmate and bundled him off to Boston for advanced degrees in chemistry and guidance control systems from MIT. Still, the one thing I knew Adam and I had in common was a love of boats. Adam profusely expressed his excitement to show me his latest, moored at the Bainbridge Island Marina and Yacht Club.

Getting off the ferry, I ran into rush hour and casino traffic on my way south to Bainbridge Island. Adam, still in a white lab coat, stepped from his vehicle when I pulled into the marina parking lot. Once a tall lanky kid with wire-rim glasses and an unruly mop of dark brown hair, Adam was now a tall, lanky man with wire-rim glasses and a bald spot in the middle of his dark brown and graying hair. We shook hands, and we were about to hug when Adam realized he still had on his lab coat. He wriggled out of the coat, balled it up, and backed away from me, motioning with one hand for me to stay put. He pointed his remote-control entry device at a dark blue SUV with plain white government plates, clicked it, then scurried over to the vehicle, threw his labcoat in, and scurried back to me for a hug. Adam had not been the most graceful social creature at the academy, and that hadn't changed.

"You wanna grab something to eat first?" Adam asked.

"Dinner here at the marina sounds good."

"I was thinking about getting sandwiches and chips from the health food store, then bringing them back down to the boat."

I chuckled to myself. A lot about Adam hadn't changed over the years.

We took my car to the health food store and returned forty-five minutes later carrying thin, white recyclable plastic sacks filled with two bags of multigrain chips, four natural sodas, three tofu sandwiches, and one turkey sandwich for me. Planning ahead for lunch until the end of the week is how Adam described our shopping junket.

His electronic passkey unlocked the gate above the slips. We walked down a metal gangway banked steeply on the low tide. From the other side of the harbor, a ferry's deep-throated horn announced its departure for Seattle.

Judging by first impressions, you'd expect a slightly goofy guy like Adam to have a slightly goofy boat. But when we stopped in front of the *Sisyus*, my heart skipped a beat. I ran my hand over her hull and looked up.

"Forty-eight-foot custom steel pilothouse trawler," I said.

"Fifty feet. Steel."

"Single diesel."

"Gardner 6XLB. One twenty-seven horsepower, capable of a hand-crank start."

"Stop, you're killing me. Get-home engine?"

"Hydraulic from a PTO off the main or the generators."

I set my plastic bag on the dock box in front of the boat.

"Martec folding prop on the get-home?"

"What else but?"

"Bow thruster?"

"Also hydraulic."

"Way cool." I walked the length of the boat. "Paravanes. A crow's nest. A sat phone. What'd I forget? Oh, yes, what's *Sisyus* mean?"

Adam smiled. "Smart."

"As in smart guy?"

He shook his head. "As in smart boat. Wait till you get inside. You'll see what I mean."

I followed Adam up the portable steps from the dock and through a sliding pilothouse door. The first thing I noticed was the sparseness of the helm. No wheel. No instrument panel. No coiled radio cords. Just a small joystick in front of a comfortable tan leather chair, and next to the joystick a wheel about six inches in diameter with a handle protruding from its rim.

Adam sat silently on the pilothouse bench behind me while I stared at the small wheel. My mind clicked through a boat's system. Then I snapped my fingers, and pointed to the small wheel.

"A Hundested variable pitched prop."

Adam bounced from his seat, jumped up and down. "Damn, Charlie, you're good. You damn sure know boats. One other main piece of equipment you missed, but you'd never know that without diving the boat. She's also got a nine-inch drop-down side-scanning sonar."

I turned my palms up. "But where's the radar, GPS, radios—where are the other instruments and electronics?"

Adam smirked again. "Place your hand down in the open space beside the joystick."

I did. Motors whirred softly. A slot several inches wide and several feet long opened up behind the joystick, from which three wide consoles rose, transforming the pilothouse of this custom-built steel trawler into the command bridge of a starship. The screen came alive with the flash of computer-drawn dials, gauges, and meters. Then a sultry semirobotic, otherworldly female voice with amplified rever-beration spoke through speakers embedded in the middle monitor.

"Hi, my name is Voz. I see you are not Commander Webster. Would you like a 3-D tour of my ship?"

I shook my head. "Voz? Adam, you've got to be kidding?"

He laughed. "Vessel Operations and Zonal Guidance Control. VOZ. IBM plus 12. HAL plus 13. Inside joke for us geeks and for fans of Arthur C. Clarke. I borrowed the voice technology from a sys-tem in my government-issue SUV."

"Voice that reminds you to close a door or put out your lights?"

Adam smiled. "Yep. We modified the voice transformation algo-rithm to make it more sexy. Works, don't you think?"

"If you go for that sort of thing."

"There's a built-in biometric palm reader in that sensor, so Voz knows if it's me at the helm. I segmented the boat's systems into dif-ferent zones of control. A close-quarter zone, a middle-range zone, long-distance zone. Then I modified some of the guidance algorithms we use at the lab to allow for complete hands-off operation of the vessel. You should see it in the close-quarter zone. I mounted sensi-tive, small radar units at the stern and the bow. All I have to do is tell Voz, 'Leave the harbor.' She'll factor wind and current into her com-putations and come up with the optimum procedure for exiting from any slip."

"But doesn't that take the fun out of operating a boat?" I asked.

Adam shot me a quizzical look. "I rarely use it."

"Then why go to all the trouble?"

"Because it could be done and no one had done it."

I shook my head, but then remembered a classmate who bragged about a low-tech approach he'd perfected, which bested Adam's night-flying infrared helicopter runs. He told Adam to have his helicopter follow him one night. We watched from Adam's monitor as this fel-low broke the academy's curfew, climbed a fence, tiptoed across the road, climbed another fence, then tiptoed across the women's cam-pus to the senior dorm. After he jimmied a door lock, we lost sight of him. Then, a few minutes later Adam's infrared cameras picked him up waving a young woman's panties while lying with her in her bed. We howled, but Adam never fully appreciated the significance of this young man's low-tech genius.

Adam and I walked down the teak steps from the pilothouse into the galley, and spread our sandwiches and chips on the table. I took a seat across from him.

"A torpedo's dropped from a plane or launched from a boat," I began.

Adam moved to the edge of his seat and leaned my way.

I continued. "It's programmed to find a target. It's outfitted with radar, sonar, GPS, and other vessel tracking systems connected to a sophisticated computer. Once it hits the water it can be left to its own devices to find the target or remotely controlled from a distant command station, like a Predator drone. Basically, it acts like a smart remote-operated vessel with a deadly payload."

Adam took a bite of his sandwich and a sip of soda. He popped a chip in his mouth and smiled. "Raytheon Mark 60. Only the list of capabilities you omitted is rather large: like the Mark 60 has special algorithms for detecting the underwater vibration signature of every vessel type known to man. It uses underwater laser radar. A target can be painted from the surface or the air once the torpedo's underway, and it will seek it out. It can return to a launch vessel safely if it should miss its target. And on and on. And, oh, yes, it's COTS."

"COTS?"

"Built with technology that's commercial off-the-shelf."

"Meaning I could buy the components from Radio Shack?"

He laughed. "Not quite, but something like that. But the Mark 60 is already old-school. Not even classified. They run about a million and a half, and were already selling contracts for them on the arms market. My lab's begun working with Raytheon on the next generation."

"Selling contracts for them? So, the Mark 60's not been deployed yet?"

"It's in final testing as far as I know. Why?"

"I may have run into one on the water up north."

Adam started to take a bite then pulled the sandwich from his mouth. "Where?"

"Whiskey Gulf."

"Once they leave my lab, that's where they go for on-the-water testing."

I took a sip of soda. "Any problems with the onboard guidance systems?"

Adam shook his head, held up a hand. "Charlie, I've said too much already. You know the answer to that question is classified."

"What I know is that a disabled sailboat entered Whiskey Gulf about three weeks ago, and it hasn't been heard from since."

Adam's arm trembled. He shrugged his shoulders. "Could have been anything. Hit a rock. Electrical fire. Propane tank explosion."

"No it couldn't have been anything, Adam. I read the Canadian Coast Guard communication log with the boat. It entered Whiskey Gulf in the fog after losing its engine, then communication with the vessel was lost. Yesterday, I was near Whiskey Gulf, also in the fog, and found fiberglass debris that appears to be from an explosion. I haven't had the fiberglass pieces analyzed yet, but I'm willing to bet they're from whatever tore that vessel apart. Then, yesterday, as I was leaving the area, not one, but two, torpedoes crossed my path. One swerved as though someone were driving it around a racetrack."

Adam placed his sandwich down, and sucked in breath. "Fog? You said the vessel entered Whiskey Gulf in fog, and you were near the test range in fog? Heavy fog?"

"Yes."

He folded both arms on the table and rested his forehead between them. He spoke into the table, muting his voice. "Heavy fog can cause GPS multipath propagation errors, and if the receiver's underwater, the chances of such multipath propagation increases. I'm not saying that's what happened, but multipath propagation is a plausible explanation for an errant torpedo."

I tamped the air down with my hand. "Can you explain multipath propagation errors in language I can understand?"

Adam lifted his head, then pulled his can of soda closer. He raised his sandwich from the white wrapping paper it was sitting on, and held it above the table. "GPS satellites transmit signals that are received by a GPS receiver unit aboard your boat." He drew a line in the air from the sandwich to the soda can.

"As long as a satellite's signal travels in a direct path straight to the receiver's antenna, your GPS unit can locate its position anywhere on the earth's surface." He pushed the soda can to a different location on the table and drew invisible lines from the sandwich there.

"But let's say something gets in the way of that signal." He crumpled the white sandwich paper with his other hand, then lifted it into the air between the sandwich and the can. "Now the satellite signal will be reflected." He bounced his finger off the edges of the crumpled paper, then ran them down to the can. "It may take longer to reach the antenna or the signal may reach the antenna with a distorted shape. Almost always it will be superimposed on other signals reaching the antenna directly and correctly. So your boat's GPS unit is then receiving two signals. One direct and undistorted. The other reflected and distorted in space or in time. Hence the name multipath. Multipath signals cause incorrect calculations of position and of speed."

He set his sandwich on the table and rested his head on his arms again.

"So heavy fog can distort a GPS signal?"

He mumbled into his arms. "So can water."

"So, you're saying that a torpedo being guided by GPS can run into several multipath problems?"

"Yes. But we've developed ways to deal with the distortion from multipath signals." Adam nodded. "Special antennae on the fish. Use of the Wide Area Augmentation System to enhance the signal accuracy. Error-correcting algorithms."

I hit the table with my fist. The soda cans jumped. Adam flinched but he did not raise his head.

"Developed but not perfected?" I asked.

He sighed.

I raised my voice. "Adam, are Mark 60s using inadequate methods of correcting for multipath propagation errors in fog?"

He still said nothing.

I yelled, "Adam?!"

He finally raised his head, shaking it.

He whispered forlornly, "Charlie, you should leave now."

Chapter 9

I DROVE NORTH from Bainbridge Island to a motel near the ferry. The following morning I parked my car in the long ferry lineup and had breakfast at a small restaurant above the ferry landing. After breakfast, while waiting for the seven-fifty sailing, I pulled the sheet music for Lady Hundson's Alman from the backseat, and propped it on the steering wheel. I pushed my seat back and hummed to myself while fingering my classical air guitar. As I plucked the invisible strings, I realized that my injured finger no longer bled.

Errant torpedoes are not simply the stuff of movies. Twenty-five years ago, when the Coast Guard retrofitted larger vessels like the *Etheridge* with antisubmarine capabilities, fleet officers learned the history and the dangers of going to sea with faulty and sometimes unpredictable fish. In 1944, the USS *Tang* launched a torpedo at a Japanese target. That torpedo circled back to strike the *Tang*. In 1954, five torpedoes from the facility where Adam Webster now worked crashed harmlessly into a Bainbridge Island beach. A naval board of investigation voted a faulty torpedo as the most likely cause of the 1968 sinking of the USS *Scorpion*. The Russian navy concluded that the 2000 sinking of its nuclear sub *Kursk* resulted from one of the *Kursk's* own torpedoes. A torpedo fired from a Taiwanese sub in 2003 went amok during a training exercise causing surface ships to scatter and the submarine to dive. And unexploded torpedoes are routinely found from warfare dating back nearly one hundred years. So why not an errant torpedo in Whiskey Gulf three weeks ago? And why cover it up?

The large green and white ferry *Walla Walla* left Kingston just before eight. After driving off at Edmonds, I pulled into a city park, pulled out my cell phone, and called Bellingham Detective Sergeant Ben Conrad. I got Ben in his car.

"Heading out to meth country to bust a lab along with ATF, DHS, FBI. Usual alphabet soup of agencies. I got about ten minutes to get there. Whaddya got?"

"Vessel registration number. Need the name and owner in a hurry."

"And you happen to know that I've got a computer in my car that connects me directly to the vehicle and vessel registration database?"

"Didn't know that."

"Give me the number."

"Shouldn't you pull over?"

"Computer's also got voice software. I speak to it, it speaks back to me. Hell, if you spoke loud enough I could probably just hold my damn cell phone up to the mike and let you speak directly with the computer. Anyway, shoot."

"W-N-7-7-2-5-6-X-B."

Ben repeated the number for his computer.

"Just be a moment . . . Here it is."

But only a garbled mechanical voice came through our cell phone connection.

"You get that?"

"No."

"Damn computer. Anyway, it said the registration number is associated with a vessel named the *Rebecca Anne* . . . Hey, is that the same boat Canadian Coast Guard's issued a warning about for the past several weeks?"

"Uh-huh."

"Janet and I went over to Sucia this weekend. Heard the broadcast all day long. Didn't the couple belong to the Kulshan Yacht Club?"

"Uh-huh."

"Lemme guess. Club hired you to investigate?"

"Uh-huh."

"Been out on a boat to inspect the site?"

"Uh-huh."

"Just what I thought. You get to run out to the islands, while I get to run out to the county to bust a meth lab."

"You wanna trade jobs?"

"I don't know, do I?"

"No."

"I'll remember that when I'm busting down the door of this lab."

AROUND ELEVEN, I exited I-5 north of Bellingham and drove east on a winding two-lane road. Several minutes later, I entered farmland cleared for miles leading up to the foothills of the Cascades. Behind the hills Mount Baker towered like a protective parent. I slowed down and scanned mailboxes until I came to one that read Morgenthaler. Then I took the next turn onto a dirt road, and after working my way up a slight rise and through a stand of cedar and fir trees, I came to a white, two-story farmhouse.

Richard Morgenthaler had run a shipyard on Bellingham Bay, until its recent collapse after more than fifty years in operation. Padden Creek Shipyard had built venerable Uniflite pleasure boats and the PBR gunboats that once patrolled the river deltas of Vietnam. The yard had also maintained and repaired generations of fishing vessels and pleasure craft. I'd hauled the *Noble Lady* out at Padden Creek several times. Renowned for his fiberglass knowledge, Morgenthaler was flown in as a consultant to yards from around the world after Padden Creek closed. If anyone could tell me what Maya Shimazu and I had found near Whiskey Gulf, Rick Morgenthaler could.

With a few of the larger fiberglass pieces tucked under my arm, I walked up to the farmhouse door and knocked. The scent of freshly turned earth surrounded me. From high in the trees, a Swainson's thrush serenaded me with its cascading, fluted song. Sarah, Richard's wife, opened the door. I'd only met her once before. She wore a paint-stained smock and had her graying brown hair tied into a bun at the back of her head. Her high, round cheekbones rose even higher into a smile.

"Hi," she said. "You're . . ." She placed a finger to the side of her head. "Noble . . . Charlie Noble. You came dressed as a one-eyed pirate to our Halloween Party last year with your partner . . ." She placed a finger to her head again, then pulled it away and snapped it. Sarah laughed. "Kate. Oh yes, I remember. She had on a skimpy bikini with skull and crossbones tattoos covering whatever the bikini missed."

I laughed. "Good memory. Is Richard home?"

She pointed to an outbuilding. "Middle one's his workshop."

A rust-colored Chesapeake retriever waddled out from the space between the door. Sarah reached down to catch it, but the moment she did the dog scampered over to me and rubbed against my legs.

"Transom," she said, "get back here."

I reached down to pet Transom, then started walking toward Rick's workshop.

Sarah yelled, "Transom!"

Transom shot Sarah a lazy glance over his shoulder, then bounded toward the door of Rick's workshop. I knocked on the door. Rick opened it, releasing a cloying smell of fiberglass and resin. He was wearing a gray and black respirator mask over his mouth and clear plastic goggles over his eyes. Transom barked at the sight. Rick opened the door a little wider, then slipped out. He pulled the door shut before stripping off his mask and goggles. The goggles left circular impressions atop the network of fine lines that radiated from the corners of his eyes, and the mask left long crisscrossed stripes on his stubbly cheeks where he'd pulled the straps tight. Transom barked again, and Rick kneeled down to pet him.

"Commander, to what do I owe the pleasure of this visit?"

He rose and pressed his fleshy palm into mine.

"Charlie, please," I said. "I've got a question that only Dr. Fiberglass can answer."

He smiled. "I'd invite you into my shop, but I'm testing out a new combination of epoxy and matt sent to me by a manufacturer. I've got the exhaust fans going. It's pretty toxic in there right now. Whaddya got?"

I handed the fiberglass fragments to Rick. He shuffled through them, turning them over. Then he whistled low.

"Late model sailboat?"

I smiled. "Uh-huh."

"What the hell happened to her? She crash into the rocks?"

"That's what I need you to tell me," I said.

"Ah. That should be easy enough." He pointed back to the workshop. "Let the fans clear things out in there and I'll have a closer look with my scope." He checked his watch. "Have you had lunch?"

"I haven't."

"Well, let's set a table for three and eat first."

Transom barked.

"Sorry, Transom. Of course, I meant a table for four."

Transom barked twice again.

"That'll give the fans plenty of time to clear out the fumes."

Sarah opened the farmhouse door, now in a long denim skirt and short-sleeve flowered blouse. She'd let down her hair and it fell to her shoulders, giving her the hint of an aging flower child. But then, Rick's graying hair tied into a frizzy ponytail and his prominent paunch gave him that aging-hippie look as well.

Sarah served bean curd, mushrooms, and water chestnuts in a black bean sauce over rice noodles, topped with bamboo shoots and a side of steamed bok choy. Transom curled next to Rick's chair, occasionally raising his head to snap up a water chestnut from Rick's hand.

"I lived with Richard in China for more than a year while he consulted at plants there." She winked. "He brought back fiberglass samples. I brought back recipes."

"And this one's a winner," I said. "Kate would love it."

After lunch, Rick pushed back from the table, grabbed the two fiberglass pieces, and disappeared from the house with Transom in tow. Sarah stood, scooped Rick's dishes from the table, then walked over to dump them in the sink. She came back for mine.

"Do you need some help?" I asked.

She smiled. "Rinse or load?"

"Load."

I stepped up beside her.

"How's Kate?" Sarah asked. She handed me a soapy plate.

"In a strange place."

"How's that?"

"An old beau who left her at the altar just resurfaced."

"And he's still interested."

"Uh-huh."

"Men." Sarah thrust a glass at me. "They don't get it."

"Lemme guess," she went on, "she doesn't want to be with him because she loves you, but seeing this jerk brought up all sorts of feelings for her, which makes it hard for her to be with you."

"Women," I said. "Do you all read from the same playbook?"

Sarah laughed. A moment later the telephone rang. She handed me a glass, and then wiped her hands on a towel. She took two steps to a desk in a nook beside the refrigerator, then lifted the receiver from the hook.

"He's here," she said. She handed the receiver to me.

"I need some questions answered," Rick said. His voice shook with the words.

I put down the receiver and headed for the workshop. To the east, beyond Rick's farm, sunlight painted the foothills a luminous green.

But clouds formed a dark backdrop behind Mount Baker, and shaded the mountain steel gray. I scanned the sky for a rainbow, then twisted the handle on Rick's shop door. A sickly sweet scent of fiberglass and resin still hung in the air. Rick stood up from a microscope. Transom barked, then rose from beneath Rick's chair. Rick lifted a fiberglass piece from his scope and waved it at me.

"You mind telling me what the hell this is?"

"All I know is that it appears to be from a boat that reported hitting something in the Strait of Georgia."

Rick laughed caustically. "Like hell it did."

"Whaddya mean?"

He shook his head. "If it hit something I'd see entry damage. Like a bullet entering a body, the impact of an object on fiberglass distorts the fibers and gel coat in a characteristic way. This is more like an exit wound. Like something exploded from inside the boat. Or . . ."

"Or what?"

He threw up his hands. "I've fired guns at fiberglass many times to see what would happen. Only a high velocity projectile could distort these fibers this way. A deadhead or even a rock wouldn't do it. Unless the boat was traveling at a hundred knots, or maybe thrown against a rock or deadhead in gale-force seas. Do you know anything about the conditions that caused this damage? Is that what we're looking at here? Boat caught in a severe storm?"

"Zero visibility. Heavy fog. No winds."

Rick shook his head. "No way. Can't be. A large, high-velocity projectile went through this fiberglass."

"You're sure?"

"I am."

"Absolutely sure?"

"Yep." He waved the fiberglass piece at me. "Where in the strait did this happen?"

I sucked in breath, then spoke slowly, "Whiskey Gulf."

Rick's jaw dropped. His eyes flashed wide. He stared at me without speaking. Finally, Transom's bark broke the silence between us.

"I'm not sure I want to know anything more," Rick said.

"Might be better if you didn't."

I scooped the large shard of fiberglass from Rick's table.

"Commander, whatever you've sailed into, I hope you'll be careful."

"Thanks for your help," I said.

I headed out of Rick's shed toward my car. I placed the fiberglass in my lap and let my fingers play around its sharp edges as I drove back to the harbor.

A large, high-velocity projectile. Rick's words played around the edges of my mind. *Surface, subsurface, and air-launched torpedoes.* Those are the hazards mariners are warned of in Whiskey Gulf; the reason they are advised to stay well clear. But nothing is launched from a ship, a sub, or a plane without knowledge of the Joint Operations Command Officer.

Back at the *Noble Lady* I jabbed at the keypad of my cell phone, punching in Jeffrey Leighton's number. While waiting for the connection, I tapped on the fiberglass remnant.

Jeff answered, "Leighton."

"Noble," I said. "Jeff, you were the JOCO during Gulf Freedom."

"I gather you had a fruitful visit to Canada," he said.

"I'm holding a piece of fiberglass that has on it the call letters of the *Rebecca Anne*. Analysis says that it's been hit by a high-velocity projectile. And I have good reason to believe there may have been an errant torpedo launched during your joint training exercise."

Leighton's long silence dwarfed the subtle background hiss of static on our call. Finally, he cleared his throat. "Commander, I'm under orders not to speak to anyone about our joint training ops with Canada."

Leighton hung up, and I called Maya Shimazu. She answered.

"You're not sitting in a natural hot spring along some beautiful stretch of the remote west coast of Vancouver Island are you?" I asked.

"You're not fantasizing about me, are you?"

"No. Roger said he'd try to kidnap you for a few days."

"Shortly after breakfast in Comox, he got a call to fly two couples to the Dean River to fish for steelhead."

"Free for dinner?"

"Roger's staying at the fishing lodge for a night then returning to-morrow with another couple, so I am free for dinner. I'm in Vancouver at the moment fulfilling my half of our bargain. Would you mind coming to Canada? I'll drive the *Princess* down to White Rock and meet you at the Giraffe about seven."

WHEN MAYA SHIMAZU strolled in to the Giraffe, a restaurant on Marine Drive, conversation stopped and heads turned. She wore black pants with black sandals, and a tailored wide-collared white blouse with hidden buttons, opened just enough to reveal a hint of her cleavage. She'd tied a black sash around her waist. An onyx pendant in the shape of a Japanese ideogram hung from a gold chain around her neck, while smaller black characters dangled from her ears. Her lips glistened deep ruby from her lipstick, and the burgundy sunglasses she'd raised to rest across her head suggested a tiara. She walked with a graceful, fluid motion toward me. I instinctively rose from my seat, to pull her chair back from the table.

Before she sat, she smiled. "You're taking a chance, you know."

I pointed to the chair. "Old school."

She smoothed her blouse beneath her before she sat, and a hint of her floral perfume drifted my way. "I like 'old school' in men."

"You look lovely," I said.

In jeans and a fitted black T-shirt, I felt outgunned by Maya's ensemble. But, thankfully, I'd also worn a lightweight tan jacket, which allowed me to hold my own.

"Thank you," she said. "It helps not to dress like a deckhand when you're out working sources."

"I'm sure your sources were in grave danger of revealing their deepest secrets when you appeared looking as lovely as you do."

Jason, our waiter, a tall man with chiseled features and a blond goatee, set two glasses of merlot and a basket of warm bread on our table. Next to the bread, he set down a plate of olive oil with a giraffe drawn in balsamic vinegar in the center, and small mounds of salt crystals around the edge. We sat by the window on an evening when the setting sun over a calm bay painted the western sky and the water in shades of orange and wine.

Jason stood for our orders. Maya got a salmon dish. I went for the halibut. I tore off a piece of bread and dipped it in the oil, vinegar, and salt. Maya did the same.

"The call letters on the fiberglass belonged to *Rebecca Anne*," I said.

She shook her head. "I'm not surprised. And the analysis of what created the debris field?"

"A high-velocity projectile."

Maya took a deep breath and held it. When she exhaled, she picked up her glass of wine.

"Whiskey Gulf is currently active with Americans, Canadians, and Bahrainis," she said.

"So the joint training exercises are continuing?"

"Officially, no. This is some sort of weapons testing or demonstration phase for the sake of the Bahrainis. And that is all my sources would reveal despite my best efforts." She smiled mischievously. "And my best dress."

Jason arrived with our dinner plates. My halibut was set atop potatoes au gratin, with fresh string beans shooting out like spokes from the potatoes, and parsley flakes sprinkled liberally over the entire dish. Maya's salmon nestled between long, thin strips of cooked carrots. A mound of rice sat at one end of the carrots, and a sauce with chunks of mango smothered her fish.

"I could not find anyone, so far, in the Coast Guard who would confirm or deny that a torpedo sank the *Rebecca Anne*, despite the fiberglass evidence."

"Which suggests that we have been effectively stonewalled," Maya said. She took another sip of wine. "However, I do intend to pursue the matter."

"By running a story based on what you know so far?"

She shook her head. "No, without more facts and with no corroboration a story at this point would be more speculation than truth."

"But you ran the first story in the *Sun* with even less than you have now."

Maya sucked her teeth. "That was a tease for the real story, which is yet to come when I get to the bottom of what happened that day, and why we encountered torpedoes off the Ballenas Islands."

"I hear persistence and confidence that you will."

She smiled. "The name Shimazu comes from a great Samurai clan of the sixteenth century. Samurai are taught that self-confidence and persistence win great battles. Charlie, if you're not planning to leave the field of this battle, I suspect that we'll see each other again soon."

I CROSSED THE CANADIAN BORDER back into Washington about ten o'clock that evening and walked aboard the *Noble Lady* about ten-forty-five. I pulled a bottle of microbrew from the fridge and sat in the dark sipping it. The *Vancouver Sun* might have deep enough pockets to pay for confidence and persistence, but I'm not sure the Kulshan Yacht Club did. I couldn't just take their money for an investigation that might drag on for months—or even longer if I went knocking on the doors of everyone in the Coast Guard I might be able to connect with this matter. The yacht club had asked me to report on my progress and I didn't want to fill them in tomorrow with tales of "multipath propagation errors" that would only propagate their conspiracy theories. But I didn't want to lie. It also surprised me that I said nothing to Maya about my evening with Adam Webster. Call it an ex-intelligence officer's gut feeling, but I had the sense throughout dinner that Maya wasn't being completely forthcoming with me.

Chapter 10

EARLY THE NEXT MORNING, I lay in my berth half-awake and restless with the covers wrapped tightly around my legs. I must have fought with them in my dreams all night. A subtle shaking still seized my body—the kind that emanates from the adrenaline rush of fighting for one's life. I closed my eyes and a dream rushed back into my mind like a flood tide sweeping to shore.

A warm, dense fog surrounded Kate and me as we laughed and hugged in the cockpit of a sailboat. Suddenly a loud explosion blew apart the boat, hurtling us high into the thick gray blanket. I plummeted head over feet toward the water, all the while reaching out for Kate. I hit the water and sank quickly, punching more than swimming as I fought back to the surface. A hot, salty smell surrounded me.

I searched for Kate, called out her name, but I couldn't find her. I swam furiously in one direction, then another, calling her name to no avail. I tread water, spinning 360 degrees, pounding the surface, making small ballistic splashes with my fists, screaming out, "No! No! No!" Then, out of the corner of my eye I noticed something float out of the fog. I raced toward it, but the closer I got the more it seemed to move away.

"Kate!"

She didn't answer.

With a Herculean effort, I pulled myself through the water. But when I reached the object I found a piece of fiberglass with the *Rebecca Anne*'s call letters. Then suddenly, a torpedo whistled by. Magically, my dream transported me back to the marina where I lay on the hard concrete dock at gate 9 alongside the *Noble Lady*. A woman's warm lips kissed mine. I smiled.

"Kate," I said softly.

But when I opened my eyes in the dream, I saw Maya Shimazu's face instead.

"Kate!"

I don't know if I called out her name for real, but I did hear something that woke me from my dream. I sat on the edge of my berth, groggy, weary, feeling fragile. I checked my watch: 0730. I picked up my cell phone and tapped in Ben Conrad's number. He answered.

"You had breakfast yet?" I asked.

"You don't sound too good," he said. "Everything all right?"

"Some things are. A lot of things aren't."

"In that case I haven't had breakfast. Where and when?"

"Old Town Café at 0800?"

"Place on Holly across from the Boss Tweed's that Janet said you liked?"

"That one."

"See you there at eight."

Still groggy, I struggled to stand. I waved off a shower, brushed my teeth, and threw on some clothes.

When I finally stepped off the *Noble Lady*, I walked into a fog-bound harbor, which only made it more difficult to distinguish whether I was really awake. Next to the *Lady*, on the spot where I lay in my dream, a seagull pecked away at the insides of a purple starfish turned upside down. The gull cocked its head, eyed me, then let go a raucous squawk. But instead of snatching the starfish and flying off, the gull dragged it under its body, squatted on its catch, and followed me with a menacing glare as I walked past it down the dock.

I stopped at the top of the gangway leading up to the parking lot. I looked but I could not even see the *Noble Lady* through the fog. I checked my watch. I had twenty minutes to get to the Old Town Café. Unless my dream had transformed me into Alice and the seagull into the Mad Hatter, who'd just murdered time and not a starfish, I could rest assured that the Old Town Café was still only ten minutes away.

So I decided to walk.

WHEN I PUSHED THROUGH the door of the Old Town Café, the eye-opening aroma of fresh-brewed coffee greeted me, finally convincing me that sleep no longer had me in its clutches. Ben sat in a wooden booth directly under the café's large plate-glass front window. I walked around to the booth. He stood as I approached. Both of us measured just over six feet. We shook hands, then pulled each other in for a bear hug. I pulled back from the hug and studied his face. Ben's weathered skin bespoke a sailor's life; his darting eyes a crime-weary detective.

I chuckled. "You colored the gray around your temples."

Ben grinned. "Funny what dating a younger woman will do, ain't it?"

"Funny," I said, though I noticed a certain lack of enthusiasm in my reply.

"Sit. Have some coffee. Then tell me what the hell's up," Ben said.

Sean, my frizzy-haired waiter friend, stood at our table a few moments after I sat down. Built like a linebacker, with the fastidiousness of a librarian, he set down a napkin and silverware with one hand, and a steaming cup with the other.

"Decaf, soy, latte," Sean said.

Ben did a double take. "How the hell'd he know what you wanted? Whaddya have personal service here?"

"Come in a lot," I said.

I'd barely finished the thought when Sean was back with a small green pad and a pencil.

"A or B?" he asked me.

Ben lowered his head and shook it.

"Okay, what's A?" Ben asked.

"Two organic eggs, sunny-side up, split order of black beans and home fries with sourdough bread." Sean rattled off the list.

"And B?"

"Order of whole grain hotcakes with organic maple syrup and organic sausage."

Ben frowned. "Everything in here organic?"

"No," Sean said.

"Good," Ben said. "Got bacon?"

"Yep, but it's organic."

Ben grumbled. "What, they feed the pigs sprouts?"

"No," Sean said. "They let them run free and make the bacon without chemical additives. Most people think it tastes better."

Ben picked up a menu from the table.

Sean's eyes twinkled. "Tell you what. If you don't like the bacon at least as much as regular bacon, I won't charge you for the order."

Ben's face lit up. "You're on. Two eggs, scrambled. Order of home fries and an order of"—he struggled to say the words—"organic bacon."

Sean broke out in a devilish smile. "Organic eggs?"

Ben grumbled again. "What the hell, yes."

Sean left. Ben smirked. "Boy, Janet's going to get a kick out of this when she hears I ordered an organic breakfast. Bud guy gone microbrew. Meat and potatoes man gone organic. Next thing you know I'll be asking the captain if I can wear Birkenstocks on the job."

I took a sip of my latte.

"So Janet was with me when you called this morning. She said that you and Kate were having a problem. That true?"

"Janet and Kate have spoken?"

"No. I asked Janet how she knew this and she said that—get this—two guys like us wouldn't call each other for breakfast unless we wanted to talk about women or business."

"Don't you just hate it sometimes?" I asked.

"What? Female intuition? Yep."

"Especially when they're right."

"Which is what? About ninety-nine percent of the time?"

I laughed. "Uh-huh. Truth is I *do* want to talk about both."

Ben threw up his hands. "Damn. See? She was right."

I wrapped both hands around my cup, lifted it, and took another sip.

"Previous beau has come back into Kate's life."

"Younger guy?"

"Uh-huh."

"Good looking?"

"Uh-huh."

"She still have feelings for him?"

"Uh-huh . . . but mixed. He's CG. Walked out on their engagement. She's angry. They're working side by side. He's apologized profusely with flowers. Wants to know if there's any way of them getting back."

"To which she said—?"

"She was confused."

"Like someone you thought was dead and buried suddenly turning up alive. I can see how that would be confusing."

"I can, too."

Sean slipped our breakfast plates in front of us almost unnoticed. Ben cut a piece of bacon, stabbed it with his fork, then scooped up some eggs before his fork disappeared into his mouth. I broke the surface of one egg and sopped the yellow with a piece of toast.

"Want my advice?" Ben said. He hadn't finished swallowing as he spoke. "Take your advice."

"What?"

He stabbed a larger piece of bacon and pursed his lips. He nodded. "Damn stuff ain't bad." He stared at me. "You remember awhile back Janet and I were having some issues? She was upset because she felt being with me was hemming her in. You know, her protests, political activity, tree-hugging stuff. And me a cop and all." Ben speared a home fry. He raised it to his mouth, then dropped it from his fork. "They got ketchup in this place?"

Sean either overheard or anticipated Ben's request. No sooner had Ben asked the question than Sean stood at the table holding a bottle. "Need ketchup?" he asked.

"Thanks," Ben said. He grabbed the bottle then stared quizzically as Sean walked away. Ben studied the label on the ketchup bottle, then roared loudly, "Hah! Something in this place that isn't organic. The goddamned ketchup's just good ol' Heinz."

Heads turned. Silence descended over the Old Town Café, followed by a wave of laughter. Ben raised his hands and blurted out. "I'm kinda new to this organic stuff . . . just learning the ropes." He shook a blob of ketchup onto his fries, speared one but held it to the plate with his fork. His voice dropped several decibels. "Now, like I was saying. When I had that problem with Janet, you remember what you said to me?"

"Some kernel of wisdom, I'm sure." I scooped up some black beans.

"Yep. You said, 'Tell her you love her, then just step back. She needs to know that and she just needs some time.' Soooo" —Ben punctuated the word with a swallow of coffee— "tell Kate you love her and just step back."

I chuckled. "Being with Janet *has* changed you, hasn't it?"

Ben threw up his hands again. "Like I told the good people here . . . I'm just learning the ropes."

I grabbed the ketchup and shook some on my fries. "Thanks, you're right."

Ben took a napkin and dabbed the corner of his mouth. "Gal problem solved. Whatever's next's gotta be easier."

"I need some background on the couple that went missing in Whiskey Gulf. All I know, all anyone seems to know, is that they came here from Florida about two years ago."

"That all? Like I said, easy. What's their names again?"

"William and Rebecca Anne Kinsley."

Ben grabbed a napkin and pulled a pen from an inside jacket pocket. He scribbled their names.

"You know where they live . . . lived?" he asked.

"Sudden Valley."

Ben rubbed his chin. "See what I can pull up. Tomorrow soon enough?"

"Club asked me to come by their meeting tonight."

"Okay, I'll get back to you by the end of the day."

"Thanks."

Sean stopped by the table. "How's that bacon?"

Ben traced a circle in the air around his plate. "Say, how much of a tip do I have to give you to put what I just ordered on the menu as C?"

Sean laughed. "I take it you liked it?"

"Damn good," Ben said.

When we finished breakfast, I picked up the bill and Ben slapped a five down on the table.

BY THE TIME I GOT BACK to the marina, the sun had burned off several layers of fog and I could just begin to see the dark outline of Lummi Island in the distance. I decided to take Ben's advice—or my advice—and call Kate. She answered with a yawn.

"Long night?" I asked.

"Vessel Traffic System picked up a large ship running without AIS. We had to scramble a crew to investigate. Turns out they'd blown a fuse and fried a circuit. The engineer had it fixed by the time the crew got there. Then about 0300, Station Seattle said they were tracking what sounded like a distress call from somewhere in Boundary Pass. So we scrambled another crew and a helo. But we didn't find anything." She yawned. "I didn't hit the sack until 0600."

"Sorry. I didn't mean to wake you. Just called to tell you I love you and I understand how confusing it must be to have Chris show up suddenly."

"I drifted off thinking about you feeling guilty about emotions popping up that I seem to have little control over."

"Let go of the guilt and get some sleep," I said.

"Charlie, you know I love you, too."

After we hung up I took a shower, then changed the bandage on my finger, which felt well enough for me to think about pulling out my guitar. But I decided not to push things. I laid out the two Dowland pieces on a music stand. I read the notes, hummed them, then closed my eyes and fingered the guitar in the air and in my mind. One half-hour into practicing, my cell phone rang.

"Noble," I answered. "Hey, Ben, that's soon."

"You call Kate?"

"I did."

"Tell her you loved her?"

"Did that, too. You give good advice."

Ben laughed momentarily, then his voice turned stern. "Now, I've got some more good advice. Leave this case alone."

"What'd you find out?"

"Zip."

"C'mon. No socials? No driver's licenses? No bank records. Phone records. Nothing in Florida?"

"Nada. Driver's license for both and that's all I could bring up."

"Strange."

"No, what's strange is what happened when I called Carl Vandeburg at the FBI. Me and Carl go way back. Do each other favors when we can. Carl got back to me immediately. 'Don't touch this one,' Carl said."

"Why?"

"Carl ran their names. He's got security clearance I don't, and he came across the reason I couldn't get anything on the Kinsleys. Access to all their records is blocked."

"At what security clearance level?"

"Only the highest Carl's ever seen."

Chapter 11

B Y MIDAFTERNOON, the morning's fog had burned away, leaving a vengeful sun, no breeze, and withering humidity— an infrequent, unholy trinity in the Northwest save for a few midsummer days like this. Most boaters here don't bother with the expense of air-conditioning for such rare use. So I yanked open all the ports and turned on the fans. I lay in my bunk, dressed only in my boxers, licking sweat off my upper lip.

A sailboat goes missing. Two governments go silent. Evidence of two lives is expunged. An errant torpedo or a cover-up? If Whiskey Gulf bordered on a hostile neighbor I could conjure up a multitude of plausible scenarios. But even post 9/11, I couldn't imagine anyone in military intelligence seriously staging a joint exercise and a false sinking as a ruse to inject two intelligence operatives into Canada. What next? Would we invade our northern neighbor? I chuckled with that thought, which brought to mind the 1990s Michael Moore comedy, *Canadian Bacon*, in which America plans just such an invasion to bolster our president's lagging poll numbers. Then, several years ago, a spate of late night "Canada invasion" jokes cropped up following the release of a classified document written in the 1930s about American war plans against Canada. I chuckled again. The bit about sending Celine Dion off to Guantanamo in a fitted orange jumpsuit stuck with me. My only problem was that every other explanation seemed equally cockamamie. I checked my watch. In less than three hours I'd have to settle on some explanation for the members of the Kulshan Yacht Club.

I PLACED ONE fiberglass piece from the *Rebecca Anne*'s hull into my backpack and left the *Noble Lady* for a walk the long way around the harbor to the yacht club meeting. I stopped at Zuanich Point hoping to find a breeze; hoping also to find an explanation I could live with. I didn't find either. Normally, a squadron of colorful kites and parafoils dash around the point. This evening, no kites flew. Instead, half-dressed bodies littered the grass in all directions soaking up the late afternoon sun like boats at anchor when no wind or current exists to keep order.

Quark the Lab curled up outside the yacht club door, her head resting on her front paws. She raised an eye and ear partway as I walked up the steps, then lowered them just as quickly. I reached down to pet her. She pulled away, stood up, and trotted off to find an even cooler place in the shade.

I stepped inside to the smells and sights of an official yacht club meeting. Not salt air and flapping sails but the confluence of aromas from potluck dishes and desserts spread over a table, and the translucent reds and pale yellows from wine splashed into clear plastic cups at each place.

I'd barely closed the door when one person after the next pushed me along until I'd reached the front of the food line. Art Grodin patted a fold-up metal chair next to him. I carried my plate of salad and lasagna there. The talk over dinner concerned rising moorage fees and the high cost of diesel. From the scuttlebutt swirling around me, apparently popular anchorages up and down the Inside Passage were pretty empty this summer.

Art leaned over and whispered to me, "We agreed not to say a word about Whiskey Gulf at dinner, so you wouldn't have to repeat yourself when you gave us your report."

I whispered back, "That's good, because it's one less time for me to fumble for an explanation."

Arthur squinted. "Fumble?"

I patted his arm. "Not over dinner, remember?" He shook his head and picked up his glass of red wine.

After dinner we stood for the Pledge of Allegiance to a dusty, slightly mildewed flag. Art set out a lone bar stool at the other end of the club from the food table.

"Mr. Noble's here to update us on his search for the Kinsleys and the *Rebecca Anne*," he said.

A round of applause followed. I heard my footsteps resound over the highly polished hardwood floor as I walked slowly toward the chair, carrying my backpack. I swung into the seat.

"I have not been able to find out definitively what happened to the *Rebecca Anne* or the Kinsleys," I said. "I do believe their boat was in Whiskey Gulf." I reached into my pack and pulled out the piece of fiberglass. "And I found pieces of fiberglass like this one bearing the *Rebecca Anne*'s call letters near the Ballenas Islands."

A voice called out, "My god, they hit a rock and sank?"

"I'm not sure they did." I took in a deep breath. "I had the sample analyzed by a fiberglass expert, Rick Morgenthaler." A number of heads nodded at the mention of his name. "And his conclusion was that it had been hit by a high-velocity projectile." A chorus of gasps rose around the room. Vince Marcellis, who now sat at the opposite end of the long room, pushed his chair back and stood up. Heads turned toward him.

"You checked with the Canadian government, I assume. What did they say?" Heads turned toward me.

"To ask the Americans in command of the joint training exercise taking place that day," I replied.

"And the Americans said—?"

"Nothing."

"Nothing?"

"Nothing."

Art jumped up. "I said it earlier and I'll say it again—it's a god-damn cover-up. Something went wrong in Whiskey Gulf. Our friends' boat was torpedoed and sunk. They were killed and now Canada and America are stonewalling on the truth."

Vince turned to Art. "Suppose it didn't happen that way. Suppose it wasn't a torpedo at all but a nuclear sub out of Nanoose Bay that surfaced underneath the *Rebecca Anne*."

"Same difference," Art said. "Military killed 'em, and now they're covering it up."

Art's wife, Connie, stood. "Maybe it's all just an elaborate cover-up. The radio call. The piece of their hull. Maybe the Kinsleys are still alive . . . And . . . And . . ."

Vince blurted out, "And what, Connie?"

"Please sit." I raised my voice. Vince, Art, and Connie sat down. Everyone turned toward me. "Vince is right . . . And what? There aren't any explanations I've come up with that make sense."

Art grumbled, "Other than a cover-up for a murder."

A woman near me raised her hand. "If the governments aren't talking, what can we do now, Mr. Noble?"

"Officially, it's still an open investigation into the disappearance of the *Rebecca Anne* in both the United States and Canada. One thing I can think of is to keep pressure on both governments for an answer to what happened."

Art jumped up. "We'll start e-mail petitions to senators and congressmen, call the newspapers, mount a protest at the Federal Building if we have to. We'll ask other yacht clubs on both sides of the border for help. Maybe hold a cross-border rally at the Peace Arch."

Vince leaped to his feet. "What then? A March on Washington?"

Art pointed at me. "You heard Charlie. All we can do is keep the pressure on. Besides, when the fox is watching the chicken coop, you need someone to watch the fox."

"And that's us?" Vince asked.

"If not us, then who else?" Art said.

I raised my voice again. "Gentlemen." Art and Vince turned away from each other and toward me. "May I suggest that you contact Coast Guard District Thirteen Headquarters in Seattle and ask for a public hearing on the disappearance of the *Rebecca Anne*. Have as many people present at the hearing as possible. Prepare a press release beforehand that states both your interest and your concerns in the matter and send that release to the Coast Guard, to our elected representatives, and to all the newspapers, radio stations, and television stations between Vancouver and Seattle." Art and Vince turned toward each other.

"Sounds like a good suggestion to me," Art said.

"Let's talk about it in the meeting," Vince said.

"I'm not sure what more I can do," I said. "But let me know if I can help you."

"Well, you certainly have our gratitude for doing what you could. And when you hand us your bill for the services you've rendered you'll also have our prompt payment," Art said.

"And perhaps you can stand by in case we need you to speak at a public hearing on our behalf," Vince said.

"Roger that," I said.

QUARK LET OUT A SOFT *WHUFF* as I walked down the yacht club stairs. Thirty yards away the heated voices of Art and Vince still wafted through the warm, moist night air. I walked the long way around to the *Noble Lady* again. I stopped at Zuanich Point, not looking for explanations this time as much as reassurance that I'd done the right thing. I thought it better to release a small tempest by revealing what I knew from the recovered piece of fiberglass, rather than unleashing a gale by repeating what I'd heard from Ben or Adam Webster. Besides, citizen pressure might go a lot further than anything else in finding answers. At any rate, other than a bill for my services to the club, my participation in the matter was through, and that felt good.

Overhead, a lenticular moon shone and stars shimmered softly. Out in the bay, tiny wavering pinpricks of starlight reflected off the dark surface of the water. Bodies still littered the large grassy area at Zuanich Point. But now they lay in pairs rather than singles, some with blankets wrapped around them, reminding me of boats rafted together at anchor.

The day's heat rose from the asphalt path as I walked toward gate 9. I'd fixed my gaze on a minivan that seemed terribly out of place. Black. Tinted windows. Government plates. Parked perpendicular to the other cars, taking up two handicapped spaces.

I decided to double back on the walkway, swing wide, and take the street into the marina parking lot. I cut through the hedges in front of a boat dealer's showroom. Stooping low, I snaked through the parking lot toward the minivan and approached the driver's window from the van's flank. I kept a car between myself and the van until the very last moment, when I dashed toward the driver's door, crouched beneath the sideview mirror, and knocked.

I braced for someone barreling out of the van with a gun drawn. But when nothing happened, I suspected I had uninvited company waiting for me at the boat.

High tide raised the marina docks almost level with the parking lot, making it harder for anyone aboard the *Noble Lady* to look out from the cockpit and see me at the top of gate 9. Still, I kept masts and superstructures of other boats on a line of sight between the *Noble Lady* and me as I walked down the ramp toward the locked gate. I punched in the code and swung back the heavy metal gate door.

A kayak and dinghy rack sat just beyond the door, and that gave me an idea. None of them were chained to the rack. I reached into cockpits until I found one that had a set of collapsible paddles. I shoved the paddle shafts together, slipped the kayak off of the rack, and let it slide gently into the water.

I paddled out and around the visitor's dock, then down the large fairway to approach the *Noble Lady* from the waterside. It's said that a safe way to approach grizzly bears is in a small boat, because these huge land predators do not perceive any threats coming from the water. As I swung wide, away from the *Lady*'s stern, I saw that she listed slightly to dockside, which convinced me of human predators aboard.

I paddled silently to the front of the boat, stopping just off the bow. I reached into my backpack and grabbed the piece of fiberglass. I snapped my wrist and flung it at the dock box. Fiberglass smacked into fiberglass with quite a clatter, bringing two men running from the cockpit. I paddled hard to the stern, leaped up, and pulled myself over the gunwales, holding the paddle and a painter, which I tied off to a cleat. I crouched low and waited in the shadows of the cockpit.

The *Noble Lady* dipped as the first man stepped back aboard. I sprang up and in one motion caught his neck in a choke hold with one arm and grabbed his gun from his holster with the other. The man still on the dock reached toward his gun. I swung the muzzle of mine toward him, then stifled a wince as a sharp hot pain shot up my arm from my hand. I hadn't squeezed a gun since injuring my finger.

"I wouldn't," I said. "You're on my boat and you're uninvited."

The man I held struggled to speak. "Commander Noble, we're CGIS."

The man on the dock held his hands out. "Going for my ID, not a weapon."

"Take it out slowly," I said.

The man on the dock reached into a pocket and pulled out a black wallet that he held up, then let flip open and down. I made out what looked like a Coast Guard Intelligence Service insignia and ID.

I pushed the man with me off the boat and onto the dock. I stood in the cockpit entryway gate and motioned with the gun, "Yours, too, son." They were only kids, and the one I'd disarmed trembled as he fumbled in his pockets for his ID. He handed it to me. I waved for the other man's ID to inspect it more closely.

"Benson and Walters," I said. "Don't you know that you never enter a boat without permission unless you're prepared for trouble?"

Benson, whose gun I held, spoke. "We're here under orders, sir."

"I don't give a damn. I'm not in the guard."

"Sir, Captain Leighton sent us for you," Walters said.

"Doesn't Captain Leighton know about calling to see if I'm in, first?"

"Sir, the captain said there was to be no unsecured communication. Our orders were to wait for you to return to your boat."

"Well, then, you should have waited at the top of the gate."

"Sorry, sir. But a boat owner left the gate open and we decided to make sure we didn't miss you by coming down to your boat." I passed their IDs back. Then I pushed the safety closed on Benson's automatic pistol and handed it to him butt first.

"What exactly does Jeff Leighton want?"

"He requests your presence aboard the *Etheridge* ASAP," Benson said.

"Regarding?"

"Sir," Walters said, "the captain informed us he was not at liberty to divulge anything further than those orders."

"Sir, would you accompany us back to the *Etheridge?*" Benson's question sounded more like a plea.

"I will, but first I need your assistance."

I stepped back into the cockpit, untied the kayak, and guided it behind the *Noble Lady's* stern. "Benson, you take the grab loop at the bow. Walters, you get the stern. We need to return this to its rack." I walked holding the kayak paddle while Benson and Walters marched before me with the boat.

As the black SUV pulled out of the marina, Benson turned around from the front passenger's seat. "Commander Noble, sir, it's an honor to be with you. The incident at the end of your career is the subject of training for every new CGIS officer now."

"It is?"

"Yes, sir. We are placed in a hypothetical situation where a superior officer issues a questionable order and we must make a choice between following that order or accepting dismissal from the guard."

"And does the choice you make then go in your record?"

"No, sir. Each officer's decision is ultimately private, though we engage in a group discussion of the exercise and the factors weighing on all sides of a decision. The exercise is called the 'Noble Option,' after the commander, sir."

"Then I won't ask which decision you chose."

"Sir, my integrity comes at a high price, just as yours did."

DING-DING . . . DING-DING.

"Attention, Captain on deck," the boatswain's mate sang upon ringing the ship's bells. Jeff Leighton awaited our shore party at the top of the gangway. He dismissed the two young CGIS officers with a cursory salute, put his arm around my shoulder, and hustled me inside a hatch.

"Jeff, what's this about?"

He barked, "Noble, save it for my quarters."

Leighton pushed open bulkhead doors, and scampered up ladders while I dogged the doors and worked hard to keep up. Many doors and ladders later, he shoved down a lever and shouldered open the door to his quarters. We walked into a spacious living room. Lights shone from the small galley and a bedroom situated off this main area. A darkened room with a half-open door in the far corner of the living room appeared to be the head.

He closed and latched the door behind us.

"I got orders earlier this evening directly from the National Marine Intelligence Center that Pete Townsend wanted to speak with you ASAP on a secure video link. Sit down there." He pointed to a stool at a desk with a computer screen and bank of three LCD monitors embedded in the wall.

Leighton spat out the words, "Hit the Enter key when you're ready to initiate the link. It may take a moment on the other end before Townsend gets on. Once you've finished, you pick up this headset and press three-four-four. That'll get me. I'll be in the officer's lounge. I'll come back for you and escort you off my ship. When I leave, you *will* shut and latch the door behind me. Understood?"

"You're not staying around?" I asked.

"Hell, I goddamn wasn't invited. And Noble"—Leighton jabbed at me with his finger—"I don't like it when a party happens on my ship"—he jabbed a finger at his chest—"and I'm not invited." He unlatched the door, then turned back toward me. "Anything else?"

"Seems pretty straightforward."

"Hell, nothing's straightforward in the Coast Guard anymore." He swung the door open and slammed it shut. Through the metal I heard him bark, "Latch the goddamn door."

Which I did.

If Leighton was goddamn angry, I was goddamn confused, and the sooner I got on the secure video link with another former CO, Pete Townsend, the sooner I'd get some goddamn answers.

I tapped the Enter key and the middle LCD monitor painted itself gray. The speakers beeped, and the gray screen changed to royal blue. At the top of the screen, the Coast Guard emblem popped up with the motto *Semper Paratus* beneath it. On the other side of the screen an animated image of the American flag waved. A message in the center of the screen read, "Receiving transmission from National Marine Intelligence Center, Suitland, Maryland, Capt. Peter Townsend, USCG."

Several minutes later, the screen flashed once before Pete Townsend's face appeared. He sat ramrod stiff behind a desk with his hands folded, flanked by the Coast Guard and American flags. A red light on the video camera above my monitor blinked.

"Charlie, are you there?"

"Hello, Pete. I am."

"Can't see you. Could you adjust your camera?"

I pointed the camera at my face.

"Better," Townsend said.

Townsend wore a blue work uniform but no hat. Clean-shaven, jaw set. Gone was the impish twinkle in his eyes, replaced by an unflinching stare into the camera. Gray had migrated further up his temples and deep furrows rippled across his brow. He narrowed his eyes to almost a squint. They tracked back and forth as though following words scrolling by on a teleprompter.

"Seventeen days ago, on my orders, the USCGC *Etheridge*, at the time the flagship of joint exercises with Canadian forces, fired a torpedo at a sailboat that had entered Whiskey Gulf and sank it."

Chapter 12

MY EYES WIDENED.

"What? Pete, I don't—"

Pete's eyes narrowed more. "Just listen, Commander. Two weeks before that I was informed by the Department of Justice that the identity and location of two high-value witnesses in the upcoming trial of terrorism suspect Sami Al-Sayed had been compromised"—his eyes returned to tracking—"Thara Al-Sayed and her domestic partner, Aaron Kane, were living in Bellingham, Washington, under the supervision of the Witness Protection Program and with the assumed names of William and Rebecca Anne Kinsley. DOJ passed this information along to me when the couple was returning from a sailboat trip to British Columbia, right at the beginning of our joint training ops with the Canadians and Bahrainis. Canadian Security and Information Services agreed to help DOJ handle the situation. I was ordered to assist the Canadians with their plan."

"So what went wrong?" I asked.

"Nothing."

"But the *Rebecca Anne* was—"

"A sailboat was sunk, Commander; a sailboat with the name and registration number of the *Rebecca Anne* painted on the hull."

I managed a snort of laughter, while shaking my head. "The Kinsleys—or whatever their names are—weren't aboard?"

Townsend inhaled. "Affirmative."

"Witness Protection has them back in custody?"

He exhaled, shaking his head. "Negative."

I squinted at the screen. "What?"

Townsend rapped his desk lightly with his knuckles. "I don't know where they are, but I do know they're not with Witness Protection. Seems DOJ didn't trust the United States Coast Guard, so they asked Canada to temporarily stash the couple while they worked out the details of a new safe house. Canadian Coast Guard hauled the real *Rebecca Anne* by crane onto a buoy tender, put the vessel in storage, and dropped the couple somewhere in British Columbia."

"Out of your hands. End of story. So why am I here on a secure video link? If you need me to keep quiet about the Kinsleys, I will."

Townsend's fist dropped to his desk. But only a dull thud came through the computer speakers. His face reddened. "Like hell it's out of my hands. It hasn't even been three weeks since Gulf Freedom. I get a message this morning from one of our assets in the Middle East that the couple's whereabouts may have been compromised again, only this time an agent's been sent from the Middle East to find and silence them."

"Pete, I'm a private citizen who was working on behalf of the yacht club the couple belonged to. Far as I'm concerned my responsibility ended about two hours ago when I told the club I'd come to a dead end." I pointed at my screen. "This is more than I want or need to know about why I came to a dead end."

Townsend's upper lip curled. "Commander, sit tight. I'm just getting warmed up."

He picked up a remote control device, pointed it at the screen, and clicked it. After a flicker, a picture from my past flashed onto the screen. I stared at myself in a full dress-white uniform with gleaming gold buttons. A rainbow of colors from a chest adorned with medals stared back. I held a cocktail glass in one hand, and had my arm around the shoulder of a younger man decked out in the dress uniform of a foreign navy.

Townsend's disembodied words animated the image. "You remember this man?"

"Remember him? Ali Sharik? Of course, he was—"

After another screen flicker the image disappeared, replaced by Pete Townsend's stern glare. "You were the U.S. Coast Guard Liaison Officer to Bahrain in 2002. You trained Sharik on setting up a Mar-intel operation in the Gulf."

"And he was an excellent student and a good friend until—"

My body grew heavy. I paused. Pete Townsend didn't speak either. I shook my head. "You've got to be kidding. Sharik's been sent after the couple?"

"That's what intel says."

"Whose intel?"

Townsend picked up his remote control device, pointed it into the camera, and clicked. The screen flashed to a fuzzy black-and-white image of two men, both well built and tall. The older man stood in front of the younger one, who whispered into the older one's ear. Both wore fitted suits, white shirts, and ties. Both had straight black hair, dark eyes, thick eyebrows, and mustaches. They could have been father and son.

"The older one's Yusuf Al Nejari, current head of Bahraini Naval Operations," Townsend said. "The younger's Mansoor Habib, Al Nejari's deputy."

The picture flashed off and Townsend reappeared.

"That picture was taken by a security camera aboard the *Etheridge* just after the two arrived for Gulf Freedom."

"And they're the source of your intel about Sharik?"

"Affirmative."

"You trust them?"

"Director of National Intelligence's office gave them the highest clearance in order to participate in the joint training ops. You know the drill. Part of all joint ops involves shared intelligence briefings, at which both real and simulated intel is passed along. At one of those briefings both Al Nejari and Habib used prearranged code words to pass along real intel about Sharik."

"Why's Sharik after this couple? What'd they see? When'd they see it?"

"Aaron Kane's a civil engineer. He'd come to Bahrain to work on the Qatar-Bahrain Friendship Bridge. Thara Al-Sayed is Sami Al-Sayed's younger sister. Aaron and Thara started seeing each other."

Townsend clicked his controller again, and a picture of a black limousine in front of whitewashed stucco walls pixelated into focus. Four burly, swarthy men in suits surrounded the limo with their hands dipped discreetly inside their coats. Each man looked off in a different direction. A fifth man, wearing a Formula One jacket, stood against the wall.

Ali Sharik bent over into the backdoor, his face turned partially to the camera, his outstretched hand grasping toward a reddish leather briefcase lying on the seat. In the shadowed interior of the limo, behind the briefcase, a hand rested on a thigh. I stared hard, trying to make out more of the mystery figure.

"This photo was taken two years ago outside of the Al-Sayed family residence near the Bahraini capital, Manama. As you can see, that's Sharik exiting the limousine."

"Guy against the wall?"

"Fawaz Al Sharani, Sami Al-Sayed's Islamic Jihad Front contact."

"What's with the Formula One jacket?"

"Bahrain hosted the first Arab Grand Prix in 2004, at their newly built multimillion-dollar racetrack."

"Lot's changed since I was there."

"That it has."

"And Mr. X?"

"IJF's contact within the Bahraini government. Something spooked him. Right after this photo was taken, everyone got back in the car and they pulled away. That night, the same limo pulled into a garage within the Al-Sayed compound."

"Lemme guess. You didn't have anyone inside, so no photo."

"Hey, it wasn't my op, Commander. I'm cribbing from someone else's homework for this briefing. Aaron Kane and Thara Al-Sayed had the misfortune of being inside the Al-Sayed residence that night, and they may have seen Mr. X."

"Which made them hot."

"State hustled them out of Bahrain into Witness Protection. Justice offered her citizenship in exchange for testimony against her brother and identification of Mr. X."

"Someone already interrogate Thara about Mr. X's identity?"

"She's playing her cards one at a time. Says she'll testify against her brother first, as a show of good faith, then after she's given citizenship she'll say what she knows about Mr. X."

"Smart gal. I'd probably do the same," I said. "And Sami Al-Sayed?"

"Used to be a political science teacher at the University of Georgia. Claims all he ever did was raise money for Islamic charities."

"Al-Sayed's in custody?"

"Has been two years without a trial."

"What ever happened to good ol' *habeas corpus?*"

"That's why he's finally being tried. District Court said try him or free him."

"So, Justice is scrambling to make their case."

"Yes."

"Sharik's not after the couple to protect Al-Sayed, he's out to protect Mr. X."

Townsend nodded. "After Sharik left the reservation he went to work for the Islamic Jihad Front."

"And I take it you want my help tracking down Sharik before he tracks down the couple?"

"You know him better than anyone in the West."

"DOJ know that he's been sent after the couple?"

"Haven't told them yet."

"Why?"

"Don't trust them."

"Canadians know?"

"Not from me."

"Where's the couple now?"

"Don't know that either."

"What!? You don't know where they are?"

"Justice didn't trust me so they didn't tell me. All the Canadians told me is they're on the water, south of Chatham Point, north of Cape Mudge."

"Big area. Why'd they even tell you that much?"

Townsend pointed to himself. "Hell, if they want my helos on stand-by air support from Port Angeles, I need to know how big an area the birds have to cover."

"Why do the Canadians need your air support if they're in charge? They've got their own air out of CFB Comox."

"Canada only agreed to provide clearance for the couple to stay in British Columbia until Justice felt it was safe to bring them back."

"Pete, what the hell is going on here? Canada provides the haven? U.S. provides the safety?"

"Worse than that. Canada provides the haven. Justice outsources the safety to a private firm, and CGIS gets blamed if something goes wrong."

"But you've got the intel."

"Welcome to the brave new world of safety and security, where outsourcing and globalization is the order of the day." Townsend narrowed his eyes. "Doesn't it just make you feel so much more safe and secure? The present Canadian government can't be seen as too close to the U.S. So they've put limits on how much help they'll provide. Post 9/11, Justice has its own intelligence arm, along with every other goddamn agency, and regardless of the DNI, who's supposed to force everyone to play nice in the intelligence sandbox, all the players still horde their own bucket of sand."

"So you work alone but together, and you need each other but you don't trust each other. That about right?"

"You get the picture. Which is why I came to you."

"Pete, I'm not stepping back into CGIS. Especially the kind of rats' nest you've just described."

"And I'm not asking you to."

"This is a favor you're calling in?"

"It is."

"For the incident on the Pine and Cedar Lakes Trail."

Townsend cocked his head. "Heard someone took out a gunman ready to pull the trigger on you."

"And I never really knew who took that gunman out."

"Angel watching your six." Townsend smiled. "*Semper Paratus*. I'll pay you at your last rank and grade."

"Why do I get the feeling you're not telling me everything?"

"'Cause I'm not till I know you're in."

"To pay back a favor to a friend? I'm in."

Townsend sighed. "Good."

"With one exception."

He barked, "What's that?"

"Another man comes along with me at the same pay."

"My authorization's only for you."

I held up a finger. "One other person, or I don't repay the favor this time."

"I assume he's qualified."

"Former Navy SEAL."

Townsend nodded. "Sounds qualified." He took out a pen. "Name?"

"Raven."

Townsend's face contorted. "That some kind of code name?"

I shook my head. "No, that's just his name."

"Knows his way around?"

"What Raven knows about the area between Cape Mudge and Chatham Point makes me look like I'm in kindergarten."

"Guess he's in then. You'll both be ghosts."

"Operating without official sanction . . . figured as much."

"You tell me what you need in terms of equipment. Fast boat? Civilian floatplane? You're the expert in those waters."

"I'll want a boat that blends into the Northwest. Looks like it belongs here. Doesn't call attention to itself."

"You got something in mind?"

"Uh-huh. Thirty-six-foot Willard Aft Pilothouse with a single engine Perkins."

"Can we charter one?"

"Only six made. Only five still afloat. And one of those five belongs to me."

Pete laughed. "I'll pay for fuel."

"My time for questions," I said.

"Shoot."

"What's all this got to do with errant Mark 60 torpedoes?"

Townsend shook his head. "Damn, you always wanted to cut to the chase."

"I'd prefer to think of it as cutting through the bullshit."

"It has to do with the outsourcing of safety and security. Bahrain has a hundred Mark 60s on order with an option for a hundred more."

"We're selling our latest weaponry to them right off the drawing board?"

"Just about. Since the U.S. wants Bahrain to pick up a major portion of Gulf security, we have to arm them. But the Islamic Jihad Front has been trying to purchase underseas weaponry on the black market for some time, and we don't want our latest weapons, especially the Mark 60, to reach them."

"Justice thinks Al-Sayed is part of this IJF attempt to procure weapons?"

"Follow the money."

"And Bahrain's already paid for their first shipment?"

"One hundred fish at a million and a half apiece. They came over to find out why the Mark 60s haven't been delivered as promised. Said we don't have to worry about the security of their stockpile."

"Which *we* don't believe?"

"I don't. So we showed them—"

"Errant torpedoes and told them you were still perfecting the multipath propagation error-correcting systems."

Townsend smiled. "Smart ass. Heard you had a chat with Adam Webster. Besides, we wouldn't want a fish circling back on a Bahraini launch vessel, would we?"

"All of which buys time to disrupt the Islamic Jihad Front's weapon procurement program."

"If Justice can prosecute Al-Sayed."

"And if the Kinsleys can be kept alive. What's the cover story on them?"

"We believe they've been kidnapped or killed by criminals operating from the British Columbia mainland. The criminals had a female accomplice who posed as Rebecca Anne Kinsley in order to make the emergency call to the Canadian Coast Guard. Triangulation of signals determined that the boat wasn't in Whiskey Gulf at all but closer to the mainland. The suspects fired a rocket-propelled grenade at the boat to sink it. With the heavy fog no one saw the fire or the smoke. We'll be issuing a statement to the press tomorrow."

"What'll the Canadians say?"

"Canadian Coast Guard has agreed to post a notice to mariners about piracy in Malaspina Strait. RCMP will issue a statement that they are investigating the case as a hijacking and murder."

"You'd better hope the press buys it."

"Think they won't?"

"I know one reporter who won't."

"There are ways to handle a situation like that if the need arises. You, however, may also have a problem, which you'll need to handle."

"What's that?"

"Sharik."

"How so?"

"Habib said he's out for more than just the couple."

"Looking to avenge his brother's death?"

"NSA intercepts of Sharik's cell phone confirm he's spoken often about going after the man who shot his brother."

"Which means he's out after me."

Chapter 13

BENSON AND WALTERS returned me to the harbor parking lot well after midnight. As I drifted off to sleep my mind replayed scenes from Bahrain. My skin felt warm from the dry heat of the desert. My nostrils flared with the smell of salt air blowing in off the gulf. My tongue tingled with the taste of cooked lamb and spicy peppers as I recalled the last meal Ali Sharik and I had together before his brother's death.

LATER THE FOLLOWING MORNING, after a protein smoothie and some time practicing Elizabethan music on my air guitar, I took the asphalt walkway that winds through Squalicum Harbor toward gate 5, where Raven lived aboard his boat.

Small, staccato bursts like the sounds of a woodpecker emanated from *Raven* as I approached the boat. The blue tarp that normally covered the rear deck had been partially pulled back. Raven sat on a stool under the sun and the building heat of the day in only his boxer shorts. Sweat glistened over his upper body. A tan line just above the elastic band of his boxers separated his dark bronze skin from his light bronze skin. He hovered over a large hunk of wood, a small hammer in one hand, an even smaller adz in the other. With his head cocked, he studied the wood, then angled the adz carefully before striking it a few times. Then he pulled back to study the wood again.

"Permission to come aboard?"

He struck the adz a few times and pulled back, saying nothing. I rapped hard on the gunwale with each word as I said, "Permission to come aboard."

Raven looked up. The jet-black tuft of his ponytail swept from around his shoulder. He pushed it away, nodded, then went back to studying the wood. I hopped over the gunwale and stepped through a litter of wood chips to a seat behind him under the blue tarp that gave shade to a small aft section of the wooden boat. The sweet, sharp aroma of cedar filled the air. Raven swiveled around. He balanced the hammer and adz on the block of wood.

I nodded to the carving. "Mask?"

He nodded back.

"Just started it?"

He shook his head, staring at me as though reading beyond my pleasantries.

"Spirits hadn't spoken to me about how to proceed until this morning," Raven said.

"What'd they say?"

"Listen to the wood, it will tell you what it wants to be."

"What'd the wood say?"

"It wanted to be a two-headed moon mask." He tapped the left side of the wood block. "Full moon." He tapped the right. "New moon. Both circles. One dark. One light. Past. Present. One full, looking back. One empty, looking forward."

I nodded. "Wanna take a trip to Desolation Sound?"

"Been waiting for you since this morning."

"Huh?" I shook my head. "Don't tell me you knew I was coming to ask you to go north with me?"

Raven smiled, exposing a gold tooth at the rear of his mouth.

"Been waiting for a way north. Spirits sent you." He chuckled. "Fast-acting spirits, huh?"

"And why do you want to go north?"

"My daughter Sarina called."

"The one who lives in Port Hardy?"

"Used to. She's married now. Lives in Campbell River. Wants me to visit."

"That's great news. You haven't been in touch with her for years."

Raven nodded. "She just had a child. Wants me to see my grandson." A hesitant smile built over his face.

"We can do that."

"When do we leave?"

"Oh-five-hundred tomorrow."

"What are we doing?"

"Looking for a couple, probably on a boat, who don't want to be found."

"Why?"

"Because someone else is looking for them and we don't want him to find them first."

"And where is this couple?"

"Somewhere between Cape Mudge and Chatham Point."

Raven picked up his hammer and tapped his palm with it. "Between Mudge and Chatham?" He shrugged. "Easy." He stared out toward the bay without a trace of sarcasm in his voice.

"Easy?"

"Only a handful of places to hide."

Raven spun back around toward his carving. He made a few quick taps with his hammer and adz. Chips of wood flew. I stood up to leave. On the left side of the mask, I just made out the beginning shape of the full moon's eye looking backward toward the past.

On the way back from Raven's, I stopped at a chandlery and picked up several gallons of oil, some oil-absorbent pads, and two fuel filters. Then I got into my car and headed to a grocery store, where I bought as much food as I thought the boat's refrigerator and cabinets could hold. When I finally got back to the boat that afternoon, I stuffed the cabinets and the refrigerator full of provisions, then flipped open my cell phone and punched in Kate's number.

"You got home late last night," she said. "I stopped by at ten-thirty and you weren't home."

"Long night on the *Etheridge*."

"With Leighton?"

"Some of the time."

"And the remainder of the time?"

"In his cabin, on his secure comm link."

"I see. And was this necessary for your investigation?"

"In a roundabout way. Can you come over tonight?" I asked.

Kate sighed. "I would love to come over, but I'm acting station CO for a few days, so I can't leave. I might be able to swing lunch for an hour tomorrow."

"Tomorrow will be too late."

Kate gasped. "It will?"

"Raven and I are headed north early tomorrow morning."

"How far?"

"Somewhere between Cape Mudge and Chatham Point."

"That seems like a great distance to travel without a specific destination. And this is also related to your investigation of the incident in Whiskey Gulf?"

"In a manner of speaking."

"Are you being cryptic because you feel distant from me? Or because you cannot tell me where you're headed?"

"I've felt distant from you ever since you walked out the other night, and I cannot tell you much about where I'm headed or why."

"I'm sorry about the other night," Kate said. "I want to talk more.

But as far as your trip north with Raven, is the Kulshan Yacht Club paying for it?"

"No."

"Then who is?"

"CGIS."

A long silence followed.

"My concern is now bordering on anxiety. Has something changed that I should know about?"

"What's changed is that my past has come back to haunt me in a way that I hadn't expected."

"I know something about hauntings from the past," Kate said. "And is this haunting a she?"

"No, it's a he, and he's related to my past service in CGIS."

"Sounds like you've gotten yourself tangled in a complicated web."

"I have."

"Is it also a dangerous web?"

"It is."

"My anxiety is now bordering on fear."

"Raven and I can handle the matter."

"I believe you can," Kate sighed. "And I'm glad that you thought to have him with you."

"And Lieutenant Commander Bad Boy?" I asked.

Kate sighed again. "I am very glad that I'm working at the station for the next several days and not on the *Etheridge*. Chris has been very prolific and very persistent in expressions of his affection for me."

"Now it's my turn at concern. And you have met his persistence how?"

"By being equally persistent that I'm in a relationship that I want with a man that I love and I have no intentions of leaving that relationship."

"My concern is ebbing, though apparently the young lieutenant commander has not received that message."

"Apparently not, which is why I will be glad when the *Etheridge* leaves in about a week. Perhaps it will also be good that you'll be away."

"Why's that?"

"I need some time away from the man I want, and this man who suddenly wants me, so that I can process the past in order to leave it behind."

"Then I look forward to being with you again on the other side of our pasts."

"Please promise me that you will be safe."

"Thinking of you will remind me to be safe."

Kate sniffed back tears as she hung up.

Chapter 14

AT FIVE THE FOLLOWING MORNING I walked upstairs into the pilothouse holding a steaming cup of coffee. From the bench behind the wheel, I watched a band of light blue brighten the eastern sky behind Mount Baker, shading the mountain's profile a dusky blue. I stared at Baker, then into my coffee, thoughts wafting through my mind like the steam swirling up from my cup.

In this morning's light, Baker's dome reminded me of a woman's breast and sent a ripple of longing up from my loins to my heart. I missed Kate. Then a twinge of inner heat singed me. *Past* reverberated loudly from within. And my coffee took on the color of Ali Sharik's angry eyes when I'd stood facing him with the news that I'd killed his brother.

"You in the wheelhouse?"

Raven's voice interrupted my thoughts, surprised me from the bottom of the pilothouse steps. I hadn't heard, seen, or felt him step aboard. I set my coffee cup on the ledge in front of the wheel, then climbed down the stairs. Raven's duffel stood near the stove, its top folded down like a crumpled stovepipe hat.

"You packed light," I said. "I don't know how long we'll be gone."

"Doesn't matter," Raven said. He shook his head. "Spirit will tell us how long to be out. Got my drum. Don't need many clothes this time of year."

"You want some coffee?"

He shook his head again. "I need to cleanse the boat, bless our path through the spirit world, before we take off."

Raven opened his duffel, pulling out his skin drum and leather drumstick. He also withdrew a bundle of sage wrapped in aluminum foil.

"I need to go down into the 'Holy Place,'" I said. "Check the oil and water, clean the intake strainer, and bless our path through the mechanical world before we take off."

Raven nodded.

I opened hatches in the galley and stateroom that gave me access to the engine. I pulled out dipsticks and wiped them dry with oil-stained rags. After unscrewing the water intake strainer, I cleaned sea-weed and green slime from its perforated walls. Low chanting and the sound of a steady drumbeat followed Raven's footsteps circling the deck. The pungent smell of burnt sage penetrated the inside air.

I closed the engine hatches and climbed into the pilothouse in time to watch Raven standing at the bow, turning in each compass direction, pausing while he raised the smoldering bundle to the dawn sky. I let him finish before turning the key and cranking the *Noble Lady*'s engine to start. He walked aft. With the engine idling, I climbed back down the pilothouse stairs into the galley, where Raven stood placing his drum and drumstick back in his duffel.

"Got your passport?" I asked.

He nodded.

"And your weapon?"

He nodded. "Have to hide them. Canada doesn't allow handguns to enter."

"We're carrying weapons entering under special authority."

He chuckled. "Whose authority?"

"Coast Guard Intelligence Service."

"Thought you'd left."

"Me, too."

"Unfinished business?"

"In a manner of speaking."

He nodded again. "Where to today?"

"Clear Canadian Customs at Bedwell, then on through Dodd Narrows. Anchor off Newcastle Island tonight. We'll do four-hour shifts. I'm up first."

Raven nodded.

"Wanna get the lines?" I asked.

He stepped through the cabin door and off the boat. When I got back into the pilothouse, I pushed the door open and stuck my head out. I didn't need to say much to Raven. I'd already pulled in the shore power cord. He undid the lines tethering the *Noble Lady* to shore. First the bow line, then the stern line, then the two midships spring lines, which he held like the reins of a horse as he walked the *Lady* back out of her slip. He threw the spring lines on deck, gave the bow a final push, then pulled himself up and under the side rails of the boat. He slipped into the pilothouse and sat on the bench behind me.

I cranked the wheel hard to port, then gave the engine a quick shot of reverse and let the *Noble Lady* glide backward. When she got to within a foot or two of the bows and sterns behind her, I swung the gear lever forward and gunned the engine. She twirled gracefully and we lumbered from the harbor. Out in Bellingham Bay, past the channel buoys, I poked my head from the pilothouse door and looked behind us, where the widening band of daylight pushed away the deep purple of night.

I pulled my head back inside. Raven sat on the pilothouse bench with his eyes closed and his head flopped down, bobbing like a buoy with the motion of the boat. I took a sip of lukewarm coffee, then switched on the VHF radio, but only static played. Radar revealed several tiny scintillating points of green light—buoys in the bay— surrounded mainly by darkness, and at the edges of the screen the jagged bright green contours of the land. I nudged the throttle ahead until the GPS unit showed us cruising at seven knots. Then I pushed a button, which set the *Noble Lady* on autopilot, and climbed down into the galley to warm my coffee.

When I got back behind the wheel, I found Raven peering out the door. I stepped over to him, and stooped slightly to get my head under the frame. The *Noble Lady* purred beneath us as we looked back at Mount Baker, now crowned in a golden light.

"She's beautiful," I said.

Raven stiffened. He brushed past me, pulling back inside. I spun around. He shook his head.

"Noble, you don't know Komo Kulshan, do you?"

"What?" I asked.

"Not she," Raven said, "he." The corners of his mouth curled upward as he emphasized the word.

"Guess I always assumed that mountains, like boats, were referred to as women."

Raven said nothing. We angled across Bellingham Bay southwest toward the southern tip of Portage Island. Raven's eyes scanned the distant southern horizon. I went back to drinking my coffee. Several minutes later he spoke.

"There," he said. He pointed south. "We can see her but not for long."

I looked to where Raven pointed. An apricot band colored a clear sky beneath a layer of clouds. "Rainier?" I asked.

"Her name is Duh-hwahk. Clear Sky," Raven said.

I nodded. "I have seen her before when it's clear about this time of the day," I said.

"Duh-hwahk," he said again. It reminded me of the crisp sound of the *Noble Lady*'s bow slapping into a wave.

"Doo-whah-kuk," I said. I winced. When I pronounced the word it sounded like the call of a sick bird.

Raven laughed. "Clear Sky," he said. "The name the Lummi call Rainier because we can only see her in a clear sky."

"So Rainier's a she and Baker's a he. I guess I don't know how to tell the sex of mountains. And I'd always heard Rainier's native name was Tahoma."

"Yes, 'Mother of the Waters,'" Raven said. "Native people from the south call her that. Lummi people called her Duh-hwahk."

"Doo-whah . . . " My mouth couldn't manage the required contortions. "You'll have to teach me how to pronounce the word sometime." I turned back toward Mount Baker. "Komo Kulshan." I nodded. "Easier."

Raven looked back, too. "It means the wounded mountain," he said. "Lummis remember when Komo Kulshan erupted, leaving a scar . . . " He paused. "My mountain." He walked over to the pilot-house bench and sat down. Low, syncopated guttural plosions escaped quietly from Raven's mouth. The back of one hand drummed against the palm of the other in rhythm with his slow chant. I stepped behind the wheel, the atmosphere inside the pilothouse now heavy like the air before a storm.

Halfway to the south tip of Portage Island, Raven's chanting stopped. I turned back. He'd closed his eyes.

"Komo Kulshan was married to two wives," he said, "as was the Lummi custom many salmon runs ago. One wife was called Duh-hwahk, Clear Sky; the other Whaht-kay, Fair Maiden. Clear Sky was the more beautiful of the two, but Fair Maiden was more gentle and kind."

Beyond the gently rippled waters ahead, Lummi Island loomed, a dark, verdant giant waking from a night's slumber. While behind me, Raven's soft voice and lazy cadence lulled me back to a time before time, when giants roamed the land. He spoke without hurrying his tale.

"Fair Maiden, through her loving ways, won Komo Kulshan's heart; but in doing so she angered Clear Sky. The two women quarreled and Clear Sky sought to turn Komo Kulshan away from Fair Maiden by appealing to him as the father of her two children. But Komo Kulshan was not easily swayed. 'I'm going away,' Clear Sky said, 'leaving you and the children behind.' She hoped to persuade

Komo Kulshan in her favor that way. 'Go if you must,' Komo Kulshan said. Though he loved his first wife, Clear Sky, pride prevented him from asking her to stay."

We'd reached Point Frances on the south tip of Portage. I punched a button to take the *Lady* off autopilot so I could steer her through this rocky stretch by hand. I swung wide of the point and headed outside of the red channel buoy at the entrance to Hale Passage. Looking up the narrow passage to the pale blue horizon over the Strait of Georgia sent a thrill through me. If Bellingham Bay is the womb, Hale Passage is the birth canal, and the Strait of Georgia the wonder world of water and islands we would soon be born into.

Raven continued his tale.

"Clear Sky also had her pride, and having said she would leave, she could not turn back. So she slowly packed her possessions—salal, salmon berries, blackberries, huckleberries, all of her seeds, bulbs, roots, berries, and her flowering plants. And still she hoped that Komo Kulshan would ask her to stay.

"Her children cried as Clear Sky left home. She traveled but a short distance, certain that, witnessing her resolve, Komo Kulshan would change his mind and ask her to stay. But he didn't. So Clear Sky traveled slowly down the mountain valley, stopping every so often, turning back to listen, but she only heard the cries of her children and never a word from her beloved.

"Once out of the valley, Clear Sky traveled south. Still, every so often she stopped, climbed a hill, and stretched up on her tiptoes as far as she could to get a glimpse of her children and their father. Finally, convinced that Komo Kulshan did not wish for her to return, Clear Sky stopped and made camp. She planted her seeds and roots. Waters gushed from her womb. And she made the land around her fertile."

We cruised between Lummi Island and the mainland. Midway up the island, I slowed to give a wide berth to the Lummi Island ferry carrying early-morning commuters to work. I mused about a mountain leaving home and heading south. Then I wondered what happened to the couple left behind. I didn't need to wonder long. The edge of Patos Island came into view, just as Raven continued his story.

"Fair Maiden lived with Komo Kulshan for many years. Then one day she said to him, 'My time to bear your child has come, and I wish to visit my mother, Whulge.' Whulge is our name for the waters of Puget Sound," Raven said.

"Komo Kulshan objected that there was no trail between them and Whulge; there was nothing but trees and rocks. But Fair Maiden insisted that her husband must make a passage for her to travel to the sea. So Komo Kulshan convened all the clawed animals—bear, cougar, beaver, raccoons, opossum, even the rats, and mice and moles. 'You must dig a ditch from here to Whulge,' he said. 'A ditch wide enough for two canoes.' The animals worked for a long while to complete the ditch. When they'd gotten all the way to the sea, Komo Kulshan brought together all the waters around him into a mighty stream that today we call the Nooksack River.

"For her long journey, Fair Maiden gathered many different foods. She traveled in a wide canoe, and once she reached the sea she stopped at several islands. She ate mussels at one island and left some mussels there. She ate clams at another island and left some there. She had devilfish and salmon berries at another island. She fed on camas while at Matia Island, which is why camas is found in plenty there. In this way, Fair Maiden left some food at each island she visited. This is why the Lummi name these islands by the food they traditionally provided.

"By the time Fair Maiden paddled to Flat Top Island, her time was near. She stood on the low-lying island for a long time, trying to choose the best place to give birth. Winds swirled around her tall figure, whipping the water into whirlpools that sucked under other native canoes. Transformer came to Fair Maiden and said, 'You must lie down to give birth. When you lie down the winds will die and no longer create whirlpools that swallow canoes.'

"So Fair Maiden lay down on her back and Transformer changed her into an island we know today as Speiden. She gave birth to a boy, also transformed into an island we call Sentinel Island, lying right next to its mother.

"Kulshan kept stretching upward, always trying to see his wives, while his three children—one boy and two twin girls—kept stretching and looking to the south to see their mother. Today, we know Kulshan's boy child as Mount Shuksan to the east, and southwest of Shuksan, we can see his two girls, the Twin Sisters. They are all stretching tall, straining to see their mother, Mount Rainier, a long journey to the south."

Raven's voice dropped. I turned back to him.

"Thanks," I said.

"Komo Kulshan's my mountain." He touched his chest. Then he began chanting and hand-drumming again.

"Your mountain?"

"I had two wives leave me."

"And you're going to see one of your children by traveling on Whulge."

"Yes. I also found my song on Kulshan."

"Found your song?"

Raven nodded. "Some other time, Noble." He closed his eyes again, and his chanting and drumming grew louder.

Chapter 15

B Y THE TIME RAVEN had finished his story, I'd turned the *Noble Lady* to port, heading her across Rosario Strait, pointed directly at Matia Island. I looked out the pilothouse side window back at Komo Kulshan and the Twin Sisters. At the south end of Matia, a slight turn to starboard took us between Sucia and Orcas Islands. We happened on a school of small black dolphins whose dorsal fins rose and fell in unison as they fed in a large tide rip. Past the dolphins and the rip, down the long stretch of President Channel, I caught a glimpse of Flat Top and Fair Maiden. I know no mountain ever stormed off in anger or walked into the sea, but I've cruised among these islands long enough to also know an intimacy with them that's hard to capture in ordinary language, and perhaps best expressed in myth.

I aimed the *Noble Lady's* bow at Skipjack Island, a lonely outpost that sits close to the watery boundary between the United States and Canada. A moderate current flowed, sucking us toward Skipjack. Beyond the tip of the tiny island, we sailed through several rings of strong currents that sent thousands of small wavelets capering around us and smacking into the *Noble Lady's* hull.

Two hours later, we'd cleared Customs into Canada at Bedwell

Harbor, and were heading north along Stuart Channel to Dodd Narrows with Raven at the helm. I stretched out on the pilothouse bench,
taking full advantage of his watch. I dropped into a deep sleep . . .

TAH-WAH-KHA-FAH! Tah-wah-kha-fah! Tah-wah-kha-fah! Blasted
from the loud hailer, setting every atom of the ship and my body in
motion. *Tah-wah-kha-fah! Tah-wah-kha-fah! Tah-wah-kha-fah!* Like
the halted bleating of an engine struggling to turn over.

"Still coming, sir."

As the young sailor turned to me, his face morphed into that of
Christopher Stanwood, Kate's former lover.

"*Tah-wah-kha-fah! Tah-wah-kha-fah! Tah-wah-kha-fah!*"

"Still coming."

Explosions erupted. Gunfire spewed. Fires burst out. A hand
grabbed my shoulder. I yelled, "*Tah-wah-kha-fah! Tah-wah-kha-fah!
Tah-wah-kha-fah!*" Then I opened my eyes to Raven reaching behind
from the wheel to gently shake me.

He whispered, "Spirit Walker, come back to my voice." He chanted
low, "Spirit Walker, come back to my voice."

Raven's voice echoed down the long dark corridors of my mind.

"Spirit Walker, follow my voice back."

My arms and legs trembled as I struggled to wake from my dream.

"Little rough back there coming through Dodd Narrows. We hit
them about an hour after slack," Raven said. "Why don't you take
over now?"

Raven stepped aside. I struggled up from the bench to the helm.
Once there, I checked *Noble Lady*'s compass and key instruments.
Ahead, I spied a small floating log and veered to starboard. Being behind the wheel of a boat centers you in the present. As we headed toward Nanaimo, I looked back at Dodd Narrows and the frothing
white crests of the standing waves we'd just fought through.

Prior to 9/11, young men and women joined the Navy or

Marines—definitely not the Coast Guard—to see combat in foreign waters. They joined the guard, as I did, primarily to protect the borders of this country rather than to invade the borders of others; to rescue mariners in trouble along America's shores, not to wage wars in foreign waters; to keep our seas safe, not from wayward bombers but from wayward boaters.

9/11 changed all of that. Though I didn't fully appreciate by how much until I found myself the acting CO of the USCGC *Nanticote*, on a six-month mission in the Persian Gulf in 2002, and the ship came under a terrorist attack.

To starboard, we passed the high green cliffs of Gabriola Island. Underneath them small tractor tugs tended a mass of log booms like spiders minding an intricate network of webs. On the other side of Northumberland Channel, plumes of white smoke rose and curled southwest into a blue sky from the stacks of the mills these spiders fed through their labor.

Beyond the mills, a British Columbia ferry sat at Duke Point looking every bit like a large apartment building turned sideways and floating. Whitecaps textured the waters of Fairway Channel just beyond Malaspina Point at the north end of Gabriola. Bent smoke and whitecaps. An afternoon nor'easter had picked up. I spun the wheel to port and turned us into Fairway Channel, exposing the *Noble Lady*'s flank to the brunt of the waves. The slap of the chop against the hull made for a bumpy ride. But in that slap I also heard, *Tah-wah-kha-fah. Tah-wah-kha-fah. Tah-wah-kha-fah.*

I looked over to downtown Nanaimo, then scanned my radar. An interisland ferry runs back and forth from Nanaimo to Gabriola Island. I didn't see the ferry against the shore and I didn't see it on the radar screen either. But just as I lost sight of Dodd Narrows at the top of Northumberland Channel, I did notice a fast-moving small target on radar that reminded me of the vessel I'd been tracking since we crossed Rosario Strait.

A turn to starboard at Newcastle Channel brought the *Noble Lady* out of the wind and my mind out of the Persian Gulf. The channel splits Nanaimo Harbor in two, where the concrete and asphalt of a major city on one side overlooks the forested shores and dirt trails of Newcastle and Protection islands on the other. The pilothouse steps creaked as Raven climbed them. He surveyed the scene beyond the boat.

"Marina or anchor?" he asked.

I patted the *Noble Lady*, then spoke to her, "Don't be offended that he mentioned a marina."

Raven smiled and stepped out of the pilothouse, walking forward toward the anchor windlass.

A bevy of boats swung at anchor in Mark Bay off Newcastle Island. I wove the *Noble Lady* in and around bows and rodes, searching for the right spot. I finally dropped the hook between a forty-two-foot Grand Banks and a restored wooden 1930s-era cutter not far from where Maya Shimazu and I had anchored several nights earlier. I shut down the engine and turned off the instruments, then I climbed down to the galley to make a very late lunch.

Raven and I sat on the fantail eating turkey sandwiches, chips, and beer. After finishing his sandwich, he took a deep breath and dropped his head. "Noble, we should pay our respects to the *Snuneymuxw*," he said.

The word registered with me as a pleasant sound, "snoo-nee-a-muk." I pointed to Newcastle Island. "First Nations people whose land this is."

Raven nodded.

So when I finished eating we lowered the dinghy from its davits and rowed the short distance to Newcastle Island. We tied up along a finger slip at the small marina that fronted the island and walked past families readying barbecues on the back of their boats. Up the ramp from the marina, I followed Raven as he strode decisively through one small field, then another, toward a freestanding totem up from the small channel that separated Newcastle and Protection islands. The totem towered twelve feet above us.

Raven closed his eyes, lowered his head, and raised his palms toward the pole, whose rough, weathered gray-cedar edges and chipped paint bespoke its age. An eagle spread its wings, carved above a standing grizzly bear, both with painted green eyes and red lips. A row of downward-pointing red triangular shapes set on white arched backgrounds adorned the eagle's wings. And the eagle's beak covered the bear's genitals on this simple but powerful totem.

Raven chanted softly for a few moments before opening his eyes.

"This carver"—Raven spoke slowly, nodding between words—"this carver not only understood his craft, he also understood the deepest sacred teachings of native people. Sun," he pointed to the eagle. "Moon," he pointed to the bear.

I'm sure Raven saw the quizzical look on my face.

"Eagle rules the sky," he pointed to the top of the pole. "It's a sun animal. Sun represents the eternal, the immortal."

He motioned to the bottom of the pole. "Bear rules the earth. Bear hibernates, then reawakens each year, like the moon, which retreats into the dark and reawakens into the light each month. Bear represents the temporal, the mortal. Like the salmon, the one life which is all life that dies only to be resurrected. Each animal guards one part of our spirit. Eagle guards the immortal. Bear guards the mortal."

He looked to me. "You understand?" he asked.

I thought for a moment. "It's more than just a welcome totem. The eagle and the bear are the keepers of the spirit."

"Hmmm. Keepers of the spirit." Raven pursed his lips and directed a penetrating stare my way. "Keepers of the spirit." He nodded. "Yes, I like that. Perhaps you do understand."

As we headed back toward the marina, we crossed a gravel path that took off to the far side of the island. "Want to stretch after almost twelve hours on the boat?" I asked.

Raven didn't answer, but when he turned right and headed down the path, I took that to mean yes. We came to a group of school-age children gathered in a line beside several picnic tables, holding paper plates with empty buns. They waited expectantly for the older woman at the head of the line, dropping hot dogs into their buns, after stabbing them with a fork from a blackened fire pit grill. Red, yellow, blue, and orange dome tents covered the large field beyond the tables. Beyond this group of school-aged campers, we passed a young man and woman pulling on hiking boots in front of a tent pitched in a numbered gravel campsite.

With each yard we gained toward the east side of the island, I lost more of the sight and sense of Nanaimo. From the eastern shore of Newcastle, I could not see the city's majestic buildings, but I could see a majestic line of snowcapped coastal mountains that rose into an evening sky along the British Columbia mainland thirty miles away, across the Strait of Georgia. Waves washed against rocks far from shore. A Swainson's thrust called out, the sound of its fluted arpeggio lingering almost long enough for its next call to play atop its first.

A foul, sulfurous smell of tide flats wafted through the air as we walked north along the shore. Then our trail turned into the sweet, piquant, cherry smell of a cedar forest. A deer scampered across our path. Overhead, the wings of a large bird beat the air with a series of loud whooshes. Another Swainson's thrush called out. And Raven stopped to pick a ripe salmonberry.

Suddenly, a woman's scream broke the tranquility. She screamed again, "Please, someone help! He's been shot!"

Raven and I cast a momentary glance at each other, then took off. A hundred yards down the trail, and just beyond a bend, a woman shepherded a group of children off to one side. Two young girls who couldn't have been more than twelve hugged each other and cried. A blond-haired boy pointed to the other side of the trail and insisted to a group of friends, "He's dead. I'm telling you he's dead."

We walked over to the woman, who was dressed in hiking shorts with binoculars slung around her neck. She looked to be in her midthirties, with long dark hair and a purple sweatband wrapped around her forehead. Her body trembled. She had her cell phone out but struggled to punch in numbers.

"Miss Garrelson," a boy called out, "don't worry. I just called 9-1-1."

"What happened?" I asked.

She pointed. A body lay sprawled in the brush on the other side of the trail. Raven walked over to it.

"I thought maybe he'd had a heart attack." Garrelson's voice shook. "So I . . . I bent down to help him. Then . . . Then . . ." She flung her arms around me, sobbing. "My god, I'm responsible for these children, and that man's . . . that man's been shot."

I looked over to Raven. He shook his head, then waved me over. My stomach tumbled at the sight of the trim man lying on his back, one side of his head blown off. Bits of brain flung onto nearby bushes, a dime-sized wound beneath the one graying temple that remained. Blood oozed from the wound. But most strangely, the man had on no clothes, just a T-shirt and boxers.

Raven whispered, "Body's still warm."

I went back to Miss Garrelson. "Did you see anyone else on this trail?"

She took a deep breath. "We came past here about twenty minutes ago. It was getting late, so I decided to turn back to camp rather than walking further. Sam," she pointed to the young blond kid, "Sam needed to pee. He started to run into the bushes then ran out, yelling for me. 'A body,' he said. 'A dead body.'"

"Did you hear a shot?"

"No."

"See anyone?"

"No."

I turned to the children. "Did anyone see someone else on the trail?"

In unison, they sang out, "No."

"Did anyone hear a gunshot?"

"No."

Raven pulled me aside. "No one passed them. No one passed us. Trail splits off back there." He pointed. "Must have gone up that trail. Twenty minutes? We might catch up."

I turned back to Miss Garrelson. "Can you wait here with the children until the police arrive?"

She winced. "You're not going to leave us, are you?"

"We might be able to catch up with whoever did this."

"Please don't go. I'm frightened for the children that someone's roaming this island with a gun."

Just then, the couple we'd seen in front of their tent turned around the bend. I raced over to them. The woman reared back. I grabbed the man's arm and pulled him over. "I need your help. Someone's been shot, and we need to go after the shooter." I pointed to Miss Garrelson. "She needs someone to stay with her and these children until the police arrive."

The man threw up his hands, nodded his head. "We'll stay." He tamped down the air. "We'll stay." He waved his companion over.

Raven had already taken off down the trail that split north from the one we'd followed to the body. I ran hard to catch up. When I reached him he slowed to a fast walk.

"What do you make of that?" I asked.

"Sniper wound."

"Tide's out. No planes flew over. Only birds singing, just like now. We would have heard a gunshot."

Raven nodded. "Unless it was silenced. Noble, I didn't want to say it back there but that man had a small tattoo on his shoulder with the letters R-C-M-P."

"A police officer?"

"Uh-huh."

We fast-walked about a hundred yards farther along the trail, then suddenly Raven's arm flew out. Even though he was almost a foot shorter than me he wrestled me to the ground and dove down beside me.

"What the—?"

A finger flew to his lips. He whispered, pointed overhead. "Birds stopped singing."

A moment later, a tiny puff of air exploded overhead and a bullet pinged as it bit the ground to our right.

Chapter 16

A DULL THUD FOLLOWED a cascade of tiny zips as another bullet ripped through a succession of leaves to our left. A third shot whistled closer right. Then a fourth hit back in the brush—even closer yet. I tapped my chest and pointed ahead. I tapped Raven's shoulder and pointed behind. In the rapidly waning light, we slithered along the trail's edge as a bullet hit the spot where we'd just been.

Next, a volley of shots whined overhead and randomly through the brush. I crawled into the brush and propped my back against a large Douglas fir. I peaked around its trunk. A few more shots helped me locate the shooter.

I called out to Raven, "Rock outcrop, about fifty yards in."

Several shots burrowed into the tree trunk.

Raven yelled back, "See it."

The next shots tried to locate him.

Multiple targets in low light don't provide a shooter many options. When I heard someone crashing through the brush away from us, I knew which one our gunman had taken. I crouched and ran back to the trail. Raven met me there. He held me back for a moment. We listened. The crashing had crossed the trail and now came from our right, moving toward the shoreline.

We both stood and ran.

Dim light made the trail harder to keep and the shooter's path harder to find. From the top of a small rise I could see a smaller trail leaving ours, angled out toward a tiny cove. I pointed. We ran down the rise, and turned to head in that direction. An outboard engine screamed to life. I couldn't see the boat, but I heard its sound, swallowed by the dusk and by the sea.

WHEN WE GOT BACK to the campers, bright white lights and pulsing red and blue lights lit the area like a movie set. Two men rolled a stretcher with a large black plastic bag up to the back of an ambulance, swung the doors open, collapsed the legs, and lifted it inside.

A man's gruff voice called out of the darkness, "Stop!"

A moment later, a circle of flashlights surrounded us, blinding me. An officer shoved a gun barrel into my face, while another did the same to Raven. Two officers stepped from the circle, grabbed our arms, ratcheting them down, around, and behind us, then jerking them up behind our backs.

"Those are the men I was telling you about."

I couldn't see Miss Garrelson, but I could hear her voice.

Officer Gruff Voice stepped forward. "Names?"

Behind the lights, I could barely make out his face. He appeared to be about my height and maybe half again as wide.

"Noble," I said. "Charles Noble."

"Raven," Raven said.

"Fuck kinda name is that?"

"Mine," Raven said.

"Fucking see about that. You got some ID?"

"No," Raven said.

"I don't either," I said.

The officer tapped the barrel of his gun on Raven's chest. "So, Chief, where ya from?"

"Raven. My name is Raven."

He grabbed Raven's shoulders and pushed him back hard against the men holding his arms. My arms flinched. I tried to wriggle free. The officers restraining me hiked my arms up even higher behind my back. I winced. Gruff Voice turned to me.

"What? You wanna piece of me?"

"I wanna know why we're being restrained."

"Because I've got a dead officer and you two just walked out of the woods from who-the-hell-knows-where without any ID." He punctuated his words with muzzle jabs into my chest.

Miss Garrelson called out, "They were trying to help us."

Gruff Voice turned. "That's what they say. You keep out of this." He turned back to me. "You come over to the island on the ferry? What, you a drug dealer? Chief here's your buy? Dorland happened along at the wrong time?"

"We're up from the States on a boat," I said. "And Chief over there has a name. It's Raven."

"Fucking wise guy. What boat? Where?"

"In Mark Bay. Thirty-six-foot white trawler."

"Registration number?"

"Whiskey November Four Fiver Four Eight Juliet Bravo."

"Eric, you get that down?" Gruff Voice said.

"Yeah," Eric said.

"Call it in to Customs." Gruff Voice turned to me. "For your sake you'd better be telling the truth."

"And for your sake, you might want to send some officers about a mile north along that cut-off trail." I nodded my head back over my shoulders. "I'm sure you'll find the same slugs there that you'll find in Dorland."

Gruff Voice shoved his barrel into my gut. I flinched to double over, but the men behind me held me straight. "That so? What? Now you some kinda cop?"

"Sarge," Eric said, "you'd better come have a talk with Customs."

Sarge chuckled. "Fucking got you now."

Sarge walked off into a path of a bright floodlight beaming down from the roll bar of a jeep. A barrage of incredulous, high-pitched imprecations spewed from beyond the light. Several minutes later, Sarge walked back over to us. I blinked my eyes shut as he shined a high-powered flashlight into them. Heat from the light burned my eyelids. Sarge turned the light away. I opened my eyes. He trained his light on a sheet of paper with a low-res computer photo of me. He moved to Raven and did the same.

Sarge strolled back over to me. "Exactly what kind of official business are you two on?"

"Officially, official business," I said.

"Fucking wise guy."

"No, fucking pissed off guy who tried to help the RCMP catch a killer."

"Dorland's death have something to do with why you're up here?"

"I don't know," I said.

"You mean you won't say."

"I mean I don't know. And I won't say a damn thing more until you release us."

"When I'm ready." He wagged his pistol in my face. "You have anything to do with Dorland's death, and I won't give a damn about 'official business.' I'll come after you myself. Understand?" A fine spittle sprayed forth with his words.

The officers behind me released my hands, then shoved me forward. I stumbled into Sarge. He pushed me back and brandished his pistol at me again.

"That's right," I said. "The Mounties always get their man."

RAVEN AND I SAT on the fantail of the *Noble Lady*. The obsidian waters of Mark Bay reflected points of light from the stars, from Nanaimo, and from the masts of boats swaying gently with us at anchor.

"You think that shooting had something to do with why we're here?" Raven asked.

"I could certainly make up a story about why it does."

"You mean, the shooter needed an officer's uniform in order to make it easier to find the people we're looking for."

"Uh-huh."

"Shooting had the feel of a professional?"

"I believe 'asset' is the current euphemism the intelligence community is fond of."

"Noble, you haven't told me whom we're after, or who is after the whom we're after."

"You haven't asked."

"I'm asking."

"Can it wait until tomorrow?"

"It can."

No sooner had Raven stepped inside the cabin when my cell phone rang. He stepped back out with my phone.

"Kate," he said.

The large bright neon-blue letters of Kate's name scrolled across the tiny window visible through my closed phone. I flipped the phone open.

"Hi," I said.

"I love you, I miss you, and I'm worried," Kate said. Her words came in rapid-fire succession.

"First things first?" I asked.

"Last things first," she said.

"I see. So you are worried about me because—?"

"I didn't say I was worried about you."

"I'm confused," I said.

"I'm worried about us," she said.

"I see. Should I also be worried?"

"Yes."

"And does this have something to do with your importune suitor?"

She laughed. "Importune?"

"I believe it means to urge with troublesome persistence."

"Well 'The Importune Suitor' sounds like a movie title."

"I could find other words to describe him."

"You needn't bother. And yes, in a way, my worry has to do with him."

"I'm listening."

"After several days of beating up on myself for the feelings that surfaced when Christopher suddenly appeared, I realized those feelings weren't really about him, they were about us."

"About us?"

"Well . . . about where he and I were in our relationship before he disappeared. And where you and I are in our relationship when he suddenly reappeared."

I lay down across the foam cushions on the fantail and propped my feet on the wooden caprail. "Sounds complicated."

"Yes . . . and no."

"Sounds confusing."

"Yes . . . and no."

"I'm confused."

"It's rather simple. Chris and I were engaged to be married, and he walked out on me without a word."

"That much I've got."

"What angered me most was the lost opportunity."

"Most people would not consider marriage an opportunity," I said.

"Not the marriage, Charlie."

"Not the marriage?"

Kate huffed. "No, not the marriage."

"My confusion is rising."

"Chris and I promised each other that we would support the other person in discovering and pursuing whatever was most meaningful and purposeful in their life, whether that was a career inside the guard or something totally different."

"And you are afraid that I won't support you in pursuing what's most meaningful and purposeful in your life?"

"No. I'm afraid our relationship will proceed as it has been—comfortably and steadily—unless we do something radical in pursuit of that meaning and purpose."

"I see. You do know that most ordinary people would welcome comfortable and steady as meaningful and purposeful pursuits in a relationship?"

"Yes, but I'm not most ordinary people."

"I do know that."

"Don't be facetious."

"I'm not being facetious in the least. It is precisely because you are not ordinary that I love you."

"Please, don't throw me off track. Love was our third topic. Worry the first."

I smiled. "In that case, I'm curious what would classify as radical in pursuit of meaning and purpose in our relationship."

"Well, for instance, we have spoken about undertaking a circumnavigation."

"That would be a radical and lovely idea."

"That's just it."

"What?"

"It's only an idea, and that's not radical. We need to make plans, have goals, develop timetables. Say, for instance, that in five years' time we'll cast off."

"You're serious?"

"I am. I need to have something to look forward to in my life beyond my next promotion."

"Plans like that take time and money, and probably a bigger boat than the *Noble Lady*."

"Well, there you go. That's exactly what I'm talking about. Making plans. Saving money. Getting a bigger boat. Cashing out and living aboard."

I bolted upright. "Did I just hear you say 'bigger boat' and 'living aboard'?"

"You did."

"And you're worried that I would not want those things?"

"No, I'm worried that if we do not plan for those things they will always remain ideas and never become realities."

"Raven would say that nothing goes according to plan, and that making too many plans encumbers the magic of the unexpected."

"Of course, there's always the unexpected, the journey not the destination. But without a destination, without some plans, the magic has no place to materialize, the unexpected no place to crop up."

"It sounds like we have a lot to talk about when I return."

"Which brings me to our second topic—that I miss you and I look forward to your return so we can talk about all these things and more. And that brings me to our first topic—that I love you precisely because you can listen to me rant about my worries and stay present despite your rising confusion."

I sighed, then lay back down on the cushions. "Which brings me to our fourth topic—it's not only my confusion that is now rising."

"Unfortunately, our fifth topic will have to wait until the next time we are together."

Chapter 17

B Y THE TIME I WALKED UP from my stateroom into the galley at six-thirty, Raven already had the blinds up, a pot of coffee brewing, and the bed converted back into a settee. He paced the fantail, his cell phone tight at his ear.

In the eastern sky above Protection Island, a low-lying layer of clouds stalled, tinged pink underneath by the early morning sun. I climbed the pilothouse stairs and stepped outside. Salt air mixed with a slight odor of diesel exhaust as, one by one, boats weighed anchor and headed south along Newcastle Channel, like an audience exiting a theater after a play. Though I hadn't checked the current table, this could mean only one thing: In about an hour the rapids at Dodd Narrows would go slack.

The pilothouse steps creaked. I stuck my head back inside.

"Someone in Nanaimo I need to see," Raven said. "Like you to meet her, too."

"We've got a long day ahead on the water."

"She'll meet us in her shop at eight. Shouldn't take us longer than an hour."

I nodded. "Okay." Then I reminded myself that life often seemed to unfold at a slower pace around Raven, who had little regard for timetables and plans. Time for him was less a measure of when he needed to be somewhere than of what he needed to be doing at any given moment.

ON OUR WAY OVER to Nanaimo by dinghy, we dodged the what-me-worry fast boats and the slower stragglers limping south toward Dodd Narrows. We also dodged the morning fleet of canary-colored floatplanes, zooming in out of the sun to land in Newcastle Channel then whip water behind them on their way to the floatplane dock in the middle of the harbor. Once inside the harbor breakwater, we scampered down a fairway past the remnants of the Nanaimo fishing fleet and tied up underneath the lattice metal ramp leading up from the docks to the harbormaster's office.

As we stepped from the dinghy, a rancorous chorus of seagulls hopped along the pier and hovered, wings flapping, a few feet in the air ahead of us. Like rowdy spectators at a prizefight, they seemed to cheer on two gulls fighting on the dock below over an orange starfish breakfast by tugging on the starfish's opposing arms.

With twenty minutes before our appointment, Raven and I had a less boisterous breakfast of scrambled eggs and coffee cake at an outdoor café above the harbor. Afterward, we strolled a few doors down to a storefront underneath a sign reading Art of the Salish. A matching pair of three-foot-high carved raven masks stared at each other across the gallery's entryway from its two large storefront windows. A Closed sign hung in front of shuttered door blinds. Raven pushed the door open and disappeared inside. When I walked past the unseen line that connected the long beaks of each carved raven, it felt as though I'd broken through an invisible laser beam that guarded the store.

Inside, the gallery reminded me more of a sanctuary than a retail outlet. A subtle smell of cedar scented the air. From a wall straight ahead, two masks—one female, the other male—stared at me from the depths of deeply recessed eyes. Both had jet-black faces and bright ruby lips opened as though forever chanting haunting "Ooooohs." A constellation of smaller masks surrounded this pair like supplicants in obeisance to a goddess and a god.

A red and yellow woolen cape caught my attention in the midst of several racks of clothes. Silver and gold glittered from the glass jewelry case the cash register sat on. From behind the case, a door brushed carpet with a gentle *whoosh* as it opened. A woman stepped out, the shock of her full mane of white hair arresting. She matched Raven in height. The taupe cape wrapped around her shoulders had dark brown images of humans paddling long canoes and could have been plucked from the store's racks. Underneath the cape she wore a calf-length ivory linen skirt, which hid the tops of her heelless, hand-made leather boots. A hand-tooled silver pendant with a raven shape-shifting into a full moon hung from her neck, and reminded me of the logo on Raven's boat. Sunlight, filtered in alternating bands of dark and light through the store's windows, played across her face and her green eyes.

She stepped from behind the counter, and she and Raven entered an extended embrace. Before letting go, the woman looked up from his shoulder at me, her gaze foreign yet familiar, welcoming yet wondering. I didn't look away. She backed away from Raven, still staring at me. Then she smiled.

"Spirit Walker?" she asked.

"I see the name has preceded me."

"Raven has told me about the black man whom he calls Spirit Walker." She pointed to the large male mask staring out from her wall. "You know Bukwas?" she asked.

"I don't."

"He's the Wild Man of the Woods. A deity of the Kwakiutl linked with the underworld of the dead—especially the spirits of the drowned, who hover near him. Mysterious. Elusive. He roams the edge of the dark forest." She touched her pendant. "Raven told me last night that he first met you when you were called to help release the spirits of drowned girls. Bukwas," she said, her vowels sounded softly.

"And her?" I pointed to Bukwas's companion.

"Dzunukwa," she said. "Also Kwakiutl. Also a Spirit Walker. The Wild Woman of the Woods."

Raven chuckled. "Maybe his name should be Bukwas."

The woman stared at me, shook her head. "Bukwas? Nah. That's his journey, not his name."

Raven nodded.

I shook my head in confusion, then stuck out my hand to the woman. "Name's Noble. Charlie Noble."

She broke into a belly laugh. "Raven, you didn't tell me he was named after the galley stovepipe on a ship." Then she shook my hand, more vigorously than I'd expected. "Georgia," she said. "Georgia Hope. My daddy fished. On cold nights he always said his 'Charlie Noble' was his best friend. He named me after the strait."

She turned to Raven, then hauled off and threw a punch that landed softly on his shoulder. "Where's my necklaces?" She fingered the one around her neck. "My carvings? My customers want more. What the hell're you doin' down there in Bellingham anyhow? Screwing around? You oughta be workin'."

Raven shrugged his shoulders and turned up his hands, looking every bit the naughty child just caught and disciplined by an adult. I stifled a laugh. I couldn't recall hearing anyone ever speak to Raven like this. She punched a key on the cash register, setting off a bell's soft *ting* and sending the drawer open. She pulled out a wad of colorful Canadian bills and handed one to Raven. "You're going to stop in Campbell River and see Sarina, yes?"

He nodded. She handed him a second bill.

"And you're going to buy her and your grandson something nice, yes?"

He nodded again. She handed him a third bill.

"And you're going to see Simone, yes?"

He hesitated. She held back the next bill.

"She came down from Port Hardy for the birth. You two never got divorced. You have loose ends to tie up. And now you both have a new grandchild. You're going to see your wife, yes?"

Raven sucked in a breath. He lowered his head. Georgia put the wad of bills on top of the register. She lifted Raven's head by his chin.

"I didn't say you needed to get back together with her. I only said you need to talk."

He nodded slowly. She picked up the wad and peeled off another bill for him.

"Consider that a down payment on two silver necklaces and one mask that you owe me," she said. "And I need 'em before the end of boating season."

Raven nodded. Georgia handed him another bill.

"And this is just 'cause I love you and I know you need the help." She kissed Raven on the cheek.

I could have sworn his bronze skin turned a shade darker. He stuffed the bills into his pocket and shuffled out the door. I followed, but before I reached the door Georgia had clapped me on the shoulder. She twisted the door latch, locking Raven out.

"You look after him, eh?" she said. "He's a good man deep down. A spirit man. But he's not so good when it comes to the practical matters of living in the world. Children need food and clothes and a home. Simone left him 'cause he wasn't much good at providing for her or the kids."

"I'll do what I can," I said.

"You look after yourself, too," she said.

Georgia's voice dropped low and soft. She stared at me through eyes that had narrowed slightly. "Spirit Walker, eh? Spirit tells me there are things you should know."

She closed her eyes, dropped her head slightly, then suddenly opened her eyes wide. My body flinched. I caught a distorted reflection of the female mask in her eyes.

"I see your hand reaching through a veil of water to pull someone from their side to yours." She lowered her head again, then raised it.

Closed her eyes, then opened them. She turned to the masks on the wall. "Bukwas laughs as he welcomes two souls. Dzunukwa screams, for she can only rescue one."

RAVEN SAT SILENTLY behind me. I steered the *Noble Lady* to starboard around Oregon Rock in the middle of Newcastle Channel, hugging the Newcastle Island shore.

"Who is she?" I asked.

Raven said nothing for a long while, then finally, "My sister."

"Your sister?"

"Half-sister. Same father."

"And what she said was true? You're still married?"

"On paper."

"And in spirit?"

"Depends."

"On what?"

"Which part of my spirit I ask."

"You want to talk about it?"

"Not now."

"Fine with me."

We turned to starboard at the north end of Newcastle Channel just as the *Queen of Vancouver* revealed herself from behind a point on her way into Departure Bay to our left. I looked at the ferry, then across the channel to Jesse Island. The *Queen* made at least twelve knots into port. Eight knots didn't give us enough margin of safety, so I pulled the throttle down and waited to cross the *Queen*'s wake.

We turned to port at Horswell Channel and carved a path through the rocks out to the strait where a light northerly blew. To windward, rippled waters gave birth to island profiles stacked atop each other in ever-lightening shades of smoky blue. To leeward, Komo Kulshan stuck his snowy head above the mountains and the sea, like a bald eagle surveying the world from a lofty perch.

"West or east side story?" I asked.

"Doesn't matter."

"West side," I said.

Suddenly, Raven blurted out. "When I got home from the first Gulf War, my soul wasn't right. I couldn't hear well from too many dives and too many explosions. I couldn't sleep. My brother had just died from a drug overdose. I walked around with my diving knife in an ankle sheath. I bolted from sleep with a recurring dream: trying to swim to the rescue craft plucking SEALs from the water, afraid it would leave the Indian behind. I drank. Then I hit her."

"Post-traumatic stress disorder. Did you get help?"

He sighed. "I went to the VA Hospital. They gave me a prescription for tranquilizers and told me not to hit my wife again. But I did, and I knew something was not right with my soul. So I went away alone for several months into the woods on Komo Kulshan. I fasted. I made my own sweat lodge. I prayed. I found my song. I drummed it. I sang it. I danced it. But when I returned, she had taken my daughter and gone back to her people here in Canada. I don't blame her. I was not right with my soul."

Raven slipped from the pilothouse bench and climbed down into the galley. Several minutes later, the sounds of drumming and chanting wafted up from the *Noble Lady*'s rear deck.

I turned my focus from Raven's beat to the *Noble Lady*'s radar. Four rings behind us, about eight nautical miles away, just heading north from Horswell Channel, I saw what appeared to be a familiar small green blip.

The VHF crackled with notices to shipping from the Canadian Coast Guard, warning of a twelve-inch deadhead in Howe Sound. *Sea Legs* called *Just in Time* to arrange for a cocktail hour meeting in Pender Harbor. I punched the button marked WX and fiddled with the station selector until I got a clear weather broadcast: ten to fifteen knot northwesterlies north of Nanaimo along the Strait of Georgia, rising to twenty-five to thirty knots overnight. Then, at the end, came a familiar warning: "Whiskey Gulf is active today from 0600 to

1600 hours with surface, subsurface, and air-launched torpedo fire. Whiskey Gulf is considered extremely dangerous, and all mariners are advised to stay well clear. Any mariners with concerns, contact Winchelsea Control VHF channel ten."

The letters WG sat in the middle of a five-sided area scribed across the chart on my computer screen. Out the starboard pilot-house window I looked across to the invisible, watery boundaries of Whiskey Gulf and up Malaspina Strait between Texada Island and the British Columbia mainland.

A couple in a sailboat had gone missing. Two governments had covered up the truth. A foreign agent had been dispatched to find and silence them; an agent whose brother I'd killed. Raven and I needed to find that couple before he did. I feared that our search might also lead him to the couple. I picked up my cell phone and gave Pete Townsend's office a call. An ensign put me through.

"Noble, you a psychic?"

A momentary image of Georgia Hope flashed across my mind. "Why?"

"Just thinking I needed to call you. Where the hell's Nanaimo?"

"Seventy miles south of Cape Mudge."

Townsend grumbled, "Wherever the hell that is. Look, RCMP lifted a set of prints from a crime scene on some small island near the city. From shell casings, I think. Got word you were involved. We had forensics analyze the prints right away. Came from at least two people. Never guess who one set belonged to."

"Ali Sharik," I said.

Townsend chuckled. "A psychic," he said.

Chapter 18

FOUR HOURS NORTH from Nanaimo, traveling the west side of the Strait of Georgia, placed us in the middle of Baynes Sound about an hour south of Tribune Bay. The *Noble Lady* punched through three-foot chop. Raven still sat on the rear deck.

I stared at the dark blue-green land mass directly ahead of us. My late wife, Sharon, and I had first taken the *Noble Lady* to Tribune Bay almost eight years ago. I was in love with Sharon. I fell in love with the *Noble Lady* during that trip. The year after that, Sharon died of cancer in my arms one evening in Tribune Bay. And five years after that I fell in love with Kate in the same spot. Tribune Bay was more than a safe anchorage from north and west winds; it was a measure of my life, and a harbor for my heart.

The cabin door swung open, then slammed shut. Raven called up into the pilothouse. "My watch." He bounded up the stairs with a zest that had been absent before.

"You feeling better?" I asked.

"Drumming, chanting, praying. Always seems to help."

He looked outside, beyond the boat.

"Heading into Tribune Bay for the night?" he asked.

"Kinda makes sense," I said. "We could keep on until Campbell

River or the Gorge but what's the use? I'd rather get an early start tomorrow."

"Good to stay in the bay," Raven said.

"Why?" I asked.

"So I can meet Sharon."

Raven took the wheel. I took the bench seat. He punched a button on the instrument panel, taking the *Noble Lady* off autopilot. He grasped the wheel with both hands.

"I like to feel a boat with my hands," he said. "Sense her underneath me."

I nodded.

An hour later we slipped into Tribune Bay, gliding by the high cliffs to starboard and the rocky ledge to port. The water changed from chop, to ripples, to gently undulating seas as Hornby Island lent us leeward protection.

"Could fit a hundred boats in here," Raven said.

"Glad there's only a handful today."

"You got a favorite spot?"

I stood and walked beside him, pointed to our port side. "About fifty yards inside that point."

He chuckled softly. "Point separates Big Trib from Little Trib Bay," he said. "Ever been there?"

"To the beach on Little Trib?"

"Uh-huh."

"And seen everyone's everything swaying in the breeze?"

"You've been there."

"Kate and I once sunbathed on Little Trib. Two guys in front of us played Hacky Sack nude. A police officer, fully dressed and armed, walked down the beach. One of the guys stopped him and said, 'I've often wondered what it'd be like to see you patrolling the beach wearing just your gun belt and gun.' The officer turned and said, 'I'll have to try it some time.'"

"Probably will," Raven said. "Canadians aren't as uptight as Americans."

"Which is why Little Trib is a public nude beach."

Raven turned us gently to port, wove between the anchor lines and bows of several sailboats. He lined up parallel to the rock ledge, went a little farther toward the beach, then hit the switch to lower the anchor as he slowly backed down. Sand grabbed the anchor and held it. I stepped out on the foredeck with the anchor bridle. A gentle northerly carried the sounds of conversation and music from Tribune Bay's white sand beach out to the boat, while it wafted the pungent smoky odor of burnt cedar from small beach fires our way.

I walked back into the pilothouse. "Keep radar on for a while," I said.

I went down into the galley for two cans of beer, but when I brought them back to the pilothouse, Raven waved his away.

"After I meet Sharon," he said.

So I clambered down the stairs, then called up to Raven.

"Grab the binoculars. See if you see anything from the south heading our way."

"That small boat that's been shadowing us?"

"I tracked it for the first three hours after we turned north into the strait."

For the next hour, we took turns alternately scanning the radar screen and the southern horizon beyond the bay. Finally, I shut the radar down. Nothing of interest had appeared in either place.

As the sun colored the western sky deep orange behind the rock ledge, we lowered our dinghy from the rear deck. I waited for Raven to hand me his drum, drumstick, and sage bundle. He climbed down into the dinghy and sat quietly scanning the surface of the water while I rowed.

"These are blessed waters," he said.

"I think I told you a monk poured the remnants of a sand mandala in the bay the year before I scattered Sharon's ashes."

Raven nodded. "Yes, but even before that," he said. "To the first inhabitants this was also a sacred place, and their blessings have accumulated through the ages."

Halfway to the beach, and midway between the cliffs and the rock ledge, I stopped rowing. Raven lit the sage bundle. Then he began drumming with his eyes closed, while I waved the smoking sage over the water. I lost track of time while we drifted to the rhythms of his slow beat and the sounds of his low chanting. When he was through, he opened his eyes and slipped his drum back into his duffel. I handed him the sage, which he snuffed out in the water with a hiss.

"Thank you," he said. "For bringing me to meet this noble lady."

BACK ABOARD the *Noble Lady*, we each had a beer while I put together a dinner of baked salmon and corn. After dinner, I unrolled a chart of Desolation Sound, the area between Cape Mudge and Chatham Point, across the galley table. We weighted down the corners with beer cans.

"A lot of places to hide," I said.

Raven shook his head. "No. A lot of places to run, but not a lot of places to hide. You really think they'd use a boat as a safe house?"

"Wouldn't be the first time the Witness Protection Program used one. Easy to move from one location to the next. Easy to situate in a remote, inaccessible area. Easy to guard."

"Unless you need to guard for submarines or SEALs."

"No such thing as an impenetrable safe house. I'm thinking they stashed this couple on a boat in a deep cove," I said.

When Raven picked up his beer can, the chart's corner furled partway. He took a sip, then smoothed out the chart before resting his can on it again. "But not just any deep cove," he said. "Can't be too close to the mainland. Has to have controlled access. Not a lot of ways to reach it other than from the sea."

"That knocks out Theodosia Inlet." I pointed to a cove at the east of Desolation Sound. "Too close to the mainland. But not Pendrell Sound."

Raven nodded. He pointed to the deep gash in East Redonda

Island. "Deep. A lagoon on one side, smaller cove at the back of the sound."

"A lot of traffic there during the summer," I said.

Raven pursed his lips. "Sometimes the best place to hide is in plain sight."

I placed a red check on the chart next to Pendrell Sound.

"Gorge Harbor?" Raven asked.

"Great place, but with the marina there a boat that stayed anchored out for a long period of time would be noticed."

"Prideaux Haven?"

"Hiding in plain sight," I said. "Prideaux is synonymous with Desolation Sound. I wouldn't hide someone there, or even around the corner in Melanie Cove. Now across Homfray Channel is Roscoe Bay. That's another story. Entrance bar. Only accessible at high tide. That's the kind of controlled access I'd choose."

Raven nodded and Roscoe Bay also got a check.

"I'd choose this inlet," I said, as I tapped on Cortes Island, where another deep gash penetrated inland from the sea.

"Ha'thayim," Raven said.

"Von Donop Inlet's native name."

"You know it?" Raven said. He seemed surprised.

"Kate and I stayed there for a few days last year. We heard a wolf pack howl in the morning and saw a black bear foraging along the shore."

Raven scanned the chart. "Narrow entrance. Three miles deep. Small coves along its length. Check it."

I did. Then I held the chart corner down as I took a swig of beer. I placed my can back over the chart and ran the eraser end of my pencil up Discovery Passage from Campbell River, then across to Kanish Bay. "Small Inlet?" I asked.

"It's past the rapids," Raven said.

"But still this side of Chatham Point."

"Good hiding holes up near its head . . . Better check it."

I did that, too.

Raven ran his finger farther up Discovery Passage, circling an area east and slightly south of Chatham Point.

"I like it here," he said.

I leaned over the chart.

"Nothing there."

Raven nodded. "Exactly why I like Thurston Bay Lagoon—it's uncharted."

The Lagoon got the final check.

"Pendrell Sound, Roscoe Bay, Von Donop Inlet, Small Inlet, and Thurston Bay Lagoon. Sounds like a boater's dream trip to Desolation Sound," I said.

"Or a sailing couple's nightmare trip to hell."

I climbed back into the pilothouse, grabbed a Canadian tide table and protractor, and went back downstairs into the galley. I laid one sharp tip of the protractor against the start of the hashed legend at the bottom of the chart, then opened the instrument's legs until the other tip reached out five nautical miles. I walked the protractor from Tribune Bay up the remaining portion of the Strait of Georgia and east to Pendrell Sound. I thumbed through the tide table.

"If we leave here early tomorrow morning, we can make Roscoe near low high water in the afternoon, then leave at the high high early the following morning."

"Pendrell, then Ha'thayim next?" Raven asked.

I leaned over the chart and traced a line from the mouth of Von Donop Inlet north along Calm Channel. I stopped at Stuart Island. "After that, through the Yucultas, around to Thurston Bay Lagoon, then down Discovery Passage into Small Inlet."

"Lot of water to cover," Raven said.

"After that, we'll drop you off at Campbell River to see your grandson."

"Lot can happen between here and there."

"Expect it."

We picked up the beer cans and the chart snap-rolled in on itself from opposite directions, giving it the look of an ancient scroll. I smoothed out one side, then rolled it tightly. I scooped up the chart, tide table, and protractor, and climbed up into the pilothouse. I slipped the chart into a rack alongside others, the tide table into its place along a shelf of books, and the protractor into a leather holster attached to the pilothouse wall. When I got back downstairs, Raven had already slipped the galley table from its pedestal, and pulled the settee out into a bunk. So I walked down into the stateroom and slipped into my berth.

PULLING TAUT against the gentle sway of the boat, the anchor bridle sang to port, then to starboard, then to port again, a high-pitched soft whine from the tension rising and lowering on each bridle line. Occasionally, a low clanging rose from the sea floor, breaking the silence between whines as the turning tide twisted the *Noble Lady* slowly about her anchor, raising and lowering chain links in the sand. I drifted off to these rhythmic sounds, the lullaby of night's safe anchorage.

A dull thud thumped the hull, resounding through several layers of sleep before reaching my awareness. I rubbed my eyes. A deadhead carried in with the tide? Flotsam and jetsam swept off the beach? The second thump reached me in an instant, sprang me upright, and had me grabbing for my pistol. I ran up the steps into the salon, dressed in boxers and a T-shirt, to find Raven kneeling on his berth, dressed the same. He held back the blinds with the barrel of his pistol while he scanned the night sea outside.

I whispered, "Deadhead?"

He whispered back, "Maybe."

I tapped my chest and pointed up the pilothouse steps. He tapped his chest and pointed toward the cabin door. We crept out of the salon. Once in the pilothouse, I slid the door back open and stepped out onto the upper deck. Mast lights from the other boats twinkled as they swayed, like stars fallen from the night sky. A faint smoky odor lingered in the air, a remnant from late-night beach fires.

Raven called out in a loud whisper, "Clear."

I turned aft toward his voice when, suddenly, an outboard engine exploded to life from beneath the *Noble Lady*'s bow.

I yelled, "Boat off our starboard bow!"

The small inflatable sped into the night, heading toward the rocky point of land that separated the two bays. I raced forward to the bow, steadied my arm and my gun against the railing, but I could only see a phosphorescent churning of water and the tail of a luminous wake. I had no shot.

Raven called out, "I'll lower the dinghy."

I turned to hurry back toward him, when I heard the soft *ting* of chain against the hull. I peered over the bow down at the anchor chain, then yelled back to Raven.

"Don't."

"Why?"

"They cut our anchor chain. We're adrift and the tide's pushing us toward the rocks."

Chapter 19

I RACED BACK INTO THE PILOTHOUSE and cranked the ignition key hard. The *Noble Lady*'s engine fired to life. I threw the gearshift into forward and headed out to the open waters of Baynes Sound. Raven joined me at the helm.

"You get the feeling that someone doesn't like us very much?" I asked.

"Someone doesn't want us to get to where we're going."

"Do you think they know that we don't *know* exactly where we're going?"

"Don't think that matters to them. Getting us out of the way does."

"Three hours till daybreak. I'll take a two-hour watch. Once we're out in deeper water, we'll drift and cruise until dawn. Keep the radar on to look for targets. Get some sleep," I said.

"I'll retrieve the anchor and chain in the morning," Raven said. He climbed down the pilothouse stairs.

THROTTLING JUST ABOVE IDLE, the *Noble Lady*'s engine whispered as she meandered through the darkness of Baynes Sound. A soft glow of red, green, blue, and orange instrument lights bathed the pilot-house. A rhythmic pulse of bright green from a circle of light in-scribed on her radar screen suggested the opening and closing of an eye. From an orifice beneath her hull she called out to the water, and though I couldn't hear it, she listened and waited for the echo of her voice to return. I set her on autopilot and stepped just outside the pi-lothouse door. Beads of condensation covered her fiberglass skin as though she had night sweats.

Above us, the hazy light ribbon of the Milky Way shimmered be-hind a carpet of stars. Ahead and to port, a thin halo of light from the mainland dimly outlined the bulk of Texada Island. I looked back at the mast lights that studded Tribune Bay. If Ali Sharik was indeed out there, why cut our anchor chain? If he wanted to avenge his brother's murder, a small explosive charge affixed to the hull would have easily done the job. And if it wasn't Sharik, then who? Someone who wanted us to give up? Someone who wanted to slow us down? Someone who wanted us to speed ahead? Someone who wanted Pete Townsend and the Coast Guard Intelligence Service to look bad? Someone who didn't like the idea of Americans operating in Cana-dian waters? Someone who didn't want us to find the couple before they did?

I replayed Townsend's video communication in my mind. My body grew heavy with a sense of déjà vu. I took in a deep breath of salt air. Perhaps it was only that I had been here before, on a moonless night on the *Noble Lady*'s deck gazing at stars. In the eastern night sky, the barely perceptible glow behind Texada Island brightened, not from mainland lights but the first hints of dawn.

The *Noble Lady* rocked under me, the steps up to her pilothouse creaked. Raven stuck his head above the steps.

"My watch," he said.

"Been two hours already?"

"Uh-huh."

He stepped outside to join me. He, too, looked east.

"B-M-N-T," Raven said.

"Before military nautical twilight," I said.

"Good time to move from the water to the land," he said. "That and EENT, end evening nautical twilight. Hard to discern the horizon. Hard to distinguish features in the environment. We launched SEAL attacks then."

I stiffened. "So did he."

"Who?" Raven asked.

"Sharik's brother. He launched his attack on the *Nanticote* at BMNT."

With a feather-light touch, Raven placed a hand on my shoulder. My body relaxed.

"Think you can find our lost anchor?" he asked.

"Uh-huh."

"Think we should start in that direction?"

"Uh-huh."

"Think it's time to talk about the demons of *tah-wah-kha-fah?*"

"I do."

Raven squeezed my shoulder once before stepping inside. Then the pilothouse steps moaned low under his weight.

I swung the *Noble Lady* around and headed back in from Baynes Sound to Tribune Bay. I'd talked with Kate about being in the Gulf after 9/11 but I'd never really told her the details. Mostly, I'd spoken to the Coast Guard therapist and to Sharon, but by then Sharon could no longer talk back.

I shifted into idle as we neared the rocky ledge on the west side of the bay. I smelled the coffee before I heard Raven slide the cup along the floor behind me. He called up from the galley.

"Got a small lunch anchor?" he asked.

"Rear port lazarette."

"Line?"

"Starboard lazarette."

"I'll drag for the anchor."

"You need help lowering the dinghy?"

"Nah," Raven said. "We're close to the rocks. You stay at the wheel."

I poked my head from the pilothouse door and sucked in a breath of cool morning air, still laced with the smell of burnt wood from beach fires smoldering through the night. A splash came from the *Noble Lady*'s stern, followed by the purring of the dinghy's outboard. Once Raven cleared the bow, I ducked inside and backed the *Noble Lady* away from the rocks out thirty yards into the half-asleep, half-awake light of the bay. Twilight can be a hard time at the helm. Too light for instrument lights. Too dark for no lights at all. I could hear the dinghy motor, but I could barely make out Raven through the windshield. So I set the *Noble Lady* to idle and stepped out the pilothouse door.

Raven lined up parallel to the rock ledge. He putted out from the shore to its tip, pulling the small anchor behind him, pivoted, moved a few yards farther away, then putted back in. In brightening light, I counted ten passes like this before the dinghy motor sputtered and fell silent. Hand over hand, Raven hauled in the small anchor line, like a crabber hauling in a trap. Once it was in the dinghy, he hauled in the large anchor chain. He tied a fender to the chain.

I stepped back inside the pilothouse and eased the *Noble Lady* forward toward the white fender bobbing in the water. The outboard sprang to life and headed to meet us. Behind him Raven let out line tied to the anchor chain. I leaned out the pilothouse door.

"Tie the line off to a forward cleat. Tie the dinghy to a stern cleat. I've got an extension link. You take the wheel. I'll pull in the chain and fasten it."

With Raven at the helm, I climbed down from the pilothouse. I hunted around the rear lazarettes before finding a toolkit. Then I climbed back up into the pilothouse and stepped outside on deck. A dog barked on shore. A few anchor lights flickered off. I undid the figure-eight coil of rope around a starboard cleat. I walked the rope forward, then threaded it through the bow roller. I spun a length of rope around the winch capstan, and pressed my foot on the deck switch. The motor whined. I hauled in line. And the boat moved forward toward the anchor and the rocks.

When rope became chain, I turned to face Raven. My arm shot straight out, then I flagged it in and out slowly from my shoulder toward the rear of the boat. The *Noble Lady*'s engine engaged in reverse with a soft clunk. We backed away, and a few moments later I sliced a finger across my throat.

Undone from each other, the top and bottom halves of the extension link looked like forward and reversed Cs. I hooked the top prong of the bottom C to the end of the anchor chain I'd hauled from the water, and bottom prong of that C to the end of the chain I still had aboard. Then I pressed the top half of the extension link onto the bottom half. I grabbed a ball-peen hammer and struck the two locking studs. The *Noble Lady*'s deck vibrated with each blow and I kept hammering at the studs, well beyond the point when they'd deform to hold the new link firmly. I stopped and looked back at Raven. He stared at me intensely but without expression. I stepped on the footswitch and drew in the remainder of the chain. When the anchor struck the steel guard plate on the hull with a heavy clunk, I twirled my finger above my head, then pointed back, out of the bay.

WE CLEARED THE LONG, slender reef protecting the east part of Tribune Bay and turned north up the Strait of Georgia. Ahead, the rounded peak of Cape Lazo reminded me of a beluga whale's head. To the east and south, a layer of clouds trapped a thin band of pale orange light above jagged mountain peaks. I held on tightly to a second cup of coffee as I sat on the pilothouse bench behind Raven, who stood at the helm.

Images of my therapist's red hair, freckles, and dogged insistence came to mind.

"You need to talk about it," Jean had said. "You need to drop the tough-guy, I-can-handle-it, shit-happens-people-die military mentality," she said. "You killed a man. You ordered others killed. And you need to talk about it. If you don't, when you least expect it, that day will creep up from the depths of your mind and attack you, not once, but over and over again."

I squeezed my coffee cup.

Chapter 20

AFTER 9/11, I PARTICIPATED IN the formation of PATFORSWA, Patrol Force Southwest Asia, as the first Coast Guard Liaison Officer to Bahrain, stationed aboard the *Nanticote*, a hundred-ten-foot cutter. I worked hand in hand with U.S. Naval Intelligence, training the Bahraini Coast Guard in vessel interdiction and inspection. Ali Sharik was my Bahraini liaison."

An image of a dashing Arab man in his early forties flashed through my mind; his thick black eyebrows and bushy mustache matching the black patent-leather brim of his white hat. He wore full dress whites to our first meeting.

"We saluted each other the first time we met. Then he took off his hat, tucked it under his left arm, shook my hand, and kissed me on both cheeks. Sharik was smart. He spoke the King's English. And I meant that. He'd been educated at British military schools, then came to the States to get a doctorate from Harvard in Economics."

"Number one son of a wealthy family?" Raven asked.

"Uh-huh. We worked closely together. I accompanied him in Bahraini patrol boats and he came on patrol with me in Coast Guard vessels. He was stationed on the *Nanticote* during a joint naval exercise. We became friends. He once asked in his thick British accent,

'Charlie, old boy, why is it that you Americans have developed such a knack for hostility and such a lack for diplomacy?"'

"To which you answered?" Raven asked.

"That while wearing the uniform of the United States, I was not permitted to speak freely of our political leadership and our commander-in-chief."

"To which he replied?"

"With an invitation to dinner out of uniform at his family's palatial compound on a hill overlooking the Gulf."

"And the brass allowed it?"

"Encouraged it. After all, I was an intelligence officer and they were looking for on-the-ground assets they could trust in the Middle East. Sharik was young, bright, and Western-trained."

"Must have made for an interesting dinner."

"A strange dinner. Only men. We sat in heavy, high-back carved wooden chairs that Ali said had been in his family for more than a hundred and fifty years. Indonesian women served us stewed lamb with extremely hot peppers. Sharik's father, Ahmed, yelled repeatedly at the women who shuffled past us with bent, covered heads. Ali's brother, Masoud, said little. He eyed me throughout the dinner. After dinner, the father asked for his sons' thoughts about the American war on terror, lit a cigarette, and leaned back in his hand-tooled wood and leather chair to watch the two collide.

"'Islam is a religion of peace,' Ali said. 'The Holy Quran says, "Each time they kindle the fire of war, Allah extinguishes it. They rush about the earth corrupting it. Allah does not love corrupters."'

"'My brother speaks of peace,' Masoud said, 'yet he was educated in the schools of the disbelievers and wears the uniform of their war against Allah. The Quran tells us, "O, you who believe! Fight those of the unbelievers who are near to you and let them find in you hardness."'

"'I wear the uniform of the defenders of the faith and the state,' Ali said. "Permission to fight is given to those who are fought against because they have been wronged," the Quran says. I serve this country to defend against those who would wrong us.'

"'If you are a defender of the faith, then why do you associate with the disbelievers?' Masoud said. He shot a cold, hard glance my way. "'Whoever amongst you takes them for a friend, then surely he is one of them," our most holy book warns.'

"'And the Holy Quran says also, "All people are a single nation. Come to terms as between us and you,"' Ali said, 'He is my friend.' Ali looked my way.

"'"Let the believers not make friends with infidels in preference to the faithful—he who does this has nothing to hope for from Allah—except in self-defense,"' Masoud said.

"This sparring continued until Ahmed clapped his hands twice. He snapped his fingers and an Indonesian woman with her head bowed scurried in. She sat a silver tray of small coffee cups in front of Ahmed. He dismissed her with another finger snap. After he passed the silver cups around the table, Ahmed turned to me. 'And what does our foreign guest think of this discussion of the Holy Quran?'

"Masoud smiled devilishly.

"'Father,' Ali said. 'I do not think that is a fair question for Charlie.'

"I raised my coffee cup to my lips and took a small sip of the bitter, thick black liquid. 'There is a verse from the Quran I am fond of,' I said.

"Masoud set his coffee cup down. A smile like the outline of a sharp saber spread over his lips.

"'Book Two, Verse 214, if I remember correctly. "Or do ye think that ye shall enter the Garden of Bliss without such trials as came to those who came before you?"'

"Masoud's smile turned down.

"Ahmed clapped his hands. 'A wonderful recitation from our guest,' he said, though his eyes conveyed derision.

"'Thank you, Charlie, for your knowledge of our Holy Book,' Ali said.

"'Be careful of quoting from the Holy Quran,' Masoud said. 'Lest your words be visited on you through the will of Allah.' He pushed back from the table and left the room.

"The next day, I went to Ali's office to review the interdiction and inspection procedures for large tankers entering the port. He saluted me, but never again reached for my hand.

"Then one evening, several weeks later, I was acting CO of the *Nanticote* while the CO and XO were meeting at a forward operating base in Kuwait with the Commander of Coast Guard Forces in the Middle East.

"To accommodate the local men who drove supply trucks to the ship, and needed to make early morning prayers, we often ran a shift at 0400 to unload trucks. One morning at 0403, a loud blast rocked the ship, and shook me from sleep. The acting XO pounded on my door. I hopped to the door, one leg in my pants, the other out. The young officer's eyes flashed wide. He expelled short, sharp breaths, and spoke with rapid-fire words. 'Sir, goddamn local blew up a truck. Took out three crew members.'

"'Sound General Quarters. Meet me at the helm.'

"'Yes, sir.' The XO took off down the companionway.

"A moment later the *Nanticote*'s intercom cycled between siren whoops and a recorded call 'General Quarters ... General Quarters ... General Quarters.' Metal hatches slammed against metal bulkheads. Hundreds of feet drummed over metal floors.

"I slipped my other leg into my pants, whipped on a shirt, and grabbed my .45 caliber sidearm and my holster from the dresser. I raced down the companionway and climbed several ladders up to the bridge. I barked, 'Damage report,' as I entered.

"Someone yelled out, 'Seamen Ruiz, Johnson, Overlake are confirmed casualties. Seamen Finseth, Hamlin, Warwick, and Williams have been transported to sick bay. We have a six-inch diameter hole in the forward starboard side of the hull about eight feet above the waterline and ...'

"He never got to finish his report. Another blast came from dockside, throwing sailors around the helm into each other. I pulled myself up from the floor, called out to my XO, 'Hamlin, where the fuck did that come from? And why the hell haven't we stopped trucks from getting anywhere near this vessel?'

"'All vehicles have been detained at checkpoint 1,' Hamlin said.

"'Anderson, notify PATFORSWA that we're under attack.'

"'Hamlin, get an armed force on the dock immediately. I want everything, I mean every goddamn garbage can and pile of junk anywhere near this ship swept for hostiles and explosives.'"

Footsteps pounding metal floors and racing down ladders swept back into my mind. A cacophony of voices barking orders drowned out the sounds of the *Noble Lady*'s engine. The biting odor of burning metal, rubber, and plastic assaulted my nose. I squeezed my eyes closed, shook my head.

"A flash of light blinded me. Another deafening explosion rocked the *Nanticote*. But this one came from seaward. I ran to the starboard side of the helm, threw binoculars to my eyes in time to see two crewmen dive from a burning patrol boat into a fiery sea. Gunfire erupted from the ocean."

Raven turned back momentarily from the helm, his eyes wide.

"'There, sir.' Hamlin pointed out a starboard window. 'Two hundred yards off our starboard beam. Headed directly at us.'

"I raised my binoculars, this time to a fleet of dozens of rowboats, two men in each boat bearing down on the *Nanticote*. The loudspeakers blared, *Tah-wah-kha-fah. Tah-wah-kha-fah. Tah-wah-kha-fah.*

"'Ten seconds,' I said. 'If those rowboats don't stop in ten seconds, order our patrol boats in and our gunners to fire upon them.'

"Smell from the dockside explosion wafted through the helm, clawed at the back of my throat. I remember coughing, stepping to the portside window. White foam spewed from nozzles directed at a few remaining flames. Sparks flew from a torch hovering close to the hull. Men and women raced up and down the gangway.

"*Bam. Bam. Bam. Bam. Bam.* Our 50-caliber machine guns called me to the starboard side of the helm. As bullets dove into the sea, dozens of tiny water spouts capered around the rowboats. Wood and bodies splintered high into the air before splashing into the sea. A crimson sheen shimmered over the pale early-morning ocean. I feared that soon dorsal fins would dash frenzied through the carnage. Then our guns went silent. No rowboats remained afloat.

"Hamlin held up his hand. Spoke over his mike. He turned to me. 'Sir, I believe the last intruder has been taken out near the engine room. PATFORSWA wants to speak with you ASAP on a secure line in your quarters.'

"'Sweep the ship for intruders and explosive devices. Start with my quarters. Have a complete damage report ready once I get off this call with PATFORSWA.'

"I turned to exit the bridge, then pivoted around. 'And Hamlin, have comm jam all incoming and outgoing signals except the en-crypted PATFORSWA frequencies.'

"A pained expression descended over my XO's face. 'Sir, we won't be able to call our patrol boats in.'

"I jabbed a finger at him. 'Jam all frequencies and do it now!'

"'Yes, sir.'

"I raced from the bridge, slid down a ladder, skipping several treads. I pressed back against the steel companionway bulkhead to let a team with a stretcher hustling a wounded crewman squeeze past me. I turned a corner toward my quarters and a heavy metal door clunked shut. A petty officer pulled a key from the door lock. When she saw me, she snapped to attention, saluted.

"'Clean and locked, sir,' she said.

"I whipped back a quick salute. 'As you were.'

"She waved the two men with her forward and they hurried off, carrying a long metal wand and an armful of electronic gear.

"I shoved my key into the door lock, and swung open the door just as a crewman in a bloody uniform turned the corner behind me and slumped down against the bulkhead a few feet away. I stepped to-ward him.

"'Are you hurt, son?'

"The man sprang to his feet, shoved the tip of a knife into my side, caught one of my arms behind my back and shouldered me into my quarters. He stripped my .45 from its holster and threw me against the back of a couch.

"I opened my mouth to order the crewman to stand down when I realized I was staring into the dark, angry eyes of Masoud Sharik."

Chapter 21

OR DO YE THINK THAT ye shall enter the Garden of Bliss without such trials as came to those who came before you?' Masoud said. A sickening grin covered his lips.

"I moved toward Masoud. He leveled my pistol at me. I stopped.

"'How did you get onto my ship?'

"'Carrying a stretcher with one of your wounded sailors.'

"'What do you want?'

"'To watch your face as we enter the Garden of Bliss.' He ripped open his shirt. A wide leather strap held off-white blocks of a claylike material around his waist. A daisy chain of wires spiraled between the blocks ending in a bundle tucked into his pants pocket. Masoud's grin widened.

"'I held out my hand. 'It doesn't have to be this way.'

"'Praise be Allah, it does.'

"'Our mission is to help Bahrain, not to hurt it.'

"'You even believe your own lies.' Masoud shook his head slowly, his grin replaced by an icy stare. 'Do you not think I know what my brother does? Your mission is to corrupt him; to turn him against his family, his country, his faith. Your very presence here disgraces Allah.'

"'If that's the message you wish to communicate, I can arrange for a broadcast from this ship that will reach millions.'

"He checked his watch. I scanned his face. His grin returned. He patted his waist. 'Praise be Allah, this I have already arranged.'

"Masoud's lips moved slowly. He spoke silently, repetitively. His eyes closed ever so slightly. He looked at me, though his gaze, now peaceful, suggested he peered into another world far away. Suddenly, his eyes flared wide. He jammed a hand into his pocket. His gaze dropped slightly, and when it did I let my knees buckle and sent a swift kick at his other hand.

"The pistol flew from one hand, a cell phone from the other. I dove for the pistol, Masoud for the phone. I swept the pistol from the floor and shot Masoud twice in the head. Blood and bits of his brain splattered over me and the back of the couch. With another shot, I destroyed the phone."

Raven turned from the helm. He nodded. "He was expecting a call to set off the explosion."

"Or maybe he'd set the cell phone timer wrong."

"Either way, you saved the *Nanticote*."

"And created a diplomatic mess."

"How?"

"The men in the rowboats? Fishermen. All unarmed. None survived."

"They were sent as a diversion."

"Some in the media claimed I ordered the massacre of innocent civilians."

"What about the explosives, the threat to the ship?"

"PATFORSWA ordered us to say nothing about a suicide bombing attempt. The official word was only that a group of terrorists tried to take over the *Nanticote*."

"They covered it up?"

"Uh-huh."

"Out of embarrassment? Because the ship's captain wasn't aboard?"

"Maybe to curtail information about force vulnerabilities from finding its way into the hands of others like Masoud. I just don't know. The Bahraini government, however, lodged a formal diplomatic protest. They claimed the fishermen were simply protesting against the *Nanticote* because they thought our ship was driving fish from their waters."

"Did you tell Masoud's brother what happened?"

"I never had a chance to. I saw Ali when he came to pick up Masoud's remains later that day. He stared at me, shook his head, then hissed. 'You killed my younger brother, Charlie. Why?' The next day I was ordered home."

"What did your command say?" Raven asked. He turned the wheel a few degrees to starboard.

"Pete Townsend's face was red when he said, 'I'm under a gag order about this, too.' Then next thing I heard was that Ali Sharik had left the Bahraini military and was working as an operative for a terrorist group centered in the Gulf."

We crossed a mile in front of the southern face of Mitlenach Island, where thousands of white specks dotted the rocky landscape. Suddenly, the gulls took to the sky en masse like a huge living sail untethered. A cacophony of muted, raucous cries penetrated the pilot-house walls. Looking south, out the starboard side window, the bulge of Cape Lazo now appeared like an island floating in the wide expanse of the Strait of Georgia. Gray clouds hung over the shadowed peaks on the mainland side of the strait. Several miles in the distance, a tug towing a barge of lumber uncovered from the background of Savary Island, heading our way.

Raven stepped back from the helm. I stood.

"You should have told me," I said. "My watch's come and gone."

"You needed to talk more than you needed to drive. Your crew know what really happened?"

"A few maybe. But they were ordered to remain silent."

"No ceremony. No medal."

"Happens when you're in intelligence. I was never much one for medals anyway."

Raven put a hand on my shoulder. "Ceremony's not for you. Neither's the medal. They're like the drumbeat and the smoke. They're for your spirit, to release it so it can go on from that man, that day. You need that. Especially if you're about to meet his brother again."

I GUIDED THE *Noble Lady* along Baker Passage, threading the gap between Hernando and Twin islands. Directly ahead, and high above, the tall, craggy snowcapped peaks of the mainland British Columbia coastal range reminded me of a conclave of conferring gigantic crones.

I had not wanted to leave Bahrain without spending time with Ali. I always believed that once past the pain of his brother's death, he'd understand the decisions I had to make, the lives and ship I had to protect. I never got a chance to say good-bye to Ali as my friend. And now I hunted him as my enemy.

When we reached Mink Island, I turned to Raven.

"Wanna check the tides for Roscoe Bay?"

He reached behind him and pulled a book off the shelf overhead.

"We're two hours early for the low high."

"Guess it's Pendrell Sound."

"You have an idea what we're looking for?"

"With DOJ responsible for protection, my guess is we're looking for guys on boats who seem out of place up here."

Raven laughed. "You mean lawyers in suits and sunglasses at the helm of Bayliners; briefcases opened on the chart table?"

I laughed, too. "DOJ was probably smart enough to leave the lawyers at the dock and contract with a private security firm."

Raven laughed again. "Oh, you mean Rambos in camouflaged pontoon boats with Uzis up here in Desolation."

I hadn't stopped laughing. "What? You suddenly meet your 'Inner Comic'?"

Raven just smiled. And I remembered what Janet Paulsen once said about the mythic Raven—a trickster figure who appears as just the opposite of what you'd expect, as a reminder to look beneath the surface layer of things.

At the moment, Raven's humor helped with the painful memories of that fiery day in Bahrain.

"Lawyers or Rambos," I said, "pretty sure they'll stick out."

We turned to starboard to enter Pendrell Sound.

I pointed to a sign on the rocks that requested boaters to slow down below five knots because of oyster spat. "It's a strange name to call young oyster," I said.

"Even stranger that the waters inside Pendrell Sound reach into the mid-seventies this time of year, warm enough for spat to grow, or for humans to swim in. Something to do with the Japanese current," Raven said.

"North Pacific current," I said. "The Japanese current, the Kurishio, flows north along the coast of Japan, bringing warm water up from the tropics. When it hits the cold subarctic Oyashio current, it sends a warm stream heading east across the northern Pacific." I pointed right and left, down the rocky fairway into Pendrell Sound. "Summertime sun hitting these rocks at low tide combined with the NPC, voilà," I snapped my fingers. "You have water that you can swim in."

Raven chuckled. "What? You suddenly meet your 'Inner Oceanographer'?"

I shook my head but didn't turn around. "Studied oceanography at the academy."

The fairway into Pendrell Sound opened up to a slightly larger inner bay two miles wide, giving East Redonda Island a horseshoe shape on the chart. I turned to starboard to begin a counterclockwise sweep around the bay. As I did, my depth sounder plummeted until dashes replaced numbers. Not only was Pendrell surprisingly warm, it was also surprisingly deep, or what mariners call "steep-to."

Raven stood up behind me. He grabbed a pair of binoculars from the ledge above the instrument panel and stepped beside me at the helm. Sun peaked through a thin white veil covering an otherwise blue sky above Pendrell's verdant peaks. Every hundred yards or so we passed the bow of a boat that seemed to poke out from the sound's rocky walls. In these depths, boats anchored within a few feet of shore, then ran a stern line to a tree, a rock, an old logging ring on-shore to keep their anchor pulling uphill, lest they swing out toward deeper water and completely lose their set.

Children dove from the gunwales of boats, swam aft, climbed back in and up onto the gunwales for their next plunge. Blue smoke curled upward from stainless steel grills affixed on the stainless steel handrails of gleaming white boats. The scent of cooking fish hovered. Laundry hung on a line running aft from the mast of a sailboat. A woman sunbathing topless on the bow of a mock tugboat didn't bother covering up as we glided by. Instead she raised her hand and waived backwards over her head, without lifting her gaze from the pages of her book. Raven's binoculars careened in her direction.

He chuckled. "Nothing out of the ordinary so far."

Webbed bags of spatted oyster shells hung from the walls at the far end of the sound. I turned to Raven.

"I'll stick our nose into the back bay," I said. "You have a look around."

With so much of the back bay devoted to an oyster farming operation, only a few larger boats stern-tied there, and with no women sunbathing topless, it didn't take long to see there was nothing out of the ordinary in the back bay either. I spun the *Noble Lady* around, swung wide to avoid some crab pots, and headed back up the smaller west leg of East Redonda Island. I hadn't gotten far when Raven whipped open the pilothouse door and stepped out on deck. A moment later, he was back inside, pointing.

"There, just in front of the lagoon. Sleek, go-fast boat. No flybridge. No bimini over the cockpit."

He handed me the binoculars.

"And two guys with backpacks climbing into a Boston Whaler with a console and a honking big outboard," I said. "Whaler's nearly as big as their boat. Boat's not even stern-tied. They've got a small inflatable fastened to the bow. Wait. And they're using the Whaler under power to ferry themselves just a few yards to shore."

I yanked the binoculars away from my eyes and handed them back to Raven.

"Okay, those are definitely not northwest boaters, and that's out of the ordinary enough for me. Did you see that yellow sign on shore?" Raven asked.

"No."

He steadied the binoculars. "Says the trail into the forest from the beach is currently closed."

Ten minutes later we reached the *Sea Dog*. A clean-shaven man in his mid- to late- thirties with a crew cut and well-developed biceps under a tight short-sleeved shirt stepped out from inside the other boat as we glided by. I turned to Raven.

"Take the helm."

He did, and I stepped just outside of the pilothouse and waved to the fellow on the other boat. I cupped my hands around my mouth.

"You guys out fishing?"

The man seemed startled at first. His neatly creased blue jeans pressed against the back railing. His eyes hid behind a pair of wrap-around sunglasses. "Yeah, but we haven't had much luck."

"Go bottom fishing here in Pendrell?" I asked.

He mounted a weak smile. "Tried but not so much as a nibble." He raised his arms and shrugged his shoulders.

"Well, better luck tomorrow," I said.

I stepped inside. Raven chimed mockingly, "Go bottom fishing here in Pendrell?"

I chuckled, then said in my best official voice, "The best intelligence is always obtained in the least intrusive way."

"In these depths you'd have to long-line to bottom fish," Raven said.

"Uh-huh, which is precisely why I asked." I pointed to the shore ahead. "Want to pull in beyond that wooden ketch?"

A hundred yards beyond the ketch, Raven slowed to idle, then turned to port. He hit the switch that dropped the anchor, then backed down. The anchor bit quickly.

"Keep her in low reverse," I said.

I climbed down from the pilothouse and walked out into the cockpit. After fumbling around in the starboard lazarette for a few moments and pushing aside some gear, I emerged with a large spool of yellow quarter-inch polypropylene line. I raised one end of a wooden shaft that sat between two posts, slipped the spool of line over the shaft, and lowered the shaft end into its holder. I undid the lines holding the dinghy up into its davits, then lowered it to the water. Without the benefit of two pairs of hands, the dinghy hit the water with a splash. Then I climbed over the *Noble Lady*'s stern with one end of the yellow line in my hand. I tied that through an eyebolt affixed to the upper part of the dinghy's transom.

Squeaks and squeals emanated from the *Noble Lady*'s stern as the spool spun on its shaft, paying out line to me. I rowed the twenty yards in to shore, beached the dinghy, undid the stern line from the eyebolt, and carried it up the short rocky beach. I found a large driftwood log, and judging from the scars around its bare trunk, so had many other boaters seeking to stern-tie. I looped the stern line around and under the trunk, dug away some rocks and pulled the yellow line through. Then, I scampered back down to my dinghy and rowed back to the *Noble Lady*, tugging on the stern line as I did. The spool continued to complain. When I reached the *Lady*'s stern, I tied off the dinghy, then climbed back over the stern and tied off the stern line to a cleat along the caprail.

I walked inside and called up the pilothouse stairs, "Cut the engine."

Raven looked straight ahead. He must not have heard me. So, I called to him again, "Cut the engine."

Then I remembered Raven's hearing loss. I climbed up the pilothouse stairs and tapped him on the shoulder. He shifted into neutral, then shut the engine down without being asked.

Out of gear, the *Noble Lady* wanted to drift forward on the pull of her anchor, but the moment she tried, the stern line pulled tight around the driftwood log and held her in place, bow pointed out from the shore. I wrangled the bridle from an aft lazarette and slung it around the anchor. Then I let a few feet of anchor out until the bridle went taut just inches above the surface of the water.

With the *Lady* snugly stern-tied, Raven and I sat in the pilothouse, watching the go-fast boat without a bimini that we'd passed on the way in. We didn't have to watch for long. From the deep green cedar and Douglas fir forest above the waterline, three men emerged, all looking just about the same as the guy on the boat: well built, jeans and T-shirts, wraparound sunglasses. All in their late thirties. So much for individual style.

One slipped on the large, smooth, rounded rocks above the waterline while trying to untie the dinghy's painter from around a tree trunk. The others laughed. He picked himself up, and they all stepped into the Whaler. Just like before, they fired up the engine for the long trip to their boat, which twisted in the current a few yards offshore.

"Think it might be worthwhile to have a look at where those fellows came from," I said.

"Maybe worthwhile for me to stay with the boat," Raven said.

"Exactly what I was thinking."

I climbed down from the pilothouse and stepped into the stateroom to grab my .45 automatic from a drawer. Then I walked out onto the cockpit, eased the pistol into the small of my back, and the dinghy into the water on the starboard side of the boat, away from the eyes of the look-alikes on the *Sea Dog*. I stepped out of the boarding gate and into the dinghy. Keeping the *Noble Lady* between me and the boat of look-alikes, I rowed further down the shore until I tucked into a tiny cove where the look-alikes couldn't see me. I hauled the dinghy high up on the rocky shore and hitched it to a tree.

Behind me, a soft breeze sent a rich aromatic whiff of cedar my way. Below me, water licked smooth beach stones. Beneath my feet, a tiny crab emerged from one rock shelter and scurried to another. I looked out over a placid sound reflecting a gently undulating pale blue sky. For a brief moment, I just wanted to sit and take it all in with Kate by my side.

But a sharp crack broke my momentary stillness. With a splat, a clam shell dropped from high above, cracked open and oozed its semi-liquid contents over rocks several yards beyond the dinghy. A series of screeches brought two screaming gulls down from the sky, nipping at each other even before they'd reached the shell. One lunged at the shell. The other lunged at its companion. They fought and squawked, unaware of a third gull, which dove silently and stole the tasty morsel away. The pugilists squealed, taking flight after the thief.

I turned from the beach and stepped into the darkness between two tall cedar trees.

Chapter 22

A THICK FOREST of downed trees and dense underbrush lay before me. I headed inland, where the forest tempered the sound of the crackling and snapping under my feet. I pulled myself up and over fallen trunks covered with a thick green slime; pushed pale green, dew-laden Spanish moss away from my face; and picked a path through the dark reddish brown carpet of branches and brambles arranged like a network of pick-up-sticks under my feet. The sun's rays cut thin light trails through the canopy and through the mist hovering in the air. Once deeper into the forest I angled right in the direction of a hoped-for trail.

Twenty minutes later, with the front of my clothes now covered in green film, I came to an opening between the trees and took a left turn onto a narrow trail that headed even deeper into the island. A moment later, branches crackled behind me. I whipped my pistol from behind my back, crouched, and turned wide-eyed, my gaze scanning like a radar beam. Suddenly, a massive form leaped from the brush twenty yards away.

The large deer stood in the path, its dark marble eyes trained on me, small steam jets rising from each nostril. Then it bounded into the brush on the other side of the trail and bounced away, leaving only the sound of breaking branches receding into the distant woods. I returned my pistol to the small of my back.

The trail soon came to a marsh where hand-cut boards lay across a spongy bog. I followed a path of still-damp footprints, pointed in both directions over the boards. On the other side of the wetland, the trail rose through a rocky outcrop. Hand over hand, I scampered up to a thrilling view of the snowcapped mainland coastal range rising above East Redonda Island's green peaks. Ahead, a thick plateau of green reminded me of a field of nettles. A narrow footpath cut through the field. Beyond that lay a small, pastel blue dome perched beneath the trees, but not of the forest.

Brronnk. Brronnk. Brronnk. A raven's cry broke the silence, and the rhythmic swish of its wings beat through the air overhead. I chuckled. Maybe he'd flown in spirit with me. That thought had not yet left my mind when I turned to the footsteps behind me, and a rifle butt crashing into my chest.

I staggered backward and fell to my knees, then onto my back. I squeezed my eyes to fight off the searing wave of pain. When I opened them, three eyes stared back at me—two belonged to a burly, bald-headed man, the third to the barrel of his automatic weapon.

In a deep voice he yelled, "Fuck you doin' here?"

He cradled his rifle in one arm, finger on the trigger, while stroking his beard.

"Stretching my legs," I said. "Been cruising most of the day."

"Expect me to believe that?"

"Boat's down in the Pendrell."

"You work for Jacques?"

"Who the hell is Jacques?"

"Yves, then, or one of them Ontario fellas?"

"Don't have a goddamn clue who you're talking about."

"Fucking American, eh?"

"Fucking Canadian, eh?"

He slapped his other hand on the rifle and jabbed it at me as though jousting. The weapon wobbled in his unsteady hands.

Though he wore camouflage fatigues, nothing about this fellow suggested a trained professional.

"Get up," he said. He motioned across the field of green. "Think we'll go back to the tent and I'll call them."

"Call who?"

"Fucking guys that just came up here outta breath and all."

"Guys dressed in matching blue jeans?"

"Yeah."

I stood. He stepped closer. I slammed my forearm into the side of the rifle barrel, while swinging my leg to catch him just behind his knee. He arched back into a fall. One hand flew from the rifle and reached for the ground, palm out. The rifle waved wildly in the other hand. He hit the ground with a thud. I pounced on his rifle arm, pinned his wrist to the ground with my knee, and tried to twist the rifle from his grip. He held on tight. Then he swung a fist into my back and pounded me hard several times. I slammed my forearm into his throat. He coughed, then clutched his throat. I whipped my pistol from the small of my back, squeezed it through the pain of my injured finger, and jammed it into the soft flesh under the big guy's chin.

"Let go of your rifle, now!"

But he held on.

"Let go."

I dug my pistol in deeper. His head arched back.

"What's so goddamn important that you're willing to get hurt?" I asked.

"Grow op," he said. He spoke with a feeble, hoarse whisper. "It's all I got."

"Let go of your rifle. I'm not after your weed."

He exhaled and finally his grip loosened. I patted him down, then grabbed the rifle and stood up. I pulled out the magazine and ejected the chambered round. Then I stuffed the magazine and the bullet in my pocket, and flung the rifle into a sea of green plants around me.

"What's your name?" I asked.

He rubbed his throat. "Russell."

"Russell, who were those men who came up here?"

"Thought you were with 'em."

"Well you thought wrong and it cost me a sore chest and you a sore throat. Who were they?"

"Buyers from Nelson or Revelstoke. Somewhere east of here."

"In that case, I'll be getting back to my boat."

Russell shook his head, closed his eyes. I left him sitting, still rubbing his throat.

"Hey," Russell called out.

I turned around. With an underhand toss he flung a package wrapped in aluminum foil my way. I caught it.

"Take an ounce back with you for your troubles," he said.

I flipped the package back to him. I waved my hand. "Swore off it," I said.

"Too bad, man. BC Bud. It's some real good shit."

RAVEN REACHED OUT a hand for me. I grabbed it, and with the other took hold of the caprail and stepped back onto the *Noble Lady*. I winced, clutching my chest.

He nodded toward the shore. "Had a feeling something wasn't right in there," he said.

"Had a feeling that you had a feeling something wasn't right," I said.

He smiled weakly. "Maybe should have listened to your feelings sooner."

Later that evening I sat in the cockpit. My head flopped back on the caprail. A crescent moon with a coterie of early stars hovered in a dark purple sky that seemed only a few inches away from my face.

"Noble."

I raised my head to Raven, standing before me with a drum and a towel. My next inhalation brought with it an aromatic and charcoal smell of partially burnt sage.

"Your spirit needs to be welcomed home from that day. You need to cleanse to meet this man again," Raven said.

"What'd you have in mind?"

He pointed off from the stern. "Drum. Sage. Water."

I sighed. "And if I don't believe in your ritual?"

"Believe, not believe, lives here." Raven tapped his head lightly. "Spirit lives here." He tapped over his heart. "My ritual doesn't matter. You have another one, Noble? Use it."

"No, I don't have one. I really was never into rituals until I met you."

Raven chuckled. "You wore a uniform with medals across your chest. You marched in step with others. You displayed your rank based on stars, stripes, and bars. You saluted those with superior rank. You pledged allegiance to a piece of fabric. You swore an oath to uphold a two-hundred-thirty-year-old document. You paid homage to the gods Neptune and Davy Jones . . . But you weren't into rituals." He spoke those final words slowly.

I cracked a smile and nodded. "Okay, what's next?"

Next was out of my clothes and into the warmth of Pendrell Sound. I floated beside the *Noble Lady*, touching her hull while Raven sat just inside of the open boarding gate. He beat out a slow rhythm in time with the gentle rocking of the boat and my body. I don't know if it was his hypnotic drumming or the relaxation from me floating, but at one point when I closed my eyes I found it hard to distinguish where the water ended and my body began.

When Raven's drumming stopped, a hiss, then a sizzle, let me know he'd lit the sage. The pungent aroma floated above me.

"With each exhalation," he said, "feel you can let go of whatever you need to let go of from that day. Thoughts. Feelings. Situations. Circumstances. Let them leave you with the smoke."

Raven went back to drumming.

As I floated in the water, an image floated into my mind. I squeezed my eyes closed, trying at first to block it. Then I breathed deeply. Let my body relax into the water, my eyes open to the full moon and the stars. The image of Masoud's head exploding from my bullet washed over me. I exhaled that image. Still, the water now lapping my body felt like his blood. I took another deep breath, fighting the urge to bolt into the boat.

One long sharp beat from Raven's drum preceded two softer short ones. Each of his long beats brought with it the sound of my .45 firing at Masoud. And with his short beats, a vision of the grotesque death smile etched on Masoud's face; blood oozing from a dime-sized hole in his forehead. I focused hard, exhaled with the long beats, and let the sound of my gun come up from my gut and out from my nostrils into the smoke hovering above my head.

Raven's drumming receded into the background of my inner world, leaving me with the sound of my gun firing and with images of Masoud's head exploding in death. The sounds and images rose. I exhaled them hard into the smoke. But they rose again and again, like the upwelling of a violent sea, until I realized at one point that all I heard was the sound of my exhalations, sharp and long in time with the beat of Raven's drum.

The drumming stopped. My breathing relaxed.

Raven whispered, "Dip under the water several times. Each time you surface, inhale into yourself whatever you need in order to let go of that day. Get it from the water. Bring it into your spirit with your breath."

He went back to drumming.

I let my legs drop from under me, taking my body from floating to treading water. I exhaled and dipped under the black liquid blanket. One by one, a line of hands raised in sharp salute across the shiny patent-leather bills of dress-white Coast Guard hats. Then my body rose from beneath the water, and one by one, I heard voices saying, as I sucked in a breath, "Lieutenant Commander Noble. Job well done." And hands cut the air as they lowered from their salute.

I dipped under the water and rose to the voices and the salutes several times until only the sounds of my breathing, the movement of my body, and Raven's drumming remained.

A moment later his drumming stopped. He extended a hand and I climbed aboard. I toweled off and dropped into my berth, spent.

HIGH HIGH TIDE at Roscoe Bay happened at seven the following morning, but Roscoe is just across Waddington Channel from Pendrell Sound, on West Redonda Island. So we waited until six o'clock to weigh anchor. Raven took the helm for the short trip. I took the pilothouse bench behind him, clutching a cup of coffee. A steam plume rose from my cup. A steady mist fell from low-lying clouds. Squeals, then thumps, then squeals played rhythmically from the wiper blades, accompanied by the deep bass rumble of the *Noble Lady's* diesel.

Beyond the mouth of Pendrell Sound, I looked to starboard, where the dark ribbon of Waddington Channel disappeared into a veil of white smoke and a curtain of forest green. Clouds obliterating peaks compressed the world from above. A thickening mist reduced visibility below. Raven flipped a switch and the radar screen beeped, then glowed neon green. I stepped to the helm beside him, set my cup on the ledge above the screen, and focused on the circular whir of light for what it might reveal about the world outside the boat.

My eyes made small circles, following each sweep of the radar, scanning not only the screen but also, it seemed, the world inside me. Where heaviness once lay, I now detected a void. Something had gone after last night in the water. I just wasn't sure what was now in its place. I took a deep breath. Then I felt the warmth of Raven's hand on my shoulder.

One half-hour later, Raven swung the *Lady* to starboard and we dipped into an opening along the West Redonda shore. A narrow fairway led back to Roscoe Bay. Less than a half-mile past the opening the fairway narrowed even further, and the depth sounder alarm squawked. I hit a button to mute it. Raven slid the *Lady* to port around a toothlike, rocky shoal and we slipped into Roscoe Bay, where several boats swayed at anchor. I picked up the binoculars, then tapped Raven on the shoulder and pointed out the starboard window to a small cove just beyond the shoal.

Close to the rock cliff on the north side of the cove, readings from the *Lady*'s sounder plunged to more than seventy feet, which made a stern-tie seem like a wise choice. Raven dropped the anchor and kept the engine running in reverse. I climbed downstairs to don blue raingear and drop the dinghy. I hauled the yellow stern line over to the wet cliff wall and looped it through a metal eye at the end of a line another boater had affixed to a tree high atop the cliff. Once back aboard, I shed my wet parka. Raven cut the engine. I snugged the stern line and the *Lady* nestled safely into her nook.

I climbed up into the pilothouse, handed Raven the binoculars, and grabbed another pair from the shelf above the pilothouse bench. I pointed straight ahead.

"Older couple on that forty-two-foot Grand Banks in front of us," I said. "Engine's running. He's hauling in the dinghy. Looks like they're getting ready to leave."

"Lady's bringing a dinghy to shore from *Queen*, a navy and gray Nordhavn 43. One chocolate Lab at the bow ... oops, make that one chocolate Lab in the water swimming to shore," Raven said. He chuckled.

"Big Bayliner at the head of the bay. See any activity on it?"

Raven spun in that direction. "Hmmm. *My Time* from Reno, Nevada. Too early for gamblers to be awake." He turned slightly to his left. "How about that American Tug 41 *Misty Rose* just the other side of *My Time*?"

"Fellow in a heavy gray sweater just came out on deck and raised his hand like he's checking the downfall. Can't imagine using a boat like that as a command post."

"Good reason to use it," Raven said.

"Bears keeping a lookout on it and on *My Time*."

"We oughta check out Black Lake."

"One that feeds into the bay?"

"Uh-huh."

"We could also take a closer look at the other boats on our way in to shore."

The mist had thickened into an honest rain. Raven suited up in orange raingear. I lead the dinghy by its painter from the stern around to the boarding gate and hopped in to take a seat at the rear. I handed Raven the painter. He held the dinghy close while he stepped in to take a front seat. He pushed us away from the *Lady*'s hull and I pulled the starter cord, which brought the outboard to life.

I spun the dinghy around in a tight circle, then pointed us toward the head of Roscoe Bay. Rain pummeled the water. I stole a backward glance at the *Lady*. A glossy wet sheen had settled over her white hull, which stood out against the slick black rock wall behind her. Warmth filled my chest. She was my safety, my security, my way home. And I'd do anything to keep her from harm. I inhaled deeply. Those 270 young men and women needed the *Nanticote*, too, and that's why I put a bullet through Masoud Sharik's skull.

Raven tapped me on the knee, then pointed over the inflatable's rounded fabric gunwales. Beneath the rain-frenzied surface of the water, thousands of small gossamer forms beat like tiny winged hearts, gliding in all directions. Our propeller's blade churned through this mass of moon jellyfish. I mashed the red Stop button. The dinghy slowly pirouetted as it glided, no longer under power. I rocked the engine up from the water. Bits of translucent moon jelly bodies clung to the engine shaft and the plastic propeller blades. Raven slid into the middle seat and slipped the oars from their holders. The head of the bay wasn't that far away and the killing wasn't that necessary.

Raven rowed us between the Bayliner, *My Time*, and the American Tug, *Misty Rose*. The drapes were closed on the Bayliner. A fellow on the back of *Misty Rose* fumbled with a fender he'd fetched from the water—a good sign that *Misty Rose* was planning on staying in Roscoe Bay for a while. At the head of the bay, Raven set one oar inside our boat and used the other like a gondolier to push the dinghy ashore. He hopped out with the painter and yanked on it, hauling the dinghy, with me still inside, farther up the small beach. He tied the painter to a piece of driftwood. The dinghy rested next to a double-seated red and white kayak, and a blue and gray inflatable with the stenciled name, *T/T Queen*.

Raven and I set off on the Black Lake trail. We'd just started up a small ravine when the chocolate Lab came bounding around a bend, head down. She pulled up and reared back when she saw us. She barked once. We stopped. She barked several times, then looked back at the trail. She sniffed me, then barked. I reached down to pet her. She looked back at the trail again and barked. I looked over at Raven. We quickened our pace with the Lab now leading the way.

Chapter 23

SMALL STEAM PLUMES escaped from the Lab's mouth, and also from mine and from Raven's. We jogged over water-slicked rocks and splashed through puddles turned to tea from the decaying remains of leaves and trees. A steady rain drew an earthy smell up from the ground, mixing it with a hint of cherry emanating from the cedar forest to our right. To our left, raindrops fell through a layer of mist hovering just above Black Lake, then danced over the surface of the water.

The trail veered right, then dropped down a shallow gully, before heading up into the forest. Under the hood of my rain jacket, I could barely make out the sound of a voice through the patter and hiss of the rain.

"Queenie . . . Queenie."

The chocolate Lab barked, then sped up. I lost sight of her around the next turn. When Raven and I rounded the bend, the Lab stood in front of a middle-aged woman. Queenie furiously shook rain from her coat. The woman's silver hair peeked from the edges of her navy and gray rain jacket. She bent low, kissing Queenie as though she was her long-lost lover. The Lab licked the woman's face. As we neared, the woman stood to meet us. Her head rose to just above my shoulders.

The blush on her soft, rounded cheeks appeared to be earned from walking and not from paint in a make-up kit. She held a blue and gray leash in one hand.

"Ma'am, are you all right?" I asked.

"Cheryl," she said.

"Charlie," I said.

Cheryl's brow furrowed. She pointed deeper into the forest. "I'm all right, but something in there spooked Queenie."

I turned to look. Queenie had already left Cheryl's side and was now locked in deep conversation with Raven.

"Queenie loves people, as you can see." Cheryl nodded in Raven's direction. "She's not easily spooked. Just a moment ago, she sniffed the ground a few times, barked, then took off into the woods. I followed until I saw her circling a bright yellow tent pitched in a clearing of cedar trees. She barked at the tent several times. No one came out. I heard strange noises from inside the tent. That's when I called Queenie back. She came running but she wouldn't stop. She took off like a bolt of lightning down the trail."

"We'll have a look," I said.

I could hear Raven whispering to the Lab, asking what she'd seen and where. Queenie barked once at Raven, then bounded into the woods.

"Queenie!" Raven called out.

The Lab stopped and spun around.

"Here, girl."

She bounced back to Raven. He rubbed her wet coat and she shook water in every direction. Raven didn't flinch.

"You take your owner back to the boat," he said softly.

Queenie barked and sauntered over to Cheryl, who stood watching the scene with her eyes wide and mouth partially open.

"Who are you?" she asked.

Before Raven could answer, Queenie barked again, this time at Cheryl. The Lab caught the dangling end of her leash in its mouth and tugged, dragging Cheryl down the path. Raven had already started along Queenie's path into the forest. Cheryl turned back to me. She shook her head.

"I don't understand. Who is he?"

I threw up my hands. "Sometimes I don't understand either."

I felt like a ballerina or high-wire walker as I picked my way through the dense underbrush, pirouetting atop downed limbs, measuring each step carefully lest I fall through to the forest floor below. Raven stood still at the edge of a clearing. He reminded me of a dog pointing. When he raised his arm, I had to hold my laugh.

Twenty yards ahead, the bright yellow dome of a tent stood in stark contrast with the washed-out greens and browns around it. Raven cocked his head. I thought I heard sounds, too. I threw back the hood of my rain jacket and touched the handle of my pistol. It sounded like low moans emanating from the tent.

We crept forward across the soft green carpet. Raven turned as we walked, scanning the perimeter of the clearing with his gun drawn. The moaning grew louder. I tapped on the tent with the barrel of my pistol. Suddenly, the moaning stopped. I heard rustling inside the tent.

"You okay in there?" I asked.

Raven stood behind the tent, gun drawn, scanning the trees.

A young woman with short, sandy brown hair and a dimpled chin stuck her head out.

"What the hell?" she said.

From inside the tent another female voice called out. "Beth, what is it? Who's out there?"

A second young woman stuck her head out, atop the first. She also had short hair but red. And her face, flushed even brighter red than her hair, nearly hid her gathering of freckles.

She screamed, "What the hell do you want!?"

I stepped away from the tent and slowly brought my gun down behind my back, where neither of the young women could see it.

"We're looking for a couple somewhere out here who may be in trouble," I said.

The redhead scowled. "Do we look like we're in trouble?"

"Actually, no," I said.

"Then leave us alone," the redhead said. She sucked her teeth and ducked back inside the tent.

"Sorry," I said.

"Don't worry," Beth said. She nodded toward the tent. "Julie'll be just fine in a moment." Beth winked before ducking back inside the tent, too.

THE STEADY RAIN had throttled back to a constant drizzle. Moon jellies floated closer to the surface, turning the waters of Roscoe Bay an undulating, milky green. A dog barked as we glided by *Queen*, the Nordhavn 43, on our way back to the *Noble Lady*. A moment later, Queenie stepped from the open pilothouse door with her owner not far behind. The Lab barked several times at Raven until he held his palm out toward her. Then she stopped. The owner waved us over. I rowed toward them and pulled in the oars as we glided closer to the hull. Raven threw a couple of fenders over the side. He reached up and handed Cheryl our painter. She lead it through a hawsepipe, then tied it off to a large, gleaming stainless steel Sampson post aboard. Queenie paced back and forth, her body shook as though she was ready to jump into our dinghy. Raven reached up to pet her, and she relaxed.

"She likes you," Cheryl said.

Raven nodded.

"Name's Cheryl," she said.

Raven nodded again.

"And yours?"

"Raven."

"Native?"

He didn't answer or nod. He just kept stroking Queenie.

"Good with animals?" Cheryl asked.

Still nothing from Raven.

Cheryl turned to me, her face contorted. "Did you find the tent?"

"We did. Turned out to be two campers."

Her face relaxed. "Everything okay?"

"Seemed to be."

"And the strange noises?"

I smiled. "Evidence of very happy campers."

Cheryl's face contorted even more.

Raven whispered into Queenie's ear. The Lab turned and promptly waddled past Cheryl back into the pilothouse. Cheryl stared at Queenie, then at Raven, then at me.

"You two want to come aboard for drinks?" she asked.

"Love to, but we're working," I said.

"Working?"

"Surveying areas where more hiking trails could be cut in Desolation Sound."

"Lovely," Cheryl said. "That's one thing I don't like about boating here. It's hard to find places to stretch your legs. Where're you off to next?"

"Von Donop Inlet," I said.

"One of our favorites. We were there three nights ago. Back bay was crowded but still a lot of room everywhere else. Here, let me untie your dinghy."

Cheryl undid the painter and handed it back through the hawse to Raven. She leaned over the railing and spoke to him, her voice now several decibels higher. Raven held on to a stanchion.

"Don't know what you said to Queenie, but she liked it, and I thank you. Most people just pat her head and rub her belly. You two seemed to talk."

"Someone close to her died recently," Raven said. "Her spirit needed help moving through it."

Suddenly Cheryl backed against the sidewall. Her hand flew to her mouth. She started to sob. "Queenie's fourteen. Titus, her partner since she was three months old, died last week. My god, how could you have possibly known that?"

"She told me," Raven said. "Talk to her. She'll also help you through it."

Cheryl brushed away tears. Raven pushed off the hull of the Nordhavn and we slowly drifted away.

I HAD THE WHEEL, which meant I also had the choice. So I turned to port at the mouth of Roscoe Bay, which then faced us down narrow Waddington Channel, even though it would have been three miles closer to Von Donop had I turned to starboard and wrapped around the southern end of West Redonda Island. When you're boating, efficiency must yield to beauty on occasion, and the back way to Von Donop held the more stunning views. Pots clanking below vouched for Raven preparing lunch. Overhead, a patch of blue held its lonely outpost in a field of gray clouds.

I checked our radar. For more than a day I hadn't seen evidence of a small boat trailing us. Had Ali Sharik already found the couple?

Once past the mouth of Pendrell Sound, that patch of blue sky had widened enough to let a column of sunlight through, sending the water sparkling like thousands of jewels, setting the islands aglow in green, and lighting the tops of the snowcapped peaks ahead of us like massive candles.

At Walsh Cove, near Waddington Channel's northern end, the bows of a dozen stern-tied boats lined up like so many glistening arrows pointing away from the land. Dinghies skipped in and out of this flotilla, depositing passengers along the large rocks that lined the shore. I headed the *Lady* toward the east side of the channel and checked GPS. We'd lost almost two knots to the current. To port, on the rocky west shore, a woman with three children near her waved to us as we cruised by. One boy reached high with a closed fist and tugged down twice on an invisible cord. I pressed a button twice, sending two short, sharp horn blasts echoing down Waddington Channel and back, bouncing off mountains before coming to rest.

The boy waved wildly and reached up again, answering with two blasts of his air horn. Then he leaped from the rocks, flapping his arms as though trying to fly, raising a splash. Another boy and a girl followed him into Waddington Channel. The mild current swept the children south in the channel before it died out after fifty yards. They swam back to shore and climbed up the rocks, ready for another round at this natural water ride, only this time they queued behind a dozen or more adults and youth also waiting their turn.

Kate and I once stern-tied here in Walsh Cove. Somewhere downstairs I had a picture of her after she had leaped off those very same rocks. She stood on a shallow ledge while I hovered above with the camera. She threw her hair back, cupped both of her breasts, and let her face bask in the sun. I call it the "goddess shot," for it shows a woman in the full stride of her power and beauty. A pang of longing rippled through me with the memories of that day.

We popped out of Waddington Channel at Dean Point and I spun the wheel to port. Out the starboard window, a line of verdant peaks rose from Toba Inlet, the tallest capped white and piercing through the remaining, low-lying cloud cover. From the pilothouse it appeared that Toba Inlet came to a halt about eight miles in. I checked my chart. In reality, the fjord-like inlet made a dogleg to starboard and continued another twelve miles inland to a glacier-fed stream at its head. Silt from that glacier ran into the sea, which explained why the *Noble Lady* now plowed through a milky green ocean.

"Humpback! Eleven o'clock! Two hundred yards out."

I half expected to hear, "Thar she blows!"

I whipped the binoculars from a ledge above the instrument panel and scanned the water to our left. I chuckled to myself. Raven's call transported me back through time momentarily, to the decks of a four-masted wooden whaler plying the Southern Pacific in search of such leviathans.

A sea geyser erupted thirty yards off the starboard bow, followed by the arch of a small dorsal fin, then the rise of an angel-wing from the deep, which slapped down with a great splash before disappearing beneath the chalky green water.

THE PILOTHOUSE STAIRS whined under Raven's footsteps. He set a tray of tuna sandwiches down on the edge of the pilothouse bench. He handed me a sandwich but I waved it off.

Raven sat behind me eating in silence as we headed northwest along Pryce Channel. I turned to port at Deer Passage and slipped between Raza and West Redonda Island. By the time we'd made Bullock Bluff on the north tip of Cortes Island, I handed the helm over to Raven and sat down behind him to enjoy my lunch.

Before Raven turned to port at Sutil Channel, I looked up Sutil, past the Rendezvous Islands to Calm Channel. The view reminded me of standing just inside the entrance to a cathedral, peering down the length of the nave, only with low-lying clouds being this cathedral's scalloped ceiling and the green peaks on either side its tall, stained-glass windows. That impenetrable mystery beyond the altar? That gateway to a hidden kingdom accessible only by initiates of the faith? That, too, lay beyond the end of Calm Channel.

But here in my cathedral of the sea, call that altar the Yucultas, those fast-moving, salt-water rapids impenetrable to all save those initiates of the mysteries of the currents and tides. And the hidden kingdom? That land of boundless beauty that lay beyond the rapids. But try entering that kingdom at the wrong time and without the requisite initiation. Hell's abyss awaits in the arms of a whirlpool known as the Devil's Hole.

Raven turned to look up Calm Channel, too. "Leads to the rapids," he said.

"Yucultas," I said.

Raven chuckled. "Spirit Walker pronounces them right, Yew-clah-taws." He said the word slowly. "Rapids form a barrier, a gateway from one realm to another—"

I cut him off. "Which is why you always seek permission to enter them from the Spirit first."

Raven nodded. "Spirit Walker learns quickly."

"Spirit Walker has a good friend and a good teacher."

He nodded again.

Beyond the turn at the needle-nose northern tip of Cortes Island, Raven pointed us directly into Ha'thayim, Von Donop Inlet.

As we entered the inlet, he stepped away from the helm. I didn't need to ask why. I took his place as he descended the staircase and a moment later the sounds of drumming and soft chanting floated through the boat.

By the time we'd reached the narrow constricted portion of the inlet, Raven was back in the pilothouse, sitting behind me on the bench. I slid the *Noble Lady* toward the starboard side of the narrows, close to shore. I heard Raven mumble, "Uh-huh," as though he approved of my maneuver to avoid a large submerged rock that sat in the middle of the channel.

Once past the narrows, I steered us back to midchannel. To port we passed a fifty-five-foot Sea Ray at anchor, a bullet-shaped boat with a plastic and blue canvas enclosure zippered over the cockpit and helm. Raven raised an eyebrow.

"Out of the ordinary," he said.

I nodded. "See its name?"

"Nah."

I pointed beyond the boat. "Been back there?" I asked.

"Lagoon behind the small reversing rapids? No. Never enough water. You?"

"Kate and I took kayaks back there at slack last year. Quiet."

A few minutes later, Raven stood. He pointed out the port side window. "Been in there?"

"Small cove beyond the sand bar? Uh-huh. Rode out a fifty-knot gale there with fifteen other boats."

Raven nodded. "Didn't think it could hold that much."

"Very tight. I had to stern-tie."

Two dozen boats lay at anchor in the bay at the bitter end of Von Donop. Several sailboats. A matching pair of blue Nordic Tugs. Four Grand Banks rafted together that looked like stair steps ranging in size from thirty-six to forty-nine feet. A smattering of Bayliners. Even a gleaming seventy-foot yacht. I found a spot in the center of the bay and dropped the anchor, which bit quickly in the mud. Raven bridled the chain, while I lowered the dinghy.

Mist had again turned to rain. We donned rain gear before stepping into the dinghy. Raven tucked his pistol underneath his parka, which reminded me to reach back inside the cabin for my binoculars and my gun. With the tide high, we putted into and a good way up the rock and mud shore. Raven jumped from the dinghy. He stepped around three other dinghies already tethered to shore and tied our painter off to a large driftwood log.

A rivulet dug a narrow trench down from the forest to the beach. A scruffy-headed blue and gray kingfisher darted from a branch above us, squawked, and dove into the water, emerging with an empty beak. The beach trail angled sharply uphill before dipping into the forest. Raven stopped. My foot squished into the soft earth. We'd come to a wooden outhouse, from which three trails took off: one left, one right, one straight ahead.

Raven turned. "Spirit Walker knows which way?"

I pointed. "We'll take this trail."

Chapter 24

I STEPPED IN FRONT OF RAVEN and started down the trail to our left. A moist earthy smell now hung in the air. Raindrops tap-danced on the hood of my parka. Cedar and Douglas fir trees lorded over each side of the trail, their barks ebony-slick from the rain.

"Back there. That trail straight ahead went where?" Raven asked. Rain muted his voice.

"North end of Squirrel Cove," I called out.

"Trail to the right?"

"Long walk to the Squirrel Cove General Store."

The slosh of Raven's footsteps halted. I stopped walking and turned around. Raven crouched and pointed at the brush on the side of the trail.

"Animal paths all over. All the paths lead to the lagoon." He stood, pointed farther along the trail. "But the lagoon is protected by shallow reversing rapids. Only way in is by kayak or dinghy, and only at high tide. No way in for a sailboat."

"The lagoon is protected by reversing rapids," I said. "Don't even need a sailboat. Put the couple in a tent inside the lagoon. Rapids help to protect them."

"With assistance from a boat outside," Raven said. "Like that Sea Ray at the lagoon's entrance."

"Maybe," I said.

We continued walking, past the huge stump of an old-growth cedar, where rain splashed into a pool of water collecting in its hollowed-out middle. A sapling struggled for life in the center of the pool. I lost the sound of Raven's footsteps. I stopped, pivoted. He crouched by the side of the trail.

"Whaddya see?" I asked.

A finger flew to his lips. He waved me to him. When I got there I crouched down beside him. Raven pointed to the muddy ground.

"Dog. Coyote. Maybe a wolf," I said. "Hard to tell with all this rain."

Raven shook his head. He motioned twice toward the ground, slightly above the animal print. I squinted, wiped away rain dripping onto my face from the brim of my parka. I sprang to my feet, grabbed the pistol from the small of my back, and scanned the forest through the downpour. Raven popped up at my shoulder.

He whispered. "Human footprints. Less than a few hours old."

"Could be an owner walking his dog," I said.

"This far from shore? In this rain?"

"Maybe a guy out walking."

Raven didn't answer, but he did draw his gun.

Like a radar beacon, I pushed my senses through the rain curtain into the forest on all sides. Each creak of a tree trunk, crack of a branch, or crunch of leaves snapped my head and my senses in that direction. We found our footing down one side of a ravine, stepping cautiously over moss-laden rocks now mostly under water, before climbing up the other side. At the top of the ravine, my hand shot up, fist closed, arm bent in an L.

A patch of drab green about fifty yards ahead moved.

I waved Raven back down the ravine, fell to my knees, and slid down its muddy side. I poked two fingers at my eyes, held up one finger, then pointed at eleven o'clock from our position. Raven nodded.

He tapped himself, then pointed left. I nodded, tapped myself, and pointed right. I crouched below the top of the ravine and tiptoed off.

Thirty yards later I looked back. Raven had disappeared beyond a bend. After another thirty yards, I slithered up the side of the ravine, lay on my stomach, and pulled my binoculars from around my neck up to my eyes.

As I focused on the figure in the drab green rain gear, I sucked in a breath . . . and held it. The man rested against a cedar tree and held binoculars to his eyes, looking deeper into the lagoon. His bushy black mustache rested above his olive-colored skin. When he lowered his binoculars, I knew then I was looking at Ali Sharik.

Suddenly, as though he'd heard my thoughts, Sharik turned in my direction. I dropped below the rim of the ravine, pressing myself into the damp earth. My chest tightened and my breath came in short, sharp drafts. I crouched, then crept farther along the ravine, crawling up the side behind a large Douglas fir. I turned sideways, jammed my shoulder into the wet bark, and tried to meld with the tree.

A sharp crack, then an explosion erupted from the forest on the other side of the ravine. I turned in time to see a limb the size of a small tree crashing through the canopy, breaking branches, finally bouncing to rest between Sharik and me. I peeked around the other side of the tree. Sharik stared at the downed limb, then turned to train his binoculars at the lagoon. Several smaller branches fell in the wake of the larger limb. Sharik twisted left with each smaller crash. I stepped from behind the tree and picked my way through the wet underbrush toward him. My jaw clenched against the pain of grasping my pistol handle tightly. I tried to let go with only my ring finger, but that left me with an insecure grip I couldn't afford. So, again, I squeezed through the pain.

Twenty yards away, I brought my pistol up to shoulder height and trained it on Sharik. Ten yards away I stepped right, found a patch of moss to cushion the sound of my footsteps. Five yards away, Sharik whipped around to his right with his gun pointed at me. His eyes flared. He pushed back against the tree.

"Charlie!" His eyes brightened. The hiss of rain dampened the sound of his heavy British accent.

"Put your gun down, Ali."

"Charlie, fancy meeting you here."

He smiled, but his gun stayed leveled at me.

"Ali, put your gun down, now."

"I don't think you understand," he said.

"No, I don't think you do," Raven said.

Raven stood a few feet away from Sharik, his pistol pointed at Sharik's head.

Sharik laid his pistol atop a bed of cedar needles and raised both hands. "I believe we're on the same side, here. There's a couple somewhere up here in great danger unless we get to them first."

"You're working for the Islamic Jihad Front," I said.

Sharik shook his head. He smiled. "Bad intel, Charlie. I'm not working for the Front, I'm—"

The rain hid all but the soft thud of a bullet entering Sharik's forehead. His head snapped back.

I dove to the ground and crab-crawled behind a large stump. Raven ducked behind the cedar. I braced for a fusillade but none came.

Raven called out, "Shooter's gone. I'm after him. Stay." He took off, high-stepping over branches like a deer prancing through the woods.

I scrambled back to the cedar tree. Sharik's body lay crumpled against the trunk. A gurgle of blood oozing from between his lips turned pink as the rain washed it down and over his chin. His eyes were wide open, his head drooped onto his chest. Bits of bloody bone and brain stuck to the cedar trunk. I laid three fingers on the side of his neck. No pulse. I shook my head, pounded the cedar trunk.

I brought my binoculars to my eyes and peered into the lagoon. I whispered to Sharik's lifeless body. "What's going on? What are you doing here? What'd you see in there?"

I half expected, half hoped for a bright-eyed, British reply, "Charlie!"

I let my gaze slowly sweep the waters of the lagoon. Nothing. The far shore. Nothing there either. But a momentary flash of white caught my eye. I trained my binoculars at the end of the small island in the middle of the lagoon and waited. A speck of white drifted in and out of view. I waited again and scanned the waters nearby. No sign of an anchor line. Then again, the speck of white drifted into view before disappearing behind the island.

Branches crashed behind me. I spun around to see Raven jogging my way.

"Lost him . . . back at the . . . outhouse." He spoke while trying to catch his breath. "Probably took . . . the road back to . . . the Squirrel Cove store." He looked at Sharik, then dropped his head. His lips moved in silence.

"We need to call this in," I said.

"First, you need to speak to his spirit."

"Not sure what to say."

"Whatever's in your heart."

I took a deep breath, then kneeled in front of Sharik's lifeless body. I struggled for words but none came. Then I simply let go and began speaking. "I'm sorry I shot and killed Masoud. I did it to save my crew and my ship. Even though I felt your anger, I always thought you knew that. I remember standing on the deck of the *Nanticote* with you one evening. We talked about the insanity of war, how through-out human history more people have killed and been killed in the name of their religion, and their God, than for any other reason, while at the same time those religions profess brotherhood and love.

"We spoke of how war pulls families and friends apart, and you said you looked forward to a day when you no longer wore a uniform, and had more time to spend with Zafia and your children. I'm sorry that day will not come for you. We were friends, Ali, and this insane war between Islam and the West stole that friendship from us. I thought it turned you against me, but I did not see warrior's hatred in your eyes today. I saw the surprised affection of a friend. I do not understand what happened, but I promise you this: I will find out. And when I do, I will let Zafia know how and why you died."

I put my hands on Ali's shoulder and hung my head. As I closed my eyes, I freed tears, which mixed with raindrops trickling down and over my cheeks. Then I raised my head and looked a final time into the eyes of my friend before lifting my fingers and closing his eyes.

RAVEN AND I STOOD in the pilothouse of the *Noble Lady* looking out toward the trail at the end of Von Donop, where a large orange Canadian Coast Guard high-speed inflatable now bobbed. Another inflatable zoomed toward them, having just untied and pushed off from the *Noble Lady*. A red Canadian Coast Guard helicopter hovered overhead. The beat of its blades thumped through the boat and my body, churning the waters of the inlet. Ashore, a detail of four men in dark blue uniforms and baseball caps hoisted a stretcher carrying a black plastic body bag on their shoulders.

From an open door on the side of the helicopter, a man in a harness and helmet lowered a steel cable with a large hook. One of the men ashore reached up to grab the hook, then secured it to a loop on the body bag. He twirled his finger above his head. Sharik's body ascended. The man in the helmet saluted the body bag before it was hauled aboard. The helicopter soon disappeared over the tops of the trees lining the inlet.

I barked at Raven, "Check the oil, water, and transmission. Then get us out of here."

"Where to?"

"Anchor at the head of the inlet near the reversing rapids."

"To check out that white object you saw?"

"Maybe."

"Noble, you okay?"

"I need to make a call."

"To whom?"

"Pete Townsend."

"About Sharik?"

"About bad intel, and why I may have lost someone who was still my friend."

I stormed down the pilothouse stairs and into my stateroom. I grabbed my cell phone from the top drawer of the locker next to my bunk. But when I flipped it open, it didn't have any bars. I slammed it shut, then climbed back up the pilothouse stairs.

"Short call," Raven said.

"No call."

"No service?"

"Uh-huh."

"Take a deep breath. What's your heart tell you?"

I inhaled and held it. "We're being played."

"By whom?"

"Don't know. I do know that we're trying to find a couple before someone else does. Only that someone may have found them before we did, and when he found them he was killed."

"By whom? Outfit protecting the couple?" Raven asked.

"Maybe. But why didn't the shooter try to take us out, too?"

"Someone gave the shooter intel about us?"

"Maybe, but who?" I asked. I lowered my head.

"A lot of questions, not a lot of answers." Raven spoke softly. "Did you notice what Sharik wasn't wearing?"

"No. What?"

"He wasn't wearing an RCMP uniform."

My head snapped up.

"Bet the shooter was."

Raven nodded.

Rain had tapered down to a drizzle. We cruised the short distance to the beginning of Von Donop. Raven pulled the *Noble Lady* into the small cove in front of the reversing rapids. I looked around.

"Sea Ray's gone," I said.

Raven shifted into neutral, and the *Noble Lady* began a gentle pirouette in the current running from the rapids. "Stay here or try to find her?"

I pulled a current atlas down from the shelf behind the pilothouse bench and hurriedly thumbed through the pages. "Yucultas go to slack before ebb in about five hours."

"Thinking of going through and around to Thurston Bay Lagoon?"

"Or Small Inlet," I said. "We need to enter the Yucultas an hour before the ebb if we want to make it all the way through. Take us two hours to get there from here. That leaves two hours to wait, or—"

"Two hours to explore this lagoon."

"My thought exactly."

"Flood's running pretty hard. Low water flood at that. Don't know if we can get a dinghy in there."

"Don't know either but we can get kayaks in there. We'll take them to shore in the dinghy, put them together, and haul them above the rapids."

Raven smiled.

We drove the dinghy to shore and pulled it up a gravel beach, tying the painter off to a rock. We pieced the aluminum frames of the kayaks together, pulled the heavy, dark-blue fabric skin over the frames, inflated the airbags with our breath, and stuffed the paddles into the cockpits. Standing between both kayaks, I caught the grab loops at the bow, Raven at the stern, and we carried them together through the trees and out over the rocks to a tiny nook above the rapids.

We slipped into the boats. Before either of us could get our paddles into the water, the flood current began carrying us farther into the lagoon. Past the noise of the rapids, the water became glassy calm and an awesome quiet settled over the tree-lined shores; the kind of quiet that makes you think about quitting the world on the other side of the rapids and giving yourself over to the stillness. We paddled past a group of purple and orange starfish clinging to a rock just below a colony of mussels. I ducked under a cedar bough hanging low and out over the water. As we traveled farther back into the lagoon the rotten-egg smell of mud flats at low tide permeated the air.

I angled away from the shore and the smell, toward the island in the middle of the lagoon. But when my view cleared the tip of the island, what I saw on the other side caused me to stop paddling, and to shake my head in disbelief.

Chapter 25

A FULLY RIGGED SAILBOAT can't get back here," I said.

"But it did," Raven said.

I shook my head. "Can't unless someone dropped it in from the air. There's not more than eighteen inches clearance at the highest tide coming through the rapids."

Raven pointed at the sailboat. "Maybe we'd better have a look."

I called out, "Ahoy!" My voice echoed four or five times around the lagoon before finally trailing off.

No one answered.

We paddled up to the sailboat. I rapped on the fiberglass hull, which flexed slightly under my knuckles, bouncing an echo through the lagoon that returned to me without an answer. So we tied off our kayaks to cleats at the stern and stepped onto the swim step. I searched the transom, then leaned over the sides looking for the boat's name. I couldn't find one.

"The Islander," a haunting song by the group Nightwish, one of Kate's recent favorites, popped into my mind, especially the lines about a ship without a name, a sea without a shore, and the search for the one who had vanished.

Raven had already ducked into the cabin when I got there. He held a coffee cup to his cheek.

"Still warm," he said.

I checked the forward v-berth where I found two sleeping bags, zipped together, crumpled in a corner. A pair of jeans, a purple bra, and two mismatched socks lay scattered atop the v-berth's tan cushions. I looked into the head, where I found a still-open compact sitting on the ledge above the sink. On the floor, a razor, a can of shaving cream, a tube of toothpaste, and a roll of dental floss spilled out from an unzipped toiletry bag.

Footsteps walking on deck reverberated through the fiberglass hull. Above, a motor whined, followed by a sharp thud that vibrated through the boat. The sailboat listed to port. The motor whined again and the boat righted.

I stepped from the cabin, held onto the lifeline as I walked forward. Raven held a spiral-bound document in his hands. He pointed to a pushbutton switch. I nodded.

"Raised and lowered her keel?" I asked.

"Bulbous, retractable keel inset into the bottom of her hull." He held up a picture of the boat.

"Fully lowered?"

Raven flipped through a few pages. "Six-foot draft."

"Fully raised?"

"Fifteen inches."

"Guess that explains how the Kinsleys got beyond the reversing rapids in a thirty-foot sailboat."

"Twenty-six-foot sailboat," Raven said.

"Helluva place to hide," I said.

"Not any longer."

"Means they're probably on the Sea Ray we saw anchored at the mouth of the rapids."

"Headed for another safe house?" Raven asked.

"That'd be my guess."

"With the shooter in pursuit?"

"Or maybe aboard."

EXITING VON DONOP INLET, Raven turned us to starboard and headed us north along Calm Channel. I poked my head from the pilothouse door and looked back. The *Noble Lady*'s exhaust gurgled, sending a trail of bubbling frothy seawater from the stern and a slight whiff of diesel floating my way. Far in the distance, the line of peaks along Vancouver Island had already turned a deep orange-pink in the dying sunlight. Ahead, the corridor to the Yucultas wound through a number of small island passes, now shrouded in ever-growing darkness, making it hard to distinguish water from land.

I stepped back inside the pilothouse, flipped my cell phone open, and checked the bars: full service. I mashed a key with my thumb and my address book popped up. When I came to Pete Townsend's name I hit Send. An off-key medley of electronic tones played in my ear.

"Hello," a female voice said.

"Pete Townsend."

"I'll—"

Her voice degenerated into garble mixed with static, and when I searched the tiny screen for bars I found none. I slammed the phone shut and took a seat on the pilothouse bench.

"Still no reception?" Raven asked.

"I had a small window, maybe from Campbell River. Then it was gone."

"And you need to speak with Townsend because—?"

"My gut tells me he knows more about Sharik than he told me."

"And if you manage to learn the truth, that will—?"

"Help me understand why Sharik died in front of my eyes."

"So your gut's angry about Sharik's death and your lack of information. What's your heart say?"

"That he was looking to protect that couple, not to kill them."

"Trust your heart. Don't worry about the call."

"In this business people are trained to lie, to deceive hearts and minds and guts."

When Raven turned around, his laserlike stare traveled through me. "Isn't that why you're not in the business anymore?"

I nodded.

"Then trust your heart regardless of what Townsend said or says."

Raven stepped away from the wheel. "Take the helm," he said.

An hour later, the *Noble Lady* lurched toward the rocky shore of Stuart Island. I spun the wheel hard to port, then snapped it back to starboard. We'd touched the tongue of the Yucultas. Twilight made it difficult to read the water ahead, to steer by eddylines and boils, mini whirlpools, and saw-toothed overflows. So I extended my sense of touch to the outer reaches of the hull and steered by my body's reaction to the movement of the boat.

"Steer with your body, not your mind." An instructor's deep voice with its hint of a Texas drawl played in my mind. Years ago, the seasoned chief who'd piloted rescue boats over the nasty Columbia Bar for years, taught that to a group of us green ensigns.

I remember the chief's fiendish smile. "Think it sounds like New Age gobbledygook? Pick up a pen and write anything. Where's your awareness? At the end of your fingertips or where the tip of the pen meets the paper? Next time you drive a car try turning right while moving your body left. No technical reason you can't do it, but just try it. Swing a bat or a golf club. Where's your awareness? Where your body ends or where the bat or club ends?"

Then came my turn at the bar, strapped to the helm of the forty-four-foot lifeboat with twenty-foot breaking seas all around. The instructor, strapped in beside me, laughed and repeated his mantra, "Trust your body, Noble. Trust your body."

I tried steering through a gap between two breaking waves, but it felt like a giant had pulled a rug out from under the lifeboat and it careened to the point of near capsize.

The instructor laughed. "Wanna do an Eskimo Roll, do ya? Go

ahead, she'll snap back up. But if you wanna learn how to pilot this bar, go through that opening between those two rollers over there, Mr. Noble"—he pointed to a thin gap between two breaking rollers—"and dammit, let go of your thoughts. Feel the boat under you like a woman, and trust that your body knows how to respond."

I did and I piloted the lifeboat through.

We'd almost made it to the top of the Yucultas. To our left, lights glowed yellow-orange through the floor-to-ceiling windows of a fishing lodge built above the rapids, bathing the wooden window frame and wooden walls inside in a rich firelike glow. As I began to make the turn to port and enter Gillard Rapids, I felt the *Noble Lady*'s bow pulled one way, her stern the other. In the dim light I couldn't see the water. So I loosened my hips, let my knees buckle slightly, took a deep breath, and allowed my body to move with the *Lady*'s hull. I eased my death grip on the wheel, then spun it to port and to starboard as though the *Lady* and I were locked in the throes of a tango. Once past Little Gillard Island, the current eased and a glow of light from Dent Island came into view.

Sitting behind me, Raven laughed. "Spirit Walker has earned a new name."

"What's that?" I asked.

"Dances with Boats."

"Dance isn't over," I said.

"Devil's Hole's up next."

I'd timed our arrival to catch the dying flood at the Yucultas, so we'd reached Devil's Hole, in the middle of Dent Rapids, right at slack. Above us, the evening's first stars twinkled around a full moon. Ahead, a vessel's disparate eyes glowed red and green. I checked to make sure Raven had switched on our nav lights. Then I picked up the VHF radio mike.

"Vessel heading south through Dent Rapids. This is the motor vessel *Noble Lady*."

"*Noble Lady*. This is the one-twenty-foot motor yacht *Emerald Isle*. Switch and answer zero niner."

"Roger, zero niner."

I jabbed the backlit channel switch and watched the red LED numbers tumble from 16 to 9.

"*Emerald Isle*, the *Noble Lady* on zero niner. Confirming we'll be passing you red to red."

"Roger, *Noble Lady*, red to red. You have a safe cruise tonight."

"Roger, *Emerald Isle*. *Noble Lady* out. Standing by channel one-six."

A few minutes later, the glare from *Emerald Isle*'s huge port-side red light filled the *Lady*'s windshield, and from a lighted pilothouse towering above us, a silver-haired man and woman waved. After the *Emerald Isle* passed, the *Noble Lady* bumped over a washboard patch of water as we approached the beginning of Devil's Hole.

I started to remind myself to "trust my body," when I looked out my starboard side window over to the lodge on Dent Island. I slowed the *Lady* down, swooped the binoculars off the ledge above the instrument panel, and handed them to Raven without turning around.

I pointed right. "What's that over there at that dock?"

Raven stepped to the pilothouse door, opened it, and poked out his head, binoculars pressed against his eyes. He pulled his head back. "Looks a lot like that Sea Ray we saw at the mouth of the rapids back in Von Donop," he said.

I cut the wheel hard to starboard. The *Lady* bucked in the current.

"Sounds like engine trouble. We may need to pull into their dock," I said. I picked up the VHF mike, punched the channel selector until it reach 69.

"Dent Island Lodge. Dent Island Lodge. Dent Island Lodge. This is the motor vessel *Noble Lady*."

I waited. No answer. So I tried again.

"Dent Island Lodge. This is the motor vessel *Noble Lady*."

I waited again. Still no answer. So I turned to Raven. "Do you take that to mean yes?"

"Uh-huh."

While Raven hung fenders over the side, I eased the *Lady* up to the Dent Island Lodge dock behind the Sea Ray. I switched on the *Lady*'s docking lights, sending two beams blasting over the surface of the water, which turned it an eerie green and reflected a starburst of light from the highly polished transom of the Sea Ray. I waited for an armed squad to swarm from the Sea Ray or swoop down from the lodge above the dock. But not even a light went on inside the Sea Ray, and only a fire's orange flickering lit the tall windows of the lodge.

The *Lady*'s engine groaned in reverse as she swung her stern in toward the dock. Raven stepped off with a midships line in hand. I threw the *Lady* into neutral, walked out onto the bow, and threw Raven a line. By the time I'd stepped back into the pilothouse and climbed down the stairs to the cockpit, Raven had the *Lady* tied off to the dock. I opened the door and handed him a flashlight.

I patted the small of my back. "You have your sidearm?"

Raven smacked his hip.

I hopped onto the dark dock and shined my light at the windshield of the Sea Ray. The wooden dock planks creaked under us as we walked in that direction. Near the Sea Ray's stern, my foot kicked what felt like a heavy canvas bag. I stumbled, then pointed my flashlight down. Raven sucked in a breath. We froze.

A man's body lay in a pool of blood, one leg bent into his chest, as though he was crawling toward the Sea Ray. Raven kneeled and pressed his fingers against the man's neck. He shook his head, then uttered a few words under his breath.

The Sea Ray rocked as I leaped aboard. I tugged my gun from my waistband, stood to one side of the sliding door leading into the cabin, and shined my light through the glass. On a blood-soaked couch, one man's body slumped, head back, blood still dripping from his mouth, while another had keeled forward, his forehead resting in a puddle of blood on a coffee table in front of the couch. I raised my foot to the slider's handle and kicked the door open. I spun inside the cabin with my flashlight and my gun out in front. Raven pivoted inside behind me. Neither man had a pulse.

I nudged Raven and pointed to the floor with my light, which illuminated a set of bloody footprints leading down the stairs from the cabin. My pulse quickened. I pressed my back against one wall of the staircase and slid slowly down the stairs. With his back against the opposite wall, Raven followed. The blood trail led to a door on one side of the teak-paneled companionway at the bottom of the stairs.

Like a pair of uneven bookends, Raven and I stood to either side of the first door we came to, guns and flashlights held in both hands and pointed down at the floor. I nodded. Raven twirled and with a swift kick crashed the door open. I crouched as I pirouetted into the stateroom and shined my light into the darkness with my finger tugging at the trigger, my heartbeat pounding in my veins. Raven, still in the corridor, added light from his flashlight to mine.

"Clear," I said.

I turned to step back into the corridor when a dull thump came from behind the door to the master stateroom at the bow. I pointed. Raven nodded. I crept along the corridor, to my place on one side of the door.

Again, Raven kicked it in. Only it hit against an object with a resounding crack and slammed closed. I aimed my light and my pistol at the door. This time, Raven stood to one side of the door and gingerly worked the doorknob. He nodded. I threw my shoulder into the open door, barreling low into the room. As I did, a large body fell on top of me, and I tumbled to the floor. Then something hit the floor with a metallic *ting* followed by the sound of small objects scattering.

A warm, sticky wetness covered my palm as I pushed the body from me. Raven hit a switch and a blinding light burst from the ceiling. When my eyes adjusted, I found a trim, dark-haired, bearded man lying on the floor, eyes wide, with blood soaking through the front of his T-shirt at his belly. A roll of tape, a pair of scissors, and packages of bandages lay strewn on the floor around him. I searched for a pulse at his wrist and his neck but I only found a bloody handprint smeared on the front of a first-aid container lying beside him.

I pulled the edge of a sheet from the bottom berth and wiped off the blood from my hands.

"Glad I didn't get an invitation to this blood party," I said.

I grabbed the VHF mike from its holder and switched on the radio. Sixteen glowed from the orange LED lights. I brought the mike closer and pressed the red button, but before I could speak a word, two loud sharp cracks of gunfire erupted from somewhere up the hill near the lodge. My thumb recoiled from the button.

"Blood party's not over," Raven said.

Chapter 26

TWO MORE SHOTS whined in the moonlight.

"Came from outside the lodge, on the back side," Raven said.

A moment later a volley of shots answered. I counted eight.

"Two shooters," I said. "One inside, one outside."

"One experienced, one scared," Raven said.

"Where's the couple?"

"Shooter hasn't found them or he wouldn't still be here."

"Means we should get into the lodge," I said.

"Help that scared shooter out," Raven said.

We raced up the ramp. At the top, moonlight transformed the gravel walkway into a shimmering silvery path. We threw our bodies against the smooth wood and rough stone of the lodge. I reached out and yanked on a heavy wooden handle. The door rattled without opening. We slid our backs over the bottom wall to the next door, which I tried but to no avail.

I tucked my pistol and my flashlight into the small of my back and reached overhead to the outside edge of a deck running the perimeter of the lodge. My biceps flexed. My arm stiffened momentarily with a spasm of pain from my finger. But I hauled myself up, then swung myself under the deck's railing. Then I reached down with my better arm to help Raven up and onto the deck. We crawled to one corner of the deck and I peered around the side.

A tiny light flashed from the bushes down and beyond the lodge, followed by the *crack* then *chuff* of a bullet burrowing into wood. Another light flash preceded a bullet's pinging off stone. Our shooter replied with five rounds zipping through the brush. Then the deck creaked under footsteps moving our way.

I moved my head back, held out a straight arm to Raven, and waited, feeling the vibrations of the deck under my feet.

I sucked in a breath. The creaking grew louder.

When a man's moonlit silhouette rounded the corner, I lunged for his wrist, then snared his throat in the crook of my other arm. Raven leaped to his feet and spun the gun out of his hand. I tightened the vice around the man's neck.

I whispered, "We're here to help. If we'd wanted to kill you, we would have already done so. Can I let go of you without a sound?"

He nodded. I let go of my grip.

"Bend down," I said, "or whoever that is will see you in the moonlight."

"Who the hell are you?" the man asked.

"Supposed to be a couple with you. Where are they?"

"Don't know anything about a couple."

A pinpoint of light flashed from the darkness. Glass shattered, then showered over us. I grabbed the man in front of me and pulled out my flashlight to push aside a strip of glass sparkling in the moonlight, dangling from the window frame. I shoved the man inside the lodge and yanked him down in front of the stone fireplace. Raven followed us in partway but kept his back to us, with his gun pointed out through the empty floor-to-ceiling frame. Cool night air rushed into the lodge, fanning the fire in the stone fireplace.

Raven barked, "Can't see a damn thing. Put out that fire." His echo measured the volume of the great room.

"Gas fireplace," the man said.

He reached up and flipped a switch. In the sputtering flames, I caught a glimpse of his blonde, youthful looks. He couldn't have been more than midtwenties.

"Yeah," Raven said.

"About that couple," I said.

"Don't know anything about a couple," the man said.

"Fellow out there probably thinks you do know."

"Got my orders."

"Don't think this is a good time to play soldier," I said.

"Who the hell are you anyway?"

A bullet whizzed overhead, whined off the stone chimney, then wheezed to silence in the dark far side of the cavernous room.

"Can't stay here much longer," Raven said.

"Who do you work for?" the man asked.

"Independent," I said. "Like you?"

"Could be."

Two sharp cracks, then two dull thuds sounded below us.

"He's shooting open a downstairs door," Raven said.

"It's truth time," I said.

"Don't know what you're talking about," the young man said.

Downstairs, hinges creaked.

"You got a name, son?"

"TQ. You?"

"Charlie."

Out of the darkness, stairs groaned under slow, carefully measured footsteps. Raven crept from the window to us. He slid TQ's gun butt first across my chest. I grabbed it and shoved it into the young man's gut.

I whispered, "Think you can wait until I tell you to shoot?"

"You suddenly assume command?"

"You wanna get out of here alive, you'll wait until I tell you to shoot. That's an order."

The footsteps and creaks stopped. Raven whispered in my ear, "I'm going outside and down. Coming back inside behind him."

Raven moved toward the broken window. A flash of light burst from the darkness, then a spark flew from stone. An explosive clap followed, leaving the trailing echo of a *ping* hovering in the room, swallowed by darkness again. Moonlight caught Raven sliding on the seat of his pants underneath the deck's bottom rail. He held on to the rail momentarily then let go with a resultant thud. A round from the intruder's gun followed over his head as he slipped to the ground.

I tapped TQ's shoulder and whispered, "See where that light flash came from?"

He nodded.

"Put a few rounds in there, then roll over behind the corner of the fireplace."

TQ's pistol exploded in my ear. The smell of gunpowder pummeled my nostrils. After the first shot, I pushed off from the fireplace and crawled with my hand groping ahead. I aimed for a spot in the darkness to the side of the gunman opposite the broken glass. I touched a chair leg and paused. But when I let go of the leg to continue, the chair scraped slightly over the floor. Two bullets dove into the chair back, tipping it over with a crash. TQ fired back twice. I ducked even lower, pressed my body against the floor and slithered toward the wall. The intruder fired in TQ's direction. I sighted on the muzzle flash and fired. The intruder shot once toward me, then quickly back toward TQ.

Suddenly, one shot rang out from the floor below. From the darkness came the sounds of a body scurrying briefly across the floor, then another sharp crack with an echo lost in the bowels of the lodge below. A heavy sigh issued forth but from whom or where I couldn't tell. I held my breath until I heard another report from Raven's pistol.

I swept my pistol across the lodge, strained in the darkness to see. But in the dim moonlight filtering into the lodge, I could only make out the shadows of lamps, couches, and tables, along with the bizarre life-sized sculpture of a metallic grizzly bear that gleamed in the silvery light about thirty feet away. A moonlit shadow moved ten feet to the left of the bear. I swung my pistol in that direction and poised for the shot, aiming uncertainly in the darkness, when another small explosion fractured the tense silence.

It came from outside the lodge, at a distance. A cough, followed by a stutter. Then another cough. I sucked in a breath, felt everyone's breathing pause—mine, the gunman's, TQ's, Raven's—as if together our minds measured the meaning of that moment, then managed the same conclusion. Outside, the stuttering and coughing continued, spaced closer, and pitched higher until the stutters became the growl and the coughs the rumble of an outboard engine.

Downstairs, the door burst open, and a moment later footsteps crashed down the stairs. I ran to a sliding door leading out to the deck and crouched beneath the railing. I couldn't see Raven. I only heard two bodies beating through the brush. I stepped back inside.

I yelled, "Where were they?"

TQ stammered, "Boathouse on the other side of the island. False room once used by bootleggers and smugglers."

"What'd you leave there?"

"Our inflatable."

"Damn. Means they're on the water now."

"Follow me," TQ said.

He made his way in the darkness toward me, and we both ran along the deck until we reached the wooden stairs leading down. TQ leaped to the ground before he reached the bottom step. I took the stairs two at a time. We raced along a narrow path, through the brush, then up and over a rock pile. At the top of the rocks, another outboard engine exploded to life below us. Ahead I saw Raven standing on a small dock.

I jogged to the dock. The moon lit Raven's breath. He pointed beneath the rock outcrop. "Shooter must have had his boat tied up over there."

I put a hand on Raven's shoulder. He turned to me. The moon also lit the whites of his eyes.

"The *Lady* or the inflatable?" I asked.

"Both," he said. "We stand a better chance."

Raven had already started jogging up the path from the dock toward the lodge. I followed him, leaving TQ still standing on the dock.

TQ yelled, "You're crazy to go out there now. Devil's Hole has opened up."

Raven and I jogged back down to the dock on the other side of the island. I jumped aboard the *Lady* and lowered the dinghy, while Raven climbed into the pilothouse and fired up her engine. I hopped over the gunwales into the dinghy, reaching up at the last minute for a life vest.

I wrapped my hand around the starter cord and jerked the outboard engine to life. Then I zoomed along a trail of moonlight into the dark waters of Dent Rapids. I tried to reach out into the night with my hearing. I searched the dark for the sound of other outboards above the whine of my engine. But I only found the roar of the current, only felt the water's grasp on the dinghy, pulling me inexorably toward Devil's Hole.

I swung the tiller to one side, pointed the dinghy away from the pull of the water, and gunned the engine. A wave slapped over the side of the boat, drenching me. I slipped one arm into my life vest, switched hands on the tiller, then thrust the other arm into the vest. I revved the engine higher but I couldn't hold the dinghy against the pull of the current tugging me toward Devil's Hole.

There's a time not to fight the water. So I spun the dinghy around, brought the throttle down, and pointed it into the middle of the channel but angled slightly away, hoping the current's pull and spin would slingshot me north of the Devil's mouth.

A bright light washed over me from behind, eclipsing the moonlight ahead. Two blasts from the *Lady*'s horn turned me around to face her searchlight bearing down on me like the lit eye of a cyclops. I waved. Raven sounded another two short, sharp blasts. I gunned the engine, tried to maneuver out of his way, but I had little control of the dinghy.

Behind me the *Lady*'s engine screamed as Raven threw her into a full-throttle reverse. With a dancer's grace, she swung her flank toward me. Raven gunned forward and the *Lady's* stern pivoted only ten yards away. Ahead, the Devil's roar grew louder.

The *Lady's* searchlight painted me again. I turned to look. This time Raven stood off away from the brunt of the current. I followed the light as it swept the water in front of me just in time to reflect off the frothing white crest of a four-foot standing wave directly ahead of the dinghy. I slammed the tiller to one side and came at the wave from an angle. I held on to a line along the side of the dinghy as we bucked up precipitously over the top of the wave. A screaming propeller pushed air before we crashed down hard on the other side.

The Devil's roar continued.

I squeezed the tiller with one hand and wiped the stinging salt spray from my eyes with the other. Raven shined the searchlight on me again. The beam shook. Then he shifted the light to follow the rocky shore fifty yards to my right, which the current whipped me along. The beam jumped from the shore at a low-lying point ahead of me and traveled into the swirling dark waters of Dent Rapids. Beyond the point, the light reflected off one brilliant white stripe in motion, then another. Two horn blasts from the *Lady* followed. I waved high overhead, then attempted to angle my dinghy toward the reflective tape on the side of the other two small boats coming within the Devil's grasp.

When my dinghy reached the point, the rough ride smoothed out but it also quickened. I'd nipped an outer edge of the whirlpool, which spun me clockwise as if I'd stepped onto a fast-moving conveyor belt. I held on as the current whipped me around, then spit me out downstream from the other two boats, whose shadows I caught brief glimpses of in the moonlight and the flickering beam of the *Lady's* searchlight.

The ebb now pushed me north, further away from the whirlpool and the other two boats. As the Devil's tendrils loosened their grip on the dinghy, I angled in close to the Sonora Island shore on the opposite side of the rapids. The bottom of my engine shaft scraped rock. I hit the red kill button, then tipped the engine, bringing the shaft up and out of the water. I pulled an oar from its holder and pushed off the shore into the pull of a strong backeddy that shot me upstream, bouncing me off and around small headlands and large rocks in my way.

Close to the edge of the whirlpool, the backeddy petered out into a hole behind a small point of land. I lowered the engine shaft into the water and fired up the outboard, sitting at idle in calm water just outside the Devil's violent lair. I tried to find the *Lady* but I couldn't see her. A moment later, faint screams rose above the water's wail. Moonlight caught the panic-stricken faces of a man and woman whipping past me in a twelve-foot inflatable struggling to gain control of their boat. Then, like movie frames ticking through a projector, a smaller inflatable flew past me with a man at the tiller, pointing a pistol ahead.

I pulled my pistol from the small of my back, twisted the tiller handle into forward gear, and pushed off the headland into the main body of the current. But by now the gunman's inflatable was already fifty yards away. So I tucked my pistol safely behind me and used both hands in an attempt to control the dinghy. The current whipped me counterclockwise and south. As it brought me back around to the middle of the channel, it also sucked me further into the maw of the Devil.

Hold on, hold on, I kept telling myself. If I could just keep the dinghy on the outer lip of the whirlpool as we rounded its southern edge, this same current would spit me out again when we reached the northern edge. I pointed the nose of the dinghy beyond the lip of the whirlpool and gunned the engine, but that put me broadside to the current and the dinghy lifted onto its edge. My heart rate soared. I threw my weight to the opposite side of the boat and jammed the tiller over, bringing the dinghy back parallel to the current and slightly more under my control.

If three on a clock face is east and twelve is north, I waited until one-thirty before I tried the maneuver again. This time the current did spit me out north, and I rode the backeddy south again. Wet and shivering, I waited at idle, hoping the Devil had not yet swallowed his other prey.

The moment the couple whizzed by in the moonlight, I pushed off from the Sonora Island shore, which placed me twenty yards behind the gunman's inflatable by the time I entered the main body of current at nine on the clock face. The dinghy shuddered in the turbulent merry-go-round, and moonlight shone off the face of the gunman who'd suddenly turned my way.

I didn't see the muzzle flash, didn't hear the sound of his gunfire. But the swish of air by my arm and the *ping* ricocheting off the engine housing told me he'd fired a shot. I whipped my pistol from behind my back but found aiming useless in this furious water. I wasn't going to take a chance that a stray round might find the couple, so I put my gun away. And by then the gunman had already turned his pistol at the couple.

Suddenly, a water dragon's menacing hiss dwarfed the snarl of the current and a growling geyser erupted. Unable to stop, I flew past the punctured inflatable, still fizzling in the water, floating wrinkled and flat, with the Kinsleys flailing beside it.

Chapter 27

I'D JUST PASSED THE KINSLEYS when the *Lady*'s bright light flashed out of the darkness, scanning the water surface. Raven locked the beam onto the couple, who tumbled toward the blackness at the center of Devil's Hole. He drove the *Lady* between them and the Hole. She rocked violently to port. A light flashed on in the cockpit. And that's all I saw before the Devil clutched the *Lady*. She rocked so far to port again that moonlight illuminated most of the dark blue keel beneath her white hull. Then, recovering, she careened to starboard, burying her gunwales in the Devil's swirl.

Again, the spinning ebb flushed me out north. But when I looked back I couldn't see the *Lady*, only a trail of moonlight interrupted by an undulating black mass at the center of Devil's Hole.

This time I heard the gunfire, and the zip of two bullets diving into the water next to the dinghy. I swerved out of the moonlit path and into the darkness. I cut my engine and drifted with the current, cocking my ears toward the Sonora Island side of the channel and the faint sounds of an outboard engine choking to a stop.

I yanked on the starter, firing my outboard engine back to life. I headed north, guessing where to angle in toward Sonora Island to place myself beyond the gunman, if he hadn't already headed into the forest on foot. As I neared the shore, I throttled down, only to find the backeddy less forceful. So I headed south in the channel about thirty yards offshore, under power, scanning the shoreline and the water in the moonlight for signs of the gunman and his boat.

Water lapped at Sonora Island. Deep in the forest an owl screeched. A gentle breeze rustled leaves, and a subtle scraping noise, which sounded like metal over stone, seemed out of place. I angled sharply toward the shore, then, close by, cut the engine and rocked it up. With an oar, I pushed into shore, stepped from the dinghy into shallow water, and tied the painter to a large rock. I crept slowly along the shoreline, sweeping low-lying branches out of my way with my gun.

I stopped thirty yards short of a pocket beach where moonlight caught the bow of the gunman's dinghy pointed toward shore. Its stern, with the engine shaft still down, scraped over rocks as it bobbed in the water.

Dew from leaves seeped through my jacket and my shirt as I lay face down, holding my flashlight high overhead, anticipating a volley of bullets. When none came, I crawled farther toward the dinghy and held the light high again. Still no reply from the gunman, so I stood and moved deeper into the forest, flashlight in one hand held atop my pistol in the other.

I swept the forest with my light as I picked my way over downed limbs and a carpet of smaller branches. Fifty yards in, I ran into a shear rock wall thirty feet high. I shined my light down the face of the wall in both directions. It bounced off dark stone as far as I could see.

I jammed my flashlight and gun into the small of my back, turned, and high-stepped my way as fast as I could back toward the shore. I caught the gunman in the midst of untying his dinghy. I dove at his legs. He tumbled to the sand, then rolled and sent his heel smashing into my shoulder. I fell back. Instantly his muscular body fell atop me. He grabbed my throat with one hand, reached for it with the other. I brought a knee up under his chest and strained while coughing to straighten my leg. I pushed him aside momentarily and rose to my knees. Then I threw a hard right at his side, but in the dim light I missed and my hand glanced off the top of his belly. He grabbed my arm, yanked, and sent me reeling over him into the sand and rocks.

I reached behind me, but before I could wrap my fingers around the butt of my pistol, the gunman's hand came down on the side of my head. With a sharp crack, the rock he held met my skull. It stunned me without knocking me out. I grabbed for his leg and held on, but my grip faltered as the pain in my head reached a crescendo, and he wriggled free. I blinked my eyes and shook my head. By the time I'd managed to grab my gun, I shined my flashlight on the stern of his dinghy and the water thrown back from his exhaust, both disappearing around a point of land at the far end of the small beach.

I stumbled back up the shoreline to my dinghy, untied it from the log, and pushed it back into the water. Before getting in, I stooped to splash cold water on the side of my head and the back of my neck, trying to numb the pain and shock the wooziness from my body. I tumbled into the dinghy and yanked the starter cord. On the first try the engine turned over. I headed south into the night, into an expiring ebb.

But a dying devil deceives.

The moon cast its light over swirling waters, now absent a central black hole. As it tugged the ebb in the opposite direction, a series of angry standing waves rose. Beneath me, the confused current tried to tear the dinghy apart. I couldn't power through this melee, so I let the current take me, using the engine's thrust to turn the dinghy at a slight angle to each standing wave I met. At the top of a four-foot standing wave, I made out the gunman a few waves ahead, taking them head-on.

The last wave he mounted flopped him ninety degrees. Before he could right his boat to face the next wave, that wave flipped him over and flung the dinghy into the dark. After I rode up and over that wave I saw him bobbing in the moonlit foam of the spiraling current. No standing waves lay ahead, only the tug of a swirling current. I angled in his direction, holding the flashlight in my tiller hand. I shined my light on him and stuck out my other hand. For the first time I saw his face, which reminded me of a younger Ali Sharik's, with his olive-colored skin, perhaps more accustomed to the shifting sands of the desert than whirling waters of the sea. But I also recognized him from the image Pete Townsend showed me during my video briefing. This man in the water, wearing an RCMP uniform, was Yusuf Al Nejari's aide, Mansoor Habib, who'd briefed Pete Townsend on the dangers of Ali Sharik.

Habib reached out for me, grabbing my arm. I pulled him toward the side of the dinghy. But then he tugged at me as though trying to rip me from the boat. I jammed my foot into the transom, arched back, and pulled against him. He swung his foot against the side of the dinghy and jerked hard. The dinghy tipped on its side. Habib pulled harder. With my other foot, I kicked the tiller away from the tilt of the dinghy, and the thrust of the engine kept it from tipping over.

A moment of moonlight reflected a determined desperation in Habib's eyes. He yanked hard again. I fought off his pull even as my grip weakened from the rising pain in my finger. The black faces and red lips of Bukwas and Dzunukwa flashed into my mind. A deep, rolling laugh echoed through my being, followed by a banshee's haunting shriek, "Ooooo . . . Ooooo . . . Ooooo."

I couldn't hold on much longer.

Suddenly, Habib's grip lessened. I looked over the side, where moonlight now revealed the unearthly smile spread over his face. Habib cried out, a cry that merged with Dzunukwa's otherworldly shriek, like a lone wolf howling for its partner.

"Allah Akbar . . . Allah Akbar . . . Allah Akbar."

Then he ripped his hand from my arm and disappeared into the death throes of Devil's Hole.

I TIED THE DINGHY to the lodge's dock. I smiled at the *Lady* and patted her hull as I walked by. Inside the lodge, Raven had the fireplace lit and the Kinsleys huddled before the flames, swaddled in heavy blankets. I stepped from my wet clothes and he threw a blanket around me as I sat on the floor next to them.

William Kinsley turned my way, and with a shaky voice, uttered, "Thanks."

⚓

DAWN WHIPPED the Dent Island Lodge into a frenzy. A Canadian Coast Guard cutter arrived to remove the bodies of the security agents from the dock and from the Sea Ray. Raven sat in front of the fireplace talking quietly with the couple. I'd just finished sweeping the last pile of glass into a dustpan when Nick Stevens, the lieutenant in charge of the detail, entered the lodge. He'd also commanded the squad that picked up Ali Sharik's body from Von Donop Inlet yesterday. Tall, young, and clean-cut, with a ruddy complexion and dark brown hair, Stevens wore a dark blue jumpsuit and heavy, polished boots. He still had his orange life vest on. He reached out to shake my hand.

"I know it's 'Thanks,'" Stevens said. "I'm just not sure if it's 'Hope to see you again.' Bodies seem to get left in your wake."

"Next time you see me, I'll be in Von Donop with my feet up on the gunwales, a book in one hand, a can of beer in the other, and a lovely woman by my side."

Stevens smiled. "Say, you think you and Mr. Raven could help us out by bringing that Sea Ray back to Campbell River? It'd take a few calls and a lot of paperwork for us to do it."

"Raven?" I asked.

He didn't bother turning from the fire. "Sure."

"Thanks," Stevens said. He turned to walk out of the lodge.

"Lieutenant," I said. Stevens turned back around. "Yesterday the man working the helo saluted the body bag before he brought it aboard. Is that standard Coast Guard practice?"

Stevens shook his head. "He wasn't from the guard, nor was the pilot. Both worked for the Canadian Security and Intelligence Service. CSIS took jurisdiction of the body from the moment it left the ground at Von Donop. Heard they had a special cargo jet waiting on the tarmac for the body when the helo touched down."

"Thanks," I said.

"Did you know him?" Stevens asked.

"He was a friend."

"Sorry," Stevens said.

Not long after Stevens and the cutter left the lodge's main dock, a floatplane with an American pilot landed to gather the Kinsleys and whisk them away. Then, just after the late morning slack at Dent Rapids, I stood outside on a sun-drenched deck to watch a fifty-foot aluminum barge with a drop-down bow section run up onto the beach next to the dock on the far side of the island.

After the barge landed, five men walked into the lodge, each carrying a large plywood board. An older man with shaggy gray hair and wire-rim glasses walked back and forth through the window frame, now open to the outside. I came in from the deck to meet him. I extended my hand and he shook it.

"Frank Covington," he said. "And you're Noble?"

"I am."

He looked around. "Nick Stevens says I have you and a Mr. Raven to thank for things not being any worse than they are at my lodge."

I pointed to the couch in front of the fire.

Covington shook his head. "Look, anytime you two want to come up here for a few days to go fishing or have a romantic getaway with the missus, you just let me know." He pointed to the window where several of the men had already begun hammering plywood boards into place. "Coast Guard'll take care of all of this. They paid for one week's full occupancy, then told me to vacate the lodge. Said they'd take care of any damage. They're sending a crew over day after tomorrow to install new glass and fill in some of the bullet holes." He chuckled. "May want to keep a few of those. Makes for good stories to tell when guests are sitting around the fire in the evening."

Covington insisted on making lunch for Raven and me. After a meal of Dungeness crab, baked potatoes, and zucchini, I walked with Raven down to the dock and stepped onto the *Noble Lady*. While Raven stood on the dock, I checked her fluids and vital signs, then climbed up to the pilothouse to crank over her engine. I let her idle and stepped out onto the pilothouse deck.

"Slack before flood's just about now," I said.

Raven nodded.

I pointed to the Sea Ray. "Honking twin diesels. Plenty of fuel. You'll be in Campbell River by the time I get to Von Donop."

Raven nodded again.

I ducked back inside. He undid the lines, then pushed me away from the dock. I stuck my head from the pilothouse door.

"See you in Campbell River."

He nodded once more.

I backed the *Lady* away from the dock, then spun her around to head into Dent Rapids. Sunlight spangled the rapids, giving them the aura of a large, calm lake masking a hidden devil below. I tapped a touch pad on my computer that brought up an electronic chart of my course into Von Donop. As I turned to port into the placid waters of Dent Rapids, I looked over to see Raven hiking up the ramp back to the lodge. The *Lady* suddenly felt empty.

Two hours later, as I started a gentle turn to port into Ha'thayim, my VHF radio sounded.

"*Noble Lady*. This is *Sea Raven*."

I chuckled. "*Sea Raven*, *Noble Lady*. Switching to zero niner."

I punched up channel 9 and looked out of my starboard window, where a speeding white hull threw a huge rooster tail behind it.

"*Noble Lady*, *Sea Raven*. I'm headed into the Discovery Harbor marina. When you get to Campbell River tomorrow, come by."

"Roger, *Sea Raven*. Have a safe trip. *Noble Lady* out and back to one-six."

"*Sea Raven* out, standing by one-six."

I slowed the *Noble Lady* and watched *Sea Raven* zoom by. It didn't take long until only his rooster tail was visible halfway down Sutil Channel. Then I headed into Ha'thayim and, after slipping through the narrows, I anchored in the bay at the mouth of the reversing rapids.

FROM THE HILLS above the opposite side of the inlet, the howls of a wolf pack woke me the following morning. I pushed open an over-head hatch to let their yips and yowls in, and to watch the sky transition from indigo to powder blue.

Later, I ordered menu item C from the only waiter aboard, then made myself a breakfast of pancakes, bacon, and eggs—all organic, thank you—and laughed, thinking about Ben Conrad as I did.

I sat on the fantail, sipping coffee before weighing anchor for Campbell River.

At first, the outboard engine sounded like a beehive far away. Then I looked up to see the small boat buzz into the inlet, bow up, throwing a short rooster tail. The boat slowed. The bow lowered. And the rooster tail disappeared as the burgundy and white boat headed my way.

Samurai Princess came at the *Noble Lady*'s starboard side with her fenders out. She swung about sharply, then glided in gently to kiss the *Lady*'s hull.

Maya Shimazu stepped from the cabin. "Permission to tie up and come aboard?" she asked.

Chapter 28

PERMISSION GRANTED."

    I reached for her lines and tied them off to my cleats. Then I reached for her hand and helped her aboard. I offered her coffee and she took it. We sat on the fantail as the sun finally stretched above the wolf pack's hills.

"Heard you might be here," Maya said.

"You've got good sources."

She chuckled. "Don't know if Raven qualifies as a good source."

"You met him?"

"Hard to say. Felt like he met me, like he already knew me in some strange, slightly unnerving way."

I nodded. "I know the feeling."

"I'm here because I need to complete my report."

"On the couple?"

"Them. The incident. The man who was killed back there." She nodded toward the reversing rapids. "I need to inspect the site."

"I think the trail's been closed off."

She nodded again. "All of the trails in Von Donop have been closed off, until the investigation's through."

"You do have good sources," I said.

"I heard you knew that man."

"Raven say that?"

"No."

"Heard that his wife and children were immediately flown out of Bahrain into Canada for their protection."

I set my coffee cup down. "Who told you that?"

Maya stared into her cup. "Heard they landed at CFB Comox last night so that they could see the body. I also heard that they'll be in the area for a while."

"You have certainly heard a lot. And all that you've heard will be in your report?"

She lifted her cup and gently swirled it. "Yes."

"And the Canadian government's allowing the *Sun* to print all that you heard?"

She smiled into her coffee and raised her head. "I said I needed to complete my report. I didn't say it was a report destined to be published in the *Sun*."

Maya stood to leave. She reached into her pocket and withdrew a business card, which she set on the cushion beside me. Beneath the words "*Vancouver Sun*," the card read, "Maya Shimazu, Investigative Reporter." She flipped the card over and wrote down a ten-digit number.

"I've heard this telephone number will only be good for the next six hours," she said. "I've also heard there is someone in Campbell River who would like to speak with you. If you call prior to your arrival, I've heard that a meeting will be arranged."

Maya set down her coffee, stood, and stepped out of the cabin. I untied her dinghy and she pushed off the *Noble Lady*'s hull, then started her engine. Not long after that, the *Samurai Princess* disappeared into the depths of Ha'thayim.

MY CELL PHONE RANG as I swept the *Noble Lady* wide around Cape Mudge at the south end of Quadra Island. The caller ID placed the number in Maryland and I decided to let my voicemail take the call. When I checked the message, an automated voice asked me only to call a number I recognized as Pete Townsend's.

I didn't call Pete back. Instead, I tapped in the ten-digit number Maya Shimazu had given me. A man's voice directed me to the police dock at a public marina south of Discovery Harbor. I snapped the phone closed and crossed over Discovery Channel to Campbell River.

I pulled into the marina and up to the police dock, where two well-groomed, well-built men wearing sunglasses and dressed in white short-sleeved shirts with dark trousers waited to take my lines. One in front of me, one in back, they hustled me up the metal gangway from the police dock to a black limousine.

After the two men assumed stations on either side of the limousine, the driver opened his door and stepped out. Then he swung open the passenger's door and I climbed in. He closed the door behind me.

I found myself next to a woman clad in a black burka, her face barely visible through its mesh. She rested her hand gently atop mine.

"Charlie."

As Zafia Sharik's voice quivered, tears welled in my eyes.

"Ali promised me that if anything happened to him I would find a way to let you know the truth. You were his friend. And that friendship was dear to him."

Zafia's British accent was less pronounced than Ali's. She reached for the knob on the smoked Plexiglas partition that separated us from the front compartment. She slid it to one side and another man with sunglasses turned to face us.

"It's okay?" she asked.

He nodded. She slid the partition closed.

"The day of Masoud's death, Ali was contacted by the Canadian embassy in Bahrain. They asked if he would infil . . . in—how do you say it?" She motioned with her hand as though calling forth the word.

"Infiltrate?" I said.

"Yes, infiltrate the Islamic Jihad Front. Charlie, he had to pretend that he hated you that day, and it hurt him deeply." Zafia squeezed my hand. "He loved his brother, but he hated what Masoud had done. He vowed he would help to bring the war between 'brothers of all nations'—as he liked to say—to an end."

I put my other hand on top of Zafia's. "I saw that in his eyes at the end."

Zafia sobbed softly.

"When I'm settled, you will come visit us?" she asked.

"Settled where?"

"Vancouver."

"You're being relocated to Vancouver?"

"They gave me a choice and I said that since I did not know anyone in this country, I wanted to live as close as I could to my husband's American friend."

"I will come to Vancouver soon, to see you and your children," I said.

"And you'll know how to reach us?"

I patted the shirt pocket where I'd tucked Maya Shimazu's card. I nodded. "I will."

I LEFT THE POLICE DOCK and cruised the short distance north to the Discovery Harbor marina. Just before the breakwater, I radioed in for a slip assignment and got placed one dock over from the Sea Ray. After tying down the *Noble Lady*, I walked around to the Sea Ray and stepped aboard. A handwritten note taped to the sliding glass door read, "Meet us at the Discovery Harbor Bed and Breakfast in the Quadra Island Room at 4 P.M. today." Raven had signed it. I checked my watch. It was just two. So I stepped off the Sea Ray and walked back around to the *Noble Lady* to place that call to Pete Townsend.

"Job well done, Commander," Townsend said.

"And the couple?"

"Offered asylum. Justice is dropping the case against Sami Al-Sayed. So, they don't need the couple's testimony any longer."

"Dropping the case?"

"Justice said they were never after Al-Sayed to begin with, just using him to move up the Islamic Jihad Front's chain of command. Habib and Al Nejari came as a surprise. They'd been after Sharik since . . . well, you remember. Al Nejari left Canada before he could be detained. But eliminating two out of three terrorists ain't bad."

I shook my head. "So Sami Al-Sayed is being released to join his sister?"

"Being released? Hell, no. He's being deported."

"She stays, he goes back. Cruel."

"No, politics. Looks bad to free a suspect after he's been accused of being a terrorist. Better to dump him off in some other country and save face."

"Guilt or innocence play a role?"

Townsend's voice rose. "When it comes to politics?"

"Guess not."

"Helluva thing to have a friend like Sharik turn on you. You must be glad to finally have closure."

"I am. And you, Pete? Are you glad to get back to a world where no one trusts each other, and you're never sure whom to believe?"

"Glad? Don't know about that. But at least it's a world I know."

AFTER THE CALL to Pete Townsend, a ten-minute walk north of the marina put me at the Discovery Harbor Bed and Breakfast, a two-story building constructed of cedar and stone that sat on a small knoll with a commanding view of Discovery Passage. A pair of unpainted totems guarded the doors to the bed and breakfast, both carved with an orca on top, whose body slowly morphed into a bear below. I stepped across the threshold and swung the right half of the double-wide cedar door. I heard footsteps approaching from behind, so I held the door and turned.

A young native woman walked toward me, a small bag in her hands. Her long dark hair fell below her waist. She wore a low-cut tan dress that reached down to her calves, and dark brown leather boots that reached up to the dress. The red shawl around her shoulders featured embroidered images of a moon and an eagle done in a Northwest native motif. A silver pendant with the engraved dorsal fin of an orca hung from around her neck and rested over the smooth chestnut-colored skin of her chest. Matching silver earrings dangled from her lobes.

She looked at me as though she knew me. I took a chance. "Are you Raven's daughter?" I asked.

She smiled. "You must be Charlie?"

She stepped through the door and I followed. Then she turned and extended her hand to me. "No, I'm Simone." She touched her chest. "His . . . well . . . Sarina, our daughter, is in the room with our beautiful grandson, David."

Simone led me down the carpeted hallway to a heavy wooden door with the name "Quadra" burned into the wood. She knocked and Raven called from behind the door, "It's open."

I opened the door for Simone, but when I stepped into the large room I stopped, unable to move. Kate sat in a reclining chair next to a window that looked out over the waters of Discovery Passage to Quadra Island. In her arms, she cradled and rocked a baby wrapped in a light blue blanket. She looked up at me with a smile. But before I could utter a word, she stood and walked over. She handed me the tiny infant. I wrapped both arms under him.

"Charlie, meet David Daniel Woods," she said.

"Middle name's after me," Raven said.

David twitched. Then he balled his small fists, stretched his arms out, and yawned. When his eyes opened he looked up at me with a gaze that penetrated deep into my soul. I turned to Raven and nodded.

"He's your grandson all right."

Raven laughed. Then David wailed. I handed him off to Sarina, who sat beside Raven on a bed filled with unopened presents wrapped in paper decorated with hand-drawn ravens, eagles, orcas, and bears. Sarina wore a blue smock and she'd wrapped herself in a red blanket adorned with embroidered animals that matched her mother's shawl. Sarina had Raven's deep eyes and her mother's warm smile. She pushed one of her two dark braids over her shoulder, parted the blanket slightly, then slipped David inside. A moment later his wailing gave way to the contented sounds of suckling, and a blissful smile radiated over Sarina's face.

Kate locked her arm in mine, then pointed to her duffel on the floor near the door. She whispered, "I think it's time for us to leave them alone."

I spoke to Raven. "Be back this way in—" I turned to Kate.

"Two weeks," she said.

"Two weeks?"

She smiled while nodding. "Two weeks."

Raven looked up at Simone. She nodded. He pursed his lips. "Should be back from Port Hardy by then."

KATE AND I WALKED arm in arm back to the marina. Once aboard the *Noble Lady*, I threw Kate's duffel down on the cockpit sole and we sat on the cushions. She leaned her head on my shoulder, and I put an arm around her. I pulled her close. She burrowed into my side.

"Thought you were the acting CO. How'd you get a two-week leave?"

"Your buddy Pete Townsend called the District Thirteen Commandant, and the next thing I knew I was ordered to take a two-week leave, and offered a helo ride to CFB Comox."

I chuckled. "Pete's full of surprises."

"I believe he viewed this surprise as a thank you." She looked at me. "Do you know where we're going for these two weeks?"

"I do."

"Where?"

"Through the rapids and then on to an uncharted lagoon. Then several days of pampering at a lodge on Dent Island."

"Oh my, that sounds exciting. When do we leave?"

"Seymour Narrows turns slack in four hours."

"That gives us some time here at the marina. And the *Noble Lady* is ready?"

"She is."

"Her fluids are topped off?"

"They are."

"You *were* planning to check my fluids as well?"

"Do yours also need topping off?"

Kate smiled. "They do."

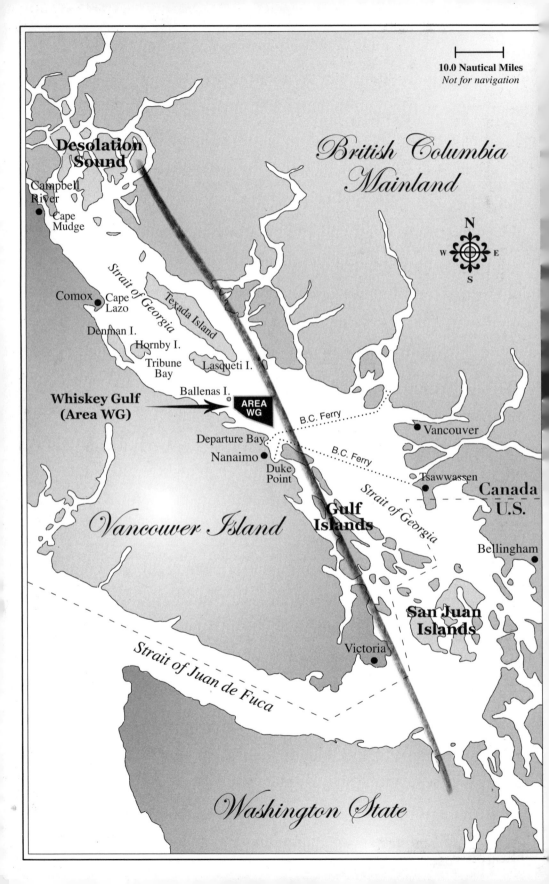